MORTON PUBLIC LIBRARY
A13002 293161
W9-BVL-714

How the Light Gets In

Also by KATY UPPERMAN

The Impossibility of Us

Kissing Max Holden

How the Light

Gets In

KATY UPPERMAN

Swoon READS

New York

A SWOON READS BOOK

An Imprint of Feiwel and Friends and
Macmillan Publishing Group, LLC
120 Broadway, New York, NY 10271

Our books may be purchased in bulk for promotional, educational, or business use. Please contact your local bookseller or the Macmillan Corporate and Premium Sales Department at (800) 221-7945 ext. 5442 or by email at MacmillanSpecialMarkets@macmillan.com.

Library of Congress Control Number: 2018955586
ISBN 978-1-250-30567-1 (hardcover) / ISBN 978-1-250-30568-8 (ebook)

Book design by Danielle Mazzella di Bosco

First Edition, 2019

10 9 8 7 6 5 4 3 2 1

swoonreads.com

For Lulu . . .

I'll love you forever.

There is a crack, a crack in everything.

That's how the light gets in.

—*Leonard Cohen, "Anthem"*

1

I never used to be the kind of girl who'd hotbox her bathroom.

Perched on the counter next to the porcelain sink, I lose myself in a haze that distorts the flower pattern dancing across the shower curtain. My bare feet bounce against the cabinet below. I absorb the staccato thumping until it permeates flesh and muscle, vibrating into my bones.

Pipe to mouth. Deep inhale. Hold the smoke until my chest sizzles. Exhale.

My junior year at North Seattle Prep ended today, and I've been drifting—a wisp of cotton in a summer breeze. The last day of school used to mean celebration. A break from the demands of private school: quadratic equations and chemical reactions and accessorizing my uniform just right. I used to spend summers with my sister, giggling over romance novels, all brawny men and luscious women. We used to shop and swim. We used to eat grilled food and drink iced mochas with extra chocolate and stay up late, gazing at the stars.

This summer, I won't spend my mornings at the pool, panting through grueling sets, and I won't squander my afternoons in a lounge chair. Instead, I'll hide out in the house. I'll avoid my parents, and I'll avoid Isaac, who's due back from his freshman year at UCSD any day.

I'll avoid life.

Pipe to mouth. Deep inhale. Hold the smoke until my chest sizzles. Exhale.

That's what I'm doing when my dad comes knocking, a sharp rap that makes me jump.

Fanning the air, I slide from the counter and empty the bowl of my pipe into the toilet, mourning the loss while the water whirlpools away. I spray perfume, splash drops into my eyes, then peek reluctantly at my reflection in the mirror. My hair looks washed out, dry as wheat, and my eyes are sunken and shadowed.

The old me is so far gone, I hardly remember her.

Dad's face crumples when I open the bathroom door. He sees her, too—the hopeless girl who stared at me in the mirror a moment ago. I sigh; a family meeting is the unavoidable next step, another pseudointervention during which Dad will threaten me with therapy.

I went once, nearly a year ago, at his insistence.

It didn't help.

We sit in his office, where the air is clear, though I'm sufficiently blazed. He's in a navy version of the standard suit he wears daily to the University of Washington, where he teaches ancient Greece using the textbooks he spent the bulk of his adult life writing. He's seated in the thronelike leather chair behind the mahogany desk, looking two parts disappointed, one part heartbroken. Mom is in the paisley wingback beside mine, her cooked-spaghetti hair held back by a thin plastic headband. She wears her favorite terry cloth robe. Once a deep crimson, now it's faded and dull, the color of rust.

Nearly a minute of silence drags by. Dad's gaze bores a hole through me. Mom picks a ragged cuticle, checked out as usual. I stare at the small cherry wood clock displayed prominently on the desk, a Father's Day gift personalized with a silver plaque. It's engraved with my dad's name—*Dr. Arthur Ryan*—and, smaller, *Love, Callie and Chloe.*

Chloe.

I concentrate on the chipped polish on my fingernails as a wave of sorrow rises in my chest. Pulling in a wheezy breath, I struggle to shove memories of my sister down.

I need out of this office, but Dad's watching me like a warden.

There are choices, and he presents them like gifts on a platter: Wild Expeditions, a Montana wilderness camp for troubled teens—*hostile, disobedient, performs below potential,* according to the glossy brochure—or Oregon with Aunt Lucy, Dad's younger sister who, early last year, bought a run-down Victorian that teeters on a coastal cliff. She's been working to renovate it into a bed-and-breakfast and, according to Dad, would love my help again this summer.

Choices.

"You've lost your motivation," he says, tapping the Wild Expeditions brochure. "I think you need distance to find it."

All at once I feel *too* stoned. Underwater, every movement slow and deliberate. Dad's muffled voice sloshes around in my head as I swallow the threat of a sob.

"That's it?" I say. "Montana or Oregon? Prison camp or indentured servitude?"

"Don't be dramatic, Calliope. Mom and I are trying to do what's best." He gestures between himself and my mom, who might as well be comatose. "You need a change of pace. Your grades have gone to hell, you've quit swimming, and more often than not, you're . . . *high*." He spits the word like it tastes rancid.

A petulant huff escapes me. "It's just weed."

Dad slams a fist down on the desk. "I won't tolerate it!"

A hand slips into mine. Cool, slender fingers, a ring with a diamond the size of a blueberry. Mom squeezes my palm; the gesture feels like solidarity, like she's worried about being sent away, too. For the first time in ages, I feel a kinship with her that extends beyond grief, beyond mutual substance abuse, beyond the crushing weight that accompanies failing Arthur Ryan.

"If you choose Montana," Dad says, "you'll fly out this weekend. If you choose to go to Lucy's—" His voice falters. He pauses until he's composed himself. "I'll drive you to Bell Cove tomorrow."

Bell Cove. A tiny Oregon beach town. I visited last summer with my sister, right after Lucy bought the Victorian she lovingly refers to as Stewart House. She'd gone through an ugly divorce the year before; her Los Angeles movie producer husband had trouble keeping his pants on, which resulted in a generous settlement, which turned Lucy into a homeowner. She invited Chloe and me to come, pitch in, swim, spend some time away from our parents, away from Seattle. We thought Lucy was glamorous, an enigma. We jumped at her invitation.

I can't go to Montana, but I can't go back to Oregon, either.

"Dad, *please*."

"I'm sorry." He glances at my glassy-eyed mom and sighs. "It's just too hard."

I get it—I do. It's torture for my parents, looking at me every day, an older, blonder version of the daughter who was taken from them. No wonder Dad's exhausted, losing weight, tense. No wonder Mom can't wade out of her merlot sea. They lost one daughter, but that doesn't mean they won't set the other loose for the family's greater good.

"There's got to be another way," I say, panic blooming in my chest. "Let me stay. I'll do whatever it takes!"

"Callie, you're not being punished," Dad says, his tone gentle now. "Mom and I love you, but something has to change. Think of this summer as an opportunity to work on yourself."

He rises from his chair and circles his desk, headed for the door. With a hand on the knob, he turns, looking far older than his forty-four years. He gives his head a sad shake. Sending me away might break him, but I know my dad—his convictions are unwavering.

"You'll let me know what you decide first thing in the morning," he says before walking out of the office.

Every night, I sneak into the memorial that was Chloe's room. I lie on her bed and pretend I can still detect her scent—clean lilac with a trace of swimming pool chlorine. I talk to her, though she doesn't talk back.

She's gone, an iridescent bubble, light and breezy, suddenly—carelessly—burst.

She doesn't talk back, but I pray for a noise, a sensation, a glimmer of light. An indication she's still with me. A sign that communicates, *I forgive you.*

I pull her crocheted blanket up and over my shoulders, the woolen yarn scratchy against my neck. If I close my eyes, I can almost convince myself that she's here, demanding I give her blanket back and then, ever so sweetly, begging me to take her out for mochas.

Her bedroom, frozen in time, has walls plastered with posters of Olympic swimmers showing off shiny medals. Its closet holds dozens of drag suits stored alongside a basket of swim caps and goggles, plus running leggings and a wealth of sneakers. Its bed is, charmingly, populated by a menagerie of stuffed animals. Her favorite, a threadbare pig called Piggy, shares the pillow on which my head rests.

"Dad thinks it's best I go away for the summer," I whisper. "He and Mom need room to be sad, to figure out how to go on. Dad thinks I do, too. Like a trip to Montana or Oregon will help me stop missing you."

At my mention of Oregon, a memory finds me: my sister and me last summer, in Bell Cove, not long after we arrived at Lucy's, before everything fell apart. We'd joined our aunt in her enormous bed, sharing a bowl of popcorn studded with M&M's, and a liter of Mountain Dew split between three tumblers. We were in the midst of an eighties movie marathon.

"I'm so glad you girls came down," Aunt Lucy said, picking a yellow M&M from the popcorn to toss into her mouth.

"So are we," Chloe said. "Bell Cove's got Seattle beat any day of the week."

I wasn't sure about that. I missed my swim team and my Acura and my boyfriend. But it *was* fun, being with my sister and my aunt. Refreshing to escape the city and its expectations.

Lucy paused the movie—one of her favorites: *Can't Buy Me Love.*

"Promise you'll come back next summer," she said. "I'd love to have you both here when I open the B&B."

Chloe, eternally impulsive, was already nodding. She'd turned fifteen a few weeks prior, and sitting beside her on Lucy's bed, I barely felt the year and a half that separated us. She'd matched my height months prior and filled out before that. Her hair was strawberry blond while mine is so pale it's nearly white, but we were sometimes mistaken for twins.

"Let's wait and see—" I started, but Lucy cut me off with a handful of popcorn to the face.

"I know summers are sacred," she said, "but it's not like I'm a tyrant when it comes to getting things done. You've had fun so far, right?"

"Right," I allowed. "But next summer's the one before my senior year. Who knows what I'll have going on?"

"Nothing more important than your aunt and your sister," Chloe said. Of course she was cool with committing to a second summer in Bell Cove. She could run and swim and bike anywhere. Plus, like me, she was romanced by the shabby, old house; the relaxed, oceanside way of life; and the almost absolute autonomy Lucy allowed us. We may have had a little home improvement to knock out in return, but compared with the rigors of school and swim team, Lucy's was a vacation. Chloe thrust her tumbler in my direction, splashing soda onto the duvet. "Next summer," she said. "Bell Cove. You and me and the B&B. Promise."

"Fine," I relented, because I'd been double-teamed by two of the most stubborn people in my world. I clanked my cup against my sister's, then my aunt's. "Next summer. Bell Cove it is."

Chloe grinned, satisfied. Lucy restarted *Can't Buy Me Love.*

An oath sworn over popcorn and Mountain Dew.

I'd keep my word regardless, but the reality is, a summer at my aunt's is a lesser evil than a summer in Montana, where I'd undoubtedly have my heart pried open and pored over by a bunch of well-intentioned strangers. The idea of stepping inside Stewart House again fills me with breathtaking anxiety, and there's no denying that Lucy and I aren't in the best place these days, but I'll go to Bell Cove.

Because she needs me.

Because my parents don't.

Because I made a promise to my sister.

Chloe was morning bedhead, races in the pool, petty arguments, and relentless laughter.

Sometimes, I'm desperate to remember, to *dissolve* into remembering. Sometimes, I want to light my memories on fire, so they burn until nothing's left but ash and despair.

Guilt is a vulture.

Guilt picks me apart.

Guilt never, ever flies away.

2

I can't remember the last time I spent three uninterrupted hours alone with my dad.

We left the Seattle skyline after a late lunch with Mom, who sat at the table rubbing her temples, nursing a hangover, no doubt. She teared up when she hugged me goodbye; I was so stunned by the uncharacteristic display of emotion, I hardly hugged her back.

Dad and I've been hurtling, meteorlike, toward Bell Cove since.

When we at last pull off the highway, he lowers the Tahoe's windows, as he did last summer, when he drove Chloe and me to Lucy's. Salty air billows through the cab, blowing my hair across my face as we roll into civilization.

Bell Cove—quaint, touristy, reeking of charm. I'd almost forgotten.

Dad, casual in khaki slacks and a white button-down, steers onto Sitka Street, Bell Cove's main drag. Chloe and I didn't spend much time in the town itself, but I remember its clean sidewalks, lined with squat buildings, tawny-shingled facades and white trim. The street signs are hunks of weathered wood painted with names like Spruce, Douglas, Cypress, and Pine. There are two stoplights on Sitka, and no golden arches or Starbucks mermaids to be seen.

Delightful, I think, blowing out a weary breath.

"Cal," my dad says, interrupting the silence that's hovered like a storm cloud since we left Seattle. "It won't be so bad."

Cal. I can read his moods by the way he addresses me. Usually, I'm Callie, but it's my full name, Calliope, pronounced sternly, when I've done something to upset him. He saves Cal for the times he's feeling lighthearted, or when he's trying to force lightheartedness.

He gives me a strained smile. "It'll be a *good* summer. Maybe you'll make some friends."

I glance out the window. Gray-haired seniors stroll the sidewalks, along with moms and dads chasing children who scamper about. New friends? Doubtful, even if I was interested.

"Lucy's excited to have you back," Dad says. "I know she's looking forward to your company. Your help, too."

He's trying so hard to be conversational, and maybe I should attempt to do my part, but I wish he'd just button it.

Through a break in the storefronts, the vast Pacific Ocean comes into view. The beach is edged with dunes, and waves crash against the sandy shore. The sky blends with the shimmering water, camouflaging the horizon line.

Last year I thought this view was beautiful.

My dad eases his foot onto the brake for yet another stop sign. "Lots of people taking advantage of the sunshine," he says as a family of four steps onto the crosswalk in front of us. They're coming in from the beach, flip-flopped feet dragging, lugging armfuls of colorful towels and plastic sand toys. They meander down Sitka. Father, mother, and two little girls, sisters, in matching swimsuits and floppy sun hats.

For a moment, my sorrow's too thick to breathe through.

Dad's noticed them, too. He grips the steering wheel so tightly the tendons in his hands go colorless. The car behind us gives a polite honk because we've been stopped too long, and he lets his foot off the brake, glancing at me with a reluctant smile.

"I wish it could be different," he says.

He wants so badly for Mom and me to take a stab at positivity. To make a go at reclaiming normalcy. To *get better*. But I don't know how to be anything but what I am: stuck. The therapist I was pushed into visiting last year spoke a lot about grief. She went on about how it's a process, an emotional journey people make at their own inconstant pace. Except, I'm not on a journey. I'm not moving at all.

Instead of traveling through grief, I've become it.

We pass the bookstore, a few art galleries, the Green Apple Grocery, and countless souvenir stores. Then the picturesque shops give way to a residential area. Manicured lawns, white picket fences, baskets of geraniums hanging from the eaves of front porches. An old man walks his well-groomed schnauzer down the sidewalk, stopping to give my father a smile and a wave as we roll past.

I slouch farther down, wary of being noticed and evaluated in my dark jeans, tar-colored tank, Black Currant nail polish, and ceaseless frown. It's only a matter of time before I'm pegged the newest, sulkiest resident of Bell Cove.

The Tahoe picks up speed as we continue south, following Sitka as it ascends a hill that quickly becomes steep. Soon, Dad makes a turn into Lucy's driveway, a bumpy lane overlaid with gravel, and then, standing among towering evergreen trees and masses of overgrown shrubs, Stewart House looms.

"Victorian" paints pictures of gingerbread shingles, fanciful turrets, and ornate moldings. Pretentious. Lucy's house—a dusty blue with white trim—has those classic characteristics, but just like last summer, it looks shabby. Chipped and faded, broken spindles across the porch railing, a network of cracks spreading across one of the attic windows.

"Hasn't changed much," Dad says, pulling to a stop behind his sister's Range Rover. He unbuckles his seat belt and states the obvious: "You and Lucy have your work cut out for you."

The front door swings open, and there she is, Lucy, stepping onto the porch, squinting through the late-afternoon light. In her midthirties, she has so many freckles her skin appears perpetually tan. Her eyes shine even bluer than mine, and red corkscrew curls waterfall down her back. If she wasn't grinning and waving zealously, I'd say she looks like Medusa.

"Shall we?" Dad asks, pocketing his keys.

I leave the Tahoe for the gravel drive, wondering whether Lucy's done anything with the house's interior since I was last here. It's weird: Now's the first time I've felt remotely interested in anything—with the exception of smoking—for a significant stretch of time. The long dormant inquisitiveness quickly morphs into discomfort, though, like shoving my foot into a shoe I haven't worn in years.

I dread stepping into Stewart House.

Still, I reach into the back seat to retrieve my suitcase, operating on autopilot. Dad expects me to take my things from the Tahoe. He expects me to move them into Stewart House. He expects me to help Lucy in all the ways that matter. He expects me to *try* to get better.

"Leave it," he says, nodding toward my bag. "I'll come back for it later."

I grab my backpack instead, which holds my laptop and a few other essentials, and force my feet to follow Dad's path through the overgrown grass leading to the house. Lucy's rocking black leggings and a yellow off-the-shoulder top. She bounds over and throws her arms around me. Her hug is warm, and her scent is familiar, lavender laced with nicotine.

"I'm so glad you're here," she murmurs, squeezing me tight. I almost smile before I remember myself and pull away.

Dad hugs her next. They're ten years apart, and while Lucy's never been geographically close, he looks out for her. In the months after her divorce, he called her all the time, and after they'd hang up, he'd have no shortage of disparaging remarks to grumble about her ex. Last summer, when she fled Seattle after Chloe's wake, hunkering down here in Bell Cove, supposedly tackling her remodel with renewed fervor, he was quick to excuse her. "This is rough for all of us," he'd say anytime I criticized her absence. "Everyone copes in their own way."

He's more gracious than I'll ever be.

"I fixed a light dinner," Lucy says now. "You'll stay, right, Arthur?"

"I suppose. I'm eager to see what this money pit looks like inside."

Lucy's grin reshapes itself into something smug. "You might be surprised." She opens the front door, white with two panels of colorful stained glass, with a flourish.

She's obviously left the outside of the house to wither over the last year, devoting her efforts to its interior. Last summer, the only rooms that were livable were Lucy's master suite and the first-floor bedroom Chloe and I shared. The foyer had been a mess, the kitchen gutted, with only a dented fridge and a hot plate, and the parlor was a particleboard shell. The rooms upstairs, which are supposed to house eventual B&B guests, had been a combined dumping ground.

Now, the walls of the foyer are paneled in whitewashed wood, and the floor is covered in glossy planks. There's a rocking chair in the corner, draped with a patchwork quilt of faded reds, whites, and blues.

"I've done a lot downstairs," Lucy tells us. "But the second floor still needs some serious attention. Callie, that's where I'll need you."

It hurts physically, standing in this house without my sister, like a piece of my soul being slowly excised. Last year she shoved me out of the way before dashing toward our room at the back of the house, whooping, ready to snag the best bed and lay claim to the majority of the wardrobe's hanging space.

Now I'll get whichever bed I want. I'll use every hanger in the wardrobe. I'll get to spend the summer an only child, exactly as I've never wanted.

Light-headed and miserable, I touch the quilt, its fabrics frayed, its seams unraveling.

I remind myself to breathe.

"Let me show you the kitchen," Lucy says.

She pushes through the double doors, and I'm taken aback by the transformation: stainless steel appliances, clean white cabinets, and countertops of black granite. Lucy, quietly satisfied by our dropped jaws, points Dad and me to the table, reclaimed wood and artfully mismatched chairs, then takes plates loaded with sandwiches, pickles, and fruit out of the fridge.

I pick at my sandwich's crust while my dad and aunt dig in.

"I've had contractors and carpenters in and out of here for months," Lucy says. "They've done everything I can't—plumbing, electrical, heavy lifting." She turns to me, her attention snagging briefly on the blemish that mars the inside of my right forearm, a pearlescent scar zigzagging halfway to my elbow. She frowns, then adjusts her line of vision, her big hoop earrings swaying. "Everything that's left will be up to you and me, Callie."

"I'll do my best," I say.

Lucy nods and eyes my dad. "How's Susie?"

"She's well," he says, putting down his sandwich. I focus on my plate; good rarely follows talk of my mom.

"I'm glad. The last time I saw her, she . . . wasn't herself."

The last time Lucy saw my mom was the day Chloe was buried. Immediately after the service, Mom got fall-down drunk and ended up passing out even before our house was clear of company. "Wasn't herself" is the understatement of the century and, God, I want to say so, but Dad ignores Lucy's flaky comment so, begrudgingly, I do, too.

My aunt bites into her pickle, then presses again about Mom. "Why didn't she come to Bell Cove today? I would've loved to see her."

Dad blinks. He almost always gives his sister a free pass, but his tone is brusque when he says, "She wasn't up for the trip."

"Ah, I see."

I need Lucy to let it go—Mom's mental health is none of her business—but at the same time, I'd like to see Dad admit the truth. Because unless staring impassively at family photos, hyperventilating at the mention of my sister, and carting around a bottomless glass of wine beginning at lunchtime and ending whenever she happens to fall into bed are *well*, Mom's not.

Unfortunately, behavior-modifying summer camp isn't an option for a woman in her forties.

Dad pushes his plate back, takes a swig from his glass of iced tea, and stands. "It's getting late. I'll grab your suitcase, Callie, and then I need to get back on the road."

"So soon?" Lucy asks.

"I don't want to be away from Susannah for too long," he says, pounding the final nail into his coffin of failed deception.

"No, of course not," Lucy says. Softly, she adds, "I'm sorry, Arthur."

Dad nods once, then looks at me. "Finish up, Callie."

I'm being treated like I'm not old enough to participate in their conversation, but its underlying theme is clear: My family is broken and in need of fixing.

3

After retrieving my suitcase, Dad gives me a long hug, murmuring, "Please, Calliope, be safe," before kissing the top of my head and climbing into the Tahoe.

Then he's off.

I stand on the porch, watching the taillights until they disappear into the trees.

Alone in Bell Cove. No Dad, no Mom.

No Chloe.

There's a tightness in my throat, one I know well. One that preludes tears.

I swallow, imagine my spine a rod of steel, and go back into the house.

Standing in the kitchen entryway, I watch Lucy line dishes in the dishwasher, then wipe down the countertops. She should've been present for my parents and me this last year. Instead, she holed up here, creating a beautiful home for herself. I don't want to be bitter. She has reasons for behaving the way she does—rationally, I know as much—but shuttering my disappointment, my *hostility*, away feels like an enormous task.

By the time she finishes lighting the jarred candle on the island and turns to face me, I've regained a fragile hold on my emotions.

She smiles. "Let me show you to your room."

It's a gratuitous offer, because I know exactly where my room is, but I don't hate the notion of her walking me down the hall, opening the door, and leading me inside.

It's different.

Where there used to be two twin beds, one is now the room's focal point, a four-poster queen dressed with a fluffy down comforter. The standing mirror I last saw in shards scattered across the floor has been replaced by a wall-mounted version, framed in filigree. There's a small writing desk, new, with a vase of flowers: tulips and daisies, baby pink roses. The wardrobe has been moved into the far corner. Maybe Narnia lies beyond its carved doors; I make a mental note to check later. Through the pair of windows, there's a wide-open view of the ocean and the slowly sinking sun.

"You have Wi-Fi, and there are fresh towels in the bathroom," Lucy tells me, turning on the lamp that sits on the nightstand. She doesn't mention the changes, the adjustments she must've made to save me the grief of remembering this room as it was when Chloe was alive.

"Okay."

"Will you be comfortable in here?"

"I think so," I say, and then I catch an unfortunate glimpse of myself in the mirror. I look rumpled and unkempt. Wasted.

I move past the lone bed to one of the windows. The glass is droopy, the view distorted: the blue plane of the ocean warped, the sharp edge of the cliff at the far end of the yard wavy. I run my fingertips over the surface, mesmerized by bubbles that look like trapped crystals.

Last summer, I was too busy to notice them.

"Windows were made differently a hundred years ago," Lucy says, stepping closer. She taps the glass with a finger. "Some consider the bubbles flaws, but I like them."

I nod, curiosity overriding my reticence. "This house is a hundred years old?"

"Nearly a hundred and twenty. Built in 1902."

A quiet mewing drifts into the room. Lucy's face lights up. "That's my Daisy. I rescued her a few months ago from the woods. Hopefully, she won't bother you."

"No, I like cats." I peek past her into the hallway, but there's no sign of Daisy.

"Anyway," Lucy says, "I've read up on the Stewart family over the last year. Joseph Stewart, the man who had this house built, was a banker from Portland. Apparently, he had quite a reputation." She walks to the bed and drops onto it with a little bounce. She's gorgeous, though in her leggings, baggy top, and bare feet, she carries an effortless air. "He picked this hill because he wanted privacy. Turns out the Stewarts were a calamity all the way up through the generations. The last of them, one of Joseph's distant nephews, died here about ten years ago."

I fold my arms and lean against the wall, feigning boredom, listening raptly.

"I hear he was a drinker," Lucy goes on. "I hear that's all he did, which explains why the house was such a mess. It was willed to one of the remaining Stewarts, a doctor who lives in Eugene, but she didn't want anything to do with it. It sat empty, neglected, for a lot of years, until she put it on the market. You'll see when we start working upstairs—she didn't even bother to clean out her relatives' belongings. There wasn't much interest until I came along."

"Why'd you want it?"

Her expression becomes pensive. "After my marriage fell apart, I needed a break from Los Angeles. I needed a project to keep myself busy. Moving to Oregon, buying this house, turning it into a B&B . . . I'm chasing a dream."

I'm wondering why she never shared any of this last summer, with Chloe and me, when a gray-and-white cat slinks up to the doorway, assesses me and the room, then gives a purposeful *meow*. Her slate eyes are marble-round, and her tail's fluffed up. She hisses once, not at me—the stranger in her home—but at the wardrobe.

"Daisy! What's gotten into you?" Lucy says, rising from the bed.

The cat backs away, then turns and bolts down the hallway, paws slipping almost comically before they find purchase on the polished hardwood.

"It's just Callie, you crazy kitty," Lucy calls after her. She shakes her head, baffled. "I'll properly introduce you two later. She's really very sweet."

I shrug. Maybe animals sense sadness the way they sense approaching storms; I wouldn't want to be around me, either.

"So what are you up for tonight?" Lucy asks. "Movie? I have some board games we could dig out. Or we could hang out with a couple of books."

A vague memory needles its way into my mind. Christmastime, several years ago, after Grandma died, but well before Chloe and I visited

Bell Cove. Lucy's husband was shooting a movie in the remote Canadian wilderness, so she spent the holidays at our house. During the ten days she was with us, she took over Mom's bedtime story routine, reading to my sister and me, the three of us in flannel pajamas, snuggled beneath a blanket on the living room couch. Lucy's curls smelled reliably of lavender, and Chloe's bony elbow always found its way into my ribs. The book was *Little House in the Big Woods*, a few chapters each night.

Once upon a time, I might have been seduced by the notion of my aunt and a stack of books in a fanciful Victorian. But this Victorian has too much history. Reliving it in jagged fragments this past hour has siphoned my energy.

I give a genuine yawn. "Honestly, I'm ready for bed."

"Oh," Lucy says, her tone betraying her disappointment. "Then how about tomorrow we have breakfast together before we start working?"

I nod. She hugs me again, but her embrace isn't as comforting as it was earlier. There's something rueful, piteous, about the way her arms encircle me now, something that makes me want to duck away from her touch.

When she steps into the hallway, I close and lock the door. Then I root through my suitcase for the meager stash of weed that escaped the search and seizure my dad carried out last night. I shove one of the heavy windows open, trying not to think about how displaced I feel, how badly I long to be at home, how desperately I miss my parents, and my sister.

I pack the bowl of the glass pipe Isaac gave me last August, a gift of contrition handed over before he moved back to San Diego to begin his freshman year of college, then draw in a stream of smoke. Closing my eyes, I hold it until my lungs burn, then blow a cloud into the darkening backyard.

For the first time all day, I don't feel like I'm floating away.

4

Daisy wanders through the crack in my door a long while later. I'm flat on my back on the bed, the *new* bed, staring at the subtly textured ceiling. She mews once before leaping up and lying down beside me. I stroke her back, glad I decided to open the door. She's a ball of soft, purring fur—nothing like the hissing creature I met earlier.

I think I like her.

I slide off the bed to check my phone—no calls, no texts, as usual—then plug its charger in and leave it to sit on the nightstand, where it'll likely remain all summer, unused. Sleepily, I change into a T-shirt and sweats. I'm pulling socks over my cold toes when Daisy lifts her head and lets out a moan. I reach out to pet her, placate her, but she's not having it. She vaults off the bed and darts out of the room, a gray streak of panic.

She's just disappeared down the dimly lit hallway when a clatter obliterates the house's silence. I whirl around to find my phone facedown on the floor, still tethered to the wall by its charger. My pulse races, thunderous in my ears. Stupid, because, holy hell, my phone fell—that's all. Stewart House is so old its floors probably aren't level.

Still, I glance around the room, making *certain* I'm alone.

A chill slithers up my spine as I notice the windows, curtains wide open. I try to remember if I pulled them shut after my smoke, before the night became so dark. I *thought* I did. But they've been open all this time, while I lay on the bed. While I changed clothes.

Stewart House is secluded, but I hate the idea of being so exposed. So vulnerable.

I hurry across the room and yank the curtains closed.

I can't shake Daisy's frantic exit or the seemingly spontaneous fall of my phone or the shiver of cold I felt a few moments ago. I consider finding Lucy, if only to share space with another human being, but quickly talk myself out of that idea.

I won't be chased out of this room I have to spend the summer in.

Throwing my shoulders back, I stride to the bathroom. Standing at the sink, I gather my hair into a ponytail and secure it with an elastic. I dig my toothbrush out of my toiletry bag and brush my teeth ferociously. With a generous squirt of cleanser, I scrub my face into a frothy mask, glowering at my reflection. Bending over, I rinse. I breathe deep, inhaling steam, letting lingering unease rush down the drain with sudsy water.

It's then, standing at the sink with my face dripping wet, that my ponytail rustles—as if a gust of wind has whipped through the small space.

I spin around, clutching my hands to where my heart sits frozen in my chest, water streaming down my face and neck, soaking the collar of my shirt.

I expect—*hope*—to find Lucy behind me.

The bathroom is empty.

I retreat to the parlor, where I spend the next half hour trying to get my blood to quit hammering my pulse points. I wrap a blanket around my shoulders, residually cold. My gaze stays fixed on the darkened hallway, watching for the slightest hint of movement.

Except, everything is still.

I keep telling myself: I smoked too much. I'm paranoid. There's no way what happened could've been real.

Right?

My grandma was a pragmatic woman, a lot like my dad, but she harbored a lifelong interest in the paranormal. There was a shelf on the bookcase in her living room that housed books with titles like *A Cultural History of the Occult* and *Apparitions: Our Silent Companions.* She used to watch shows about psychics and ghost hunters and the most haunted locations in America, and when I visited, I'd watch with her. She thought skepticism about the afterlife was the same as arrogance. Nobody *really* knows, so why not keep a mind open to possibility?

When I've climbed down from my high, when I've stopped shivering, when I'm *sure* there's no one lurking in a shadowy corner, I get up to scan the dozens of books Lucy's displayed on the parlor's built-in shelves. There's nothing about the supernatural, but I do find a tattered copy of *Little House in the Big Woods.* It's super late, but I curl up on the settee and spend some time with Laura and Mary and Ma and Pa, trying to replace my lingering restlessness with the pleasantness of their everyday

Wisconsin lives, trying *not* to think about how acutely this story is linked to my sister.

It's nearly dawn when I work up the courage to leave the parlor for my room. I steer clear of the bathroom and dive into the bed. Once I bury myself in soft cotton and down, I feel safer.

I dream of a gloomy cemetery. Headstones, ashen and crumbling, staring straight ahead. The grass is soggy, the sky liquid mercury, tossing up thunder and rain. Lightning illuminates graves, trees, bouquets of faded flowers left by long-ago mourners.

Laughter is so wrong in this place, but I hear it, cheerful and tinkling. I spin around to find the source of the sound, wet hair snaking across my face, and see my sister, wearing a yellow dress, walking among the headstones.

I call out, but she must not hear me. My feet sink into the earth as I step closer. "Chloe!"

She looks up, strawberry blond hair heavy and wet.

Sheets of rain pelt my skin. "Chloe, come here!"

For a moment, she stares.

And then, she turns and runs.

My heart splinters. My sister, my favorite person in the world, doesn't want to see me?

I follow, weaving through headstones, stepping around plaques set flush to the grass. She pulls to a stop at the edge of a grove of trees, her back heaving with the exertion of her dash. When she turns to face me, I see that her eyes, once blue like mine, have gone black. She clutches her chest, her mouth opening soundlessly.

"Chloe!" I scream into the wind.

I cover my face with my hands, raindrops mixing with tears.

It's a long time before I summon the nerve to look at her again. When I do, she's gone.

In her place stands a flower, face turned up, seeking sun.

Its petals are as red as blood.

5

I sit up in bed, the platinum light of morning washing over me.

It's been months since I've dreamed of Chloe. Of cemeteries. Of death. I wrap my arms around my middle, pinching my eyes shut.

When I open them a moment later, I find flowers on my nightstand. Red, centers of inky black. They're not in a vase like the flowers on the desk. Instead, they're tied with a long blade of grass, sitting near my phone. I pick them up and inhale the softest honey scent. They're eerily beautiful—just like the flower from my dream.

On some subconscious level, I must have noticed them before climbing into bed. I must have filed them away to conjure while I slept.

The flowers urge me up. I conduct a distanced examination of the bathroom—serene, still—before tiptoeing over the threshold and taking history's quickest shower. With the drapes in my room securely drawn, I dress for work, old cutoffs and a gray T-shirt. I consider a hoodie to cover my scar, but my aunt's acquainted with it. There's no point in suffering the humidity of this old house for vanity's sake. I tie my hair into a messy knot and, grabbing the spray of flowers, I head for the kitchen.

Lucy's up, wearing baggy jeans and an electric-pink tank. She's standing over a griddle, poking slices of French toast with a spatula. She's brewed coffee, which smells amazing. I pour myself a mug.

"You're up early," she says. "Sleep well?"

"Sure," I lie. I find a drinking glass in a cabinet near the sink and fill it with water, then submerge the flowers' stems.

"There's something about the ocean air, you know?" She gestures toward the flowers with her spatula. "Those are pretty. You like poppies?"

"I didn't realize that's what they are, but yeah. They're nice."

"There's a meadow out past the tree line where poppies bloom, hundreds of them at a time. You and I should hike out there one of these days."

"Yeah, maybe."

She goes back to the French toast, the bangle bracelets on her wrist clacking together as she works. I take a seat at the table, and after a few minutes of dense silence, Lucy slides breakfast in front of me. She plops down with a plate of her own and spears a bite. She holds it up in the air as if to exclaim, *Cheers!* "Fuel up," she says. "We've got a lot of cleaning to do."

I eat, mainly to avoid conversation. The French toast is sweet, with hints of cinnamon and vanilla, and the maple syrup drizzled over the top is delicious.

"How is it?" Lucy asks when my plate's nearly empty.

"Really good," I admit.

She flips her copper curls over her shoulder. "Your grandma taught me how to cook when I was about your age."

"Really? Dad can barely fry an egg."

"He was out of the house by then, absorbing culture in Greece."

"I don't get his obsession with that place."

Lucy sips her coffee. "It's the thing he's most passionate about. My thing used to be acting; now it's this house. Yours is swimming."

I look down at my plate, swirling my fork through sticky amber syrup, thinking about the outdoor lap pool in Bell Cove. Last summer, Lucy tried to get Chloe and me to work out there instead of in the ocean, but Chloe wasn't into it, and I never wanted to go without her.

I shiver, cold out of nowhere. Quietly, I say, "I quit swimming."

Lucy doesn't appear surprised, which means my dad told her. For a moment, I wonder if he mentioned my shitty grades and the weed, too, but for him, candor usually comes second to reputation. I doubt he wants my aunt to know how far I've actually fallen.

She gazes at me over the rim of her coffee mug. Her eyes fall to my arm. My scar, pink and prominent against my pale skin. "How come?"

"I'm not interested in it anymore. Not since . . ."

"Since Chloe died?"

I shake my head, my windpipe kinking like a hose. I don't want to have a conversation about my sister. Not with Lucy. Not with anybody.

She puts down her mug and tents her hands. "I know things at home have been intense, and I know I've been . . . away, but Chloe isn't a taboo topic. I think it might be good for you to talk about her."

I stare at my lap, praying she'll leave it alone.

"Really," she says, her voice dripping with sympathy. "I'm willing to listen."

She's dangerously close to hurdling over the line that separates inquisitive from intrusive. The tiny part of my brain that's still sensible knows her intentions are good, but the unreasonable part is screaming, *Lucy doesn't know you anymore!*

"You don't get it," I say.

"I get more than you think. In a way, I've lost my husband."

Her comment triggers an explosion of anger, and I stand so abruptly, with such force, my chair topples backward, banging against the floor. "You and your husband got *divorced*—he's alive and well. You left Seattle after Chloe's funeral. You bailed on us. On *me.* So don't pretend to understand what I'm going through now!"

Lucy stares at me, openmouthed, a flush climbing her neck.

I storm out of the kitchen before she can say another word.

6

I retreat to the porch, where the smell of cloyingly sweet French toast isn't gag-inducing. There are white rocking chairs lined in a row, as if Stewart House is an antebellum plantation instead of a beach-town Victorian. I choose the farthest rocker from the door and fall into it, fuming.

I wish I could talk to my sister about the last twenty-four hours: my strained ride with Dad, the changes inside Stewart House, my falling phone and the chilly drafts, Lucy's wacky clothes and heedless insensitivity, and Daisy, who's either hissing or purring. Chloe would ask for details about our aunt's eccentricities and her cat's mood swings, then giggle breathlessly and tease me about being scared last night. Remembering her laughter brings a torrent of emotion so powerful I have to pull my knees to my chest to contain it.

Closing my eyes, I inhale ocean air, listening to the faint sound of waves crashing against the rocks below the cliff out back.

I wonder how high we are. . . . fifty feet above the water? One hundred?

The crunching of tires on the gravel drive disturbs my relative peace. I peer through my lashes as the approaching vehicle comes into view, a cloud of dust trailing behind. It's one of those old Jeeps, a Wagoneer, I think, boxy and covered in hideous wood panels. I remain motionless, watching from my secluded corner of the porch.

The car comes to a screeching halt. A guy climbs out, wearing khaki shorts and a T-shirt the same pale blue as the sky. He slams the car door and hustles toward the house with a bounce in his step. Sinking lower into my chair, I pray he doesn't spot me; I lack the patience for a conversation with this apparently merry stranger.

As he gets closer, I see that he's younger than his car made me assume. A split second passes, during which I think, *Holy hell, he's adorable*, before recognizing what a frivolous thought that is. I have no business entertaining even the most innocent of romantic inclinations when I can barely stand my own existence. Still, I can't ignore his tall frame, his sun-bronzed skin, or his bleached hair, longish, in that shaggy, I-don't-give-a-shit style few pull off.

His footsteps fall heavy on the porch planks. He raises a fist to the front door. There's a pause, a moment of silence while I wait for his inevitable knock—which never comes. Instead, to my embarrassment, he turns and catches me staring from my remote rocking chair, as if I'm a stalker.

His smile is like a sunburst.

Heat floods my face.

He strolls over, then folds himself into the chair next to mine. His eyes are sea-glass green, sparkling in the morning light. He extends his hand in my direction and says, "Tucker Morgan. Lucy hired me as her landscape specialist, known also by its less glamorous title: yard boy."

His palm floats in front of my face while he waits for me to take a turn introducing myself. I don't, and I don't shake his hand, either.

He drops it to his lap.

It's not like I'm trying to be rude to this guy who seems generally affable, but I don't want anything to do with him.

"You're not going to tell me your name?" he asks.

I shrug. "It doesn't matter."

"Sure it does. If you're gonna be hanging around this summer, we'll probably see a lot of each other."

"What makes you think I'll be hanging around?"

He sizes me up, from the tips of my toes, higher, his eyes lingering a millisecond on my bare legs and the scooped neckline of my shirt. When he finds my scar, I wait for curiosity to seep into his expression. It doesn't, and I feel naked, suddenly, like Tucker Morgan can see all of me, inside and out.

"You look comfortable," he says. "I bet you'll be around awhile."

"Wrong. I'm visiting."

"Cool. You'll love Bell Cove."

I wrinkle my nose.

"City girl?" he guesses. When I don't confirm or deny, he continues. "I've lived here my whole life, which gives me the authority to tell you: Bell Cove is the shit."

The blind conviction in his voice gives me pause, and for the space of a second, I wonder if Bell Cove might really be an okay spot to hang out for a couple of months. Then I remember my prying aunt and my frightful night and the feeling of displacement that won't quit. I remember last summer, and the day my sister was found just down shore from Bell Cove.

This town sucks.

"Anyway," Yard Boy says, "if you get bored while you're visiting, you can, you know, tell me your name and then, if you want, maybe I can show you around town."

I'm preparing to shut him down—I don't want to hang out with him, or any boy, maybe not ever—when Lucy barges through the door, big hair and bigger jewelry. "That's a good idea!"

I tense; she's been eavesdropping. "It's not necessary."

She makes her way down the porch and leans against the rail, across from where I sit. "Sure it is. You can't sit around in the house all summer like a recluse, Callie."

"I can do whatever I want," I snap. "I came here to help you, not to explore." I look Tucker Morgan in the eye. "Not to make friends."

He's not smiling anymore.

"Oh, come on," Lucy says, tapping her coral-painted toes against mine, like we're best friends—or worse, sisters.

"I said no, okay? Would you just let it go?" I pop out of my chair, blowing past her and her stupid landscape specialist, and head for the house.

I slam the front door hard enough to rattle the stained glass in its frame.

7

I've had one boyfriend of significance, Isaac Park, who bulldozed into my world a month before the end of my sophomore year, when he and his parents moved into the home next door. The first time I saw him, he was sprawled in the grass out front, holding a beat-up clipboard, flipping through a stack of papers as a crew of movers traipsed between the huge truck parked at the curb and the house.

I spent a minute in my Acura watching the boy, who watched the crew haul cardboard boxes, sleek furniture, and an assortment of expensive-looking mountain bikes. Chloe should've been in the passenger seat, but she'd persuaded me to let her run the five miles home from the pool after swim practice because she was hard-core that way. As I sat, I cataloged my observations into what would quickly become a thick mental file: The boy's hair was dark, he was wearing gray chino shorts with a hoodie, and a pair of mirrored aviators hid his eyes.

One of the movers emerged from the back of the truck, calling out a number. Dutifully, if not apathetically, the boy drew a finger along the paperwork, then made a mark.

He was cute.

I got out of my car, slamming the door a little harder than necessary, ensuring he heard, guaranteeing he noticed.

He lifted his hand in a wave that tried and failed to be blasé. Even from behind those sunglasses, I felt his gaze track me as I moved down the driveway, along the sidewalk, and up the lawn toward where he sat.

"Neighbor?" he said.

"Neighbor," I confirmed.

"Isaac Park, formerly of San Diego."

"Callie Ryan. Lived here forever."

He appraised me without the pretense of discretion. "Getting home from school?"

"Swim practice. School let out a couple of hours ago. I go to North Seattle Prep."

"High school?"

I nodded. "Couple more years. You?"

"Just graduated."

"Lucky. We've still got weeks to go."

"Yeah, kinda nice to get a jump on summer. I'm starting at UCSD in the fall."

Back to San Diego—to attend a *university*. Two years isn't much of an age gap, but the fact that he was, for all intents and purposes, a college guy . . .

His appeal skyrocketed.

"I've heard that's a good school," I said, "though my dad's a professor at UW, so . . ."

"Go Huskies," Isaac said wryly, circling his pen through the air like a little streamer. I laughed, and he grinned, revealing a dimple that put all other dimples to shame. He pulled his sunglasses away, allowing me the full scope of his face, all tawny skin and honed angles. His eyes were deeply brown and slightly hooded, his brows thick and black as his hair. He said, "I like your smile, Callie Ryan."

He gestured to the patch of grass beside him.

I sat.

He told me about his dad, who's half Korean, half Irish, the biggest Padres fan on the West Coast; his PR firm had recently transferred him to Seattle. And then he told me about his mom, who'd been a New York City socialite until she left the East Coast for Southern California and, more recently, the Pacific Northwest. He marked numbers on the inventory as the crew marched up and down the driveway with his family's treasures. I listened, mesmerized, as he told me that he liked to read about famous athletes and that he couldn't wait to go mountain biking in the Cascades. He was an only child and glad about it, he said, and his parents were way cooler than any middle-aged duo had a right to be.

"Dad's at the office, and Mom's inside, directing traffic. Next time, I'll introduce you."

I smiled. There'd be a next time.

It's Tucker Morgan, not Lucy, who finds me in the kitchen ten minutes after my outburst. He joins me at the table, a safe two chairs away from where I sit, chipping Black Currant polish from my nails. He's plugged buds into his ears, a thin white cord trailing down, disappearing into the pocket of his shorts. Faintly, I hear the strains of "Better Man," an oldie that's easily recognizable because Pearl Jam is a Seattle institution; my parents used to listen to them, before, while working on dinner in the kitchen, or pulling weeds in the yard.

Such a good song.

As soon as the thought materializes in my head, Tucker pulls out his phone and turns off the music, tucking his earbuds into his pocket.

"So," he says. "You okay?"

I don't look at him, just continue chipping.

"No, I guess?"

In my periphery, I watch him glance around the kitchen, eyeing the poppies that remain in the center of the table, then the fruit bowl. He starts to reach for a peach before thinking better of it. "This is a nice house," he comments, his tenor like a curl of smoke in the sunlit kitchen.

God, his voice, I think, and then, *What is* wrong *with me?*

"I've never been inside," he tells me, like I care. A wayward flake of Black Currant lands on the table in front of him. Unfazed, he brushes it away. "Today's my first day of work. I'm not dreading it, to tell you the truth. Changing something neglected into something people will look at and appreciate . . . I mean, is there a better job?"

I want to tell him that, yeah, I can think of about a million, but I don't, lest he conclude that I, too, am a project in need of improvement. I'm starting to wonder how long he's going to keep up this one-sided conversation when he says, "So if Lucy can be trusted, your name's Callie?"

"Short for Calliope," I say, still focused on my fingernails.

"Greek muse or musical instrument?"

I look up, surprised he's heard of either. "Greek muse. My dad's obsessed with ancient Greece. Besides, the musical instrument is loud and big and abrasive."

His eyes spark with amusement. "Well, that's not you—not the loud or big parts, anyway."

I'm not sure why, but his comment makes me smile. The expression feels stiff, though, and I drop my gaze, embarrassed out of nowhere. My nails look horrible with their jagged patches of polish, and I hide my hands under the table, trying to recall the exact moment I stopped giving a shit about looking nice.

Tucker reaches for the peach he eyed before. It rolls in his outstretched hand. "Want one?"

"You're passing out my aunt's food now?" I ask, but I catch it when he tosses it my way.

It's good, sweet. Tucker polishes off his in all of two seconds, then places the pit on a paper napkin he snags from the stack in the center of the table. He fixes his gaze on me, and then I feel self-conscious, biting and chewing and swallowing in front of this disarmingly beautiful boy. I put my unfinished peach down next to his pit.

"No good?"

"I'm full."

"So, anyway," he says with a shrug, "I'm thinking we should start over. I mean, if you're here all summer, we're gonna run into each other sometimes and I, for one, don't want things to be uncomfortable."

The way he says all this, flashing a smile that could thaw glaciers, is too genuine to answer with irreverence.

"Okay," I say. "Let's start over."

Again, he sticks out his hand. "Tucker Morgan."

"Callie Ryan."

I slip my hand into his, surprised by the warmth of his palm, the firmness of his grip.

I pull quickly free, before I become swept away.

8

When Tucker heads outside to start taming the yard, I escape to my room. I bring the poppies and set them on my nightstand; they're too pretty to leave in the kitchen, where Lucy might enjoy them. I know I'm going to have to face her and get to doing some actual work eventually, but some time to cool off won't hurt either of us.

Everything in my room is as I left it: the wardrobe, the desk, the bed—an unavoidable reminder that I'm no longer half of a pair—and the mirror. I *hate* the mirror. It's bad enough, recalling the original and why Lucy had to replace it, but this new mirror's clear cast throws back my likeness with staggering clarity. I shirk past the sad girl's reflection, draw the curtains, and curl up on the bed, enormous and cold and lonely. The light is dim and the air is cool, and there's a constant, quiet *tap-tap-tapping.* Drafty old house, Daisy playing, wind rustling the tall trees.

I'm off course, having just encountered an intriguing boy.

The last time this happened, I couldn't wait to tell Chloe. Except, she beat me to it.

"I met someone," she'd said, bursting into my room.

She was incandescent, wearing a nightgown, an old favorite she refused to give up, her hair freshly washed and twisted into a knot. She'd been distracted through dinner, ignoring Mom's chatter about how she'd just planted summer squash and lettuce in the backyard garden, shrugging off Dad's concern about her running home from the pool by herself, but now she was focused, situating herself on the end of my bed, folding her fawn legs beneath her.

"Really?" I said, putting my bio homework aside.

"After my run. Get this—he's *our new neighbor.*"

Her eyes glittered, as if such good fortune was unheard of. Her interest in romance, in boys, was new and innocent and sweet. I wasn't about to flatten it, but I couldn't pass up an opportunity to tease her, either.

"Isaac," I said, nudging her with my foot. "Dibs."

"Callie!"

I laughed. "I talked to him when I got home from practice. He's nice, right?"

"*So* nice."

"And cute."

"*So* cute."

"And . . . old."

Chloe rolled her eyes. "Not that old."

"Ancient. He's going to college in California in the fall."

"He told me. Also, he thinks it's badass that I'm training for a triathlon."

"If only Dad felt the same."

She groaned. "He gave me such a hard time while we were doing the dishes. He was all, 'I just don't understand why you can't swim exclusively, like your sister. It's *dangerous*,'" she said emphatically, mimicking Dad's disapproving baritone with impressive accuracy. "'Cavorting around the city alone. What if you're hit by a car? And during the triathlon, what if you crash on your bike? What if another swimmer takes you under?'" She'd giggled then, as if our dad's fretting was unfounded and absolutely hilarious.

"Have you registered yet?"

"Last week. I used birthday money from Aunt Lucy for the fee." She was lucky her birthday fell when it did; fifteen was the minimum age for athletes entering the Seattle Summer Triathlon, held Labor Day weekend annually.

"Dad might be ticked," I warned.

"It'll be worth it. Swim team is cool, but I'm starting to feel like a hamster on a wheel, blowing through all those sets, going literally nowhere."

I pulled an indignant face.

"No, no," she recanted. "I love that *you* love swim team, and I think you should stick with it—you're too good to give it up."

"You're good, too. In a couple of months, you'll probably be faster than me."

She shook her head, her gaze drifting around my room, snagging on the trophies and medals displayed on the wall across from my bed. "I need something else," she said. "Something different. Something all mine."

"I get it," I told her, though I didn't. I liked that we were both swimmers, both students at North Seattle Prep, both regularly annoyed with our loving but overbearing parents.

We were the Ryan girls. A twosome.

"You could register for the triathlon, too," Chloe said. She'd detected, as usual, my hesitancy to speak the truth. Another difference: My sister favored honesty, while I defaulted to courtesy.

"No way. Dad's right: *so* dangerous."

She smiled, though her tone was apologetic. "When I said I wanted something all mine, I didn't mean—"

"No, I know. The triathlon's about you, and what a badass you're becoming."

She moved quickly, a snake's sudden strike, and poked me in the ribs. "Isaac thinks so."

Isaac did think so. Not long after, he started giving Chloe pointers on biking, going so far as to join her on some of her training rides. My parents liked that she wasn't out alone. My sister liked that she had a hot guy pedaling beside her.

I roll onto my side, uncomfortable on this unfamiliar mattress, in this unfamiliar house.

Disoriented.

Sometimes I fall into memories so vivid and powerful, so full of Chloe's spirit, I forget, for a few minutes, that she's really gone. Resurfacing—*remembering*—is the same as losing her all over again, an endless cycle of daydreams and dashed hopes.

In need of a diversion, I give myself permission to think of Tucker Morgan, all floppy hair and cheerful smiles. I waste a few minutes conjuring stories about his youth, deciding his parents were once into the grunge scene, before he crashed into their lives and forced them toward a more conservative existence. Reasonably intelligent, the Tucker of my imagination is considering college but wants to see how he feels about lawn mowers, rakes, and climbing roses before committing to higher education. And so he's taken up work as Bell Cove's most promising Yard Boy.

For the first time since arriving in Bell Cove, I relax and drift into a dreamless sleep.

9

A draft.

My whispered name.

Cold fingertips ascending my arm.

I lurch into wakefulness. The sun throws prisms of light across the floor. The curtains are wide open, though I'm sure I closed them before I lay down.

Sure.

Someone came into my room while I slept. Someone opened the drapes and breathed my name and touched my arm and then . . . disappeared?

I shudder.

My stomach rumbles.

God, I'm such a disaster.

As I swing my legs over the side of the bed, I notice a swim cap on my nightstand. It's sitting harmlessly next to the poppies, black, with my old club team's logo—a stylized swimmer racing freestyle, feet kicking up a plume of water—in shades of aqua and cerulean.

It wasn't there before I fell asleep.

Gingerly, I pick it up. I have a half dozen caps exactly like this at home. There's one in my backpack, too, plus a pair of goggles, in case hell freezes over and I decide to go for a swim.

Chloe had caps identical to this one, too.

I cross the room to the wardrobe and dig into my backpack. My fingers find silicone, and I pull out the cap I packed.

It's the other's twin.

In the chaos of my departure last summer, I must have left a swim cap behind. Or maybe Chloe left one lying around. We both used these exact caps for our ocean swims, favoring them over latex options because silicone is insulating. So this cap spent the last year at Stewart House. Lucy found it and set it out for me. Because she thought I might want it? Or because she thought it would nudge me into conversation?

A knock sounds from the hallway.

"Just a sec," I call, dropping the cap I brought back into my backpack. I hurry across the room and shove the found cap into the nightstand's drawer.

Out of sight, out of mind.

Screw Lucy and her prodding.

I open the door to my aunt and spend a second examining her expression. Is she waiting for me to mention the cap? Pour my heart out about how much I miss my sister? Yell at her, again, for interfering?

She invites me to join her for lunch.

I'm starving and she's suitably repentant, so I follow her to the kitchen for a quiet meal.

"I started upstairs while you were resting," she says, pushing the leftover bits of her tuna fish sandwich into Daisy's bowl.

"Before or after you came into my room and opened the curtains?"

She gives me a quizzical look. "I didn't open the curtains."

"I closed them before I fell asleep. They were open when I woke up."

Pity shines in her eyes. "I wouldn't invade your privacy. You're remembering wrong."

"I don't think so," I say, but now she's got me second-guessing my recollection.

I don't mention the swim cap.

She stacks our plates atop each other. "Now that you've eaten, do you feel like working with me upstairs?"

I nod, tired all over again.

Lucy looks relieved, like she was worried I'd refuse to help, forcing her to take a stab at discipline. She leaves our dishes in the sink, grabs a folder from the counter, and drags me upstairs.

Chloe and I hardly came up here last summer, but I know there are six bedrooms, and now I can see they're in the same terrible shape they were in a year ago. Ugly wallpaper, sheets draped over furniture, cobwebs dangling from corners. One room's become a storage space, stuffed with piles of junk. Lucy tells me it'll all need to be sorted and either purged or moved to the third-floor attic.

"We'll name the rooms after the six original Stewart children," she says as we walk down the hallway. "Thomas, Theodore, Gabriel, Abigail, Savannah, and Victoria. We'll do each room in a color of the rainbow, but not in a tacky, obvious way," she's quick to clarify. "It'll be lovely."

She leads me into the room she's calling the Abigail. The furniture has been pushed to the middle of the space, and the floor is mostly covered by drop cloths. The walls are bare, with the exception of bold flower-print wallpaper.

"Sit," she says, dropping down on a clear patch of floor.

I join her. She opens her folder between us. There are swatches of fabric stapled inside, along with dozens of paint samples in every imaginable shade of red. There's a detailed floor plan drawn on graphing paper, and magazine cutouts of everything from a large braided rug to prints for the walls.

"So," she says breathy and animated—nerve grinding. "This is my vision, but if you have ideas, we can make adjustments."

I don't mention that I know nothing about interior design, and I keep quiet about how I have zero stake in this house and its aesthetic. She's trying, and despite our rocky morning, I'll try, too.

I point to a paint chip. Red, like blood. "This is nice."

"You don't think it's too much for the walls?"

I shrug. "It's a big room. It could be cool."

"That's what I was thinking. Why not go all out?" Her grin becomes a grimace. "But first, we have to clean."

She shows me how to scrub the moldings with a bucket of soapy water and a thick sponge, then she tows an old boom box into the room and pops in a CD of eighties power ballads. We set to work, me scrubbing, Lucy prying nails and picture hooks from the walls with the claw end of a hammer. She pauses occasionally to dance and twirl to the dramatic strains of Bon Jovi and Mötley Crüe, her hammer doubling as a microphone. I do my best to ignore her random dance fits and focus on dipping the sponge, scrubbing, and dipping again.

Lucy lets me get away with silence for a good twenty minutes before she's compelled to start in with the questions. "So, Tucker . . . What do you think?"

"What difference does it make?"

"None, but—"

"He's here to work on the yard, right?"

She frowns. "I thought it'd be nice for you to meet someone close to your age."

"*That's* why you hired him?"

"Well, no, but—"

"I'm not interested in meeting anyone. My age or otherwise."

"You should make the most of your summer, Callie. Bell Cove's not a bad place."

Says the woman who moved here to escape Los Angeles and her messy divorce. Of course Bell Cove is appealing, compared with *her* alternative.

She dances over to dip an extra sponge in the bucket so she can help me scrub. "Did I tell you I joined a book club?" she asks over screeching guitar riffs.

"No," I say, hoping she's not about to invite me into its membership. "But that explains the library-worthy collection in the parlor."

"The moderator, Shirley, owns the bookstore in town. We can go one day, if you want."

I sigh—I can't help it—and answer with a noncommittal "Maybe."

She drops her sponge into the bucket and wipes her hands on her jeans, facing me like she's got something epic to say. "This morning, at breakfast, and on the porch . . . I know it's difficult for you, being here. You're so much like your dad when it comes to hard things—you lock your feelings up tight—but I shouldn't have pushed."

I nod, thinking about how *not* alike Dad and I are. He's been so stoic since my sister died. He goes to work and brings home dinner and rushes around to pick up the balls my mom and I regularly drop. He sees a counselor and visits Chloe at the cemetery. Nothing seems to rattle him—not Mom's drinking, not his surviving daughter using drugs in his house, not his sister, backhandedly provoking him during what was supposed to be a pleasant meal. Compared with Dad, I'm a catastrophe.

With renewed fervor, I scrub the molding around one of the Abigail's large windows. A flash of color in the yard grabs my attention. Tucker Morgan, pushing an ancient mower. I watch furtively, rubbing my sponge over an already clean patch of molding. He's making neat lines across the wild lawn, trimming it into something like a golf course green.

If I'm thinking like a normal teenage girl, I can admit that he seems nice enough. But as I told my aunt, it doesn't make a difference.

He's out of bounds.

10

The next morning, after a mercifully uneventful night and a check-in phone call with my dad, I share a subdued breakfast with Lucy. After, she clears her cereal bowl from the table and says, "I'm off to Green Apple Grocery. Would you get a start sorting up in the Gabriel? Trash the obvious junk. Stow anything interesting in the attic. I'll take a look when I get back."

I ditch my own dish in the sink and trudge up the stairs. In the stale air of the Gabriel, I pick a box, sink to the floor, and pull the cardboard flaps open. Dust plumes skyward. I sneeze. I find documents: old electric bills and bank statements addressed to Clayton Stewart, dated in the mid-2000s. This must be the man Lucy mentioned my first night back—the last Stewart to live here. The last Stewart to die here. I use a Sharpie to mark the cardboard TRASH and shove it unceremoniously aside.

The next box is full of back issues of *National Geographic*. I flip through one, glossy pages slipping through my fingers. There was a time not so long ago when I loved these magazines, their lengthy, detailed articles and gorgeous photography. My dad subscribes and saves them; there are more than a hundred lining the shelves of his office back home. But there's no room for old magazines at Stewart House. TRASH.

Box number three is a relative gold mine: a collection of old CDs. The Police, the Cure, U2, even Bon Jovi. Lucy will be thrilled; whomever this stuff belonged to must be her musical soul mate.

Under the CDs are photographs. Mostly black-and-white, old and poor quality. I shuffle through the piles, examining the old-fashioned clothing and vintage cars, looking for rhyme or reason. There doesn't seem to be an organizational system, though: Pin curls mingle with beehives, high ponytails, and flips.

At the bottom of the box, there's a manila envelope. I tear the closure, and more photos fall into my lap. These are different, full-color and more modern, probably developed at one of those drugstore processing centers nobody uses anymore. Most of the pictures are of the same two children. A little boy playing on various sports teams, dark eyes shining from beneath the bill of a ball cap, peering from behind the face mask of a football helmet. A little girl who's holding bouquets of wildflowers, sitting primly at a tea party attended by dolls. Here they are running around on the beach, and here's a family portrait, two ebony-haired children standing in front of their parents, father resigned yet commanding, mother homely and meek. The girl is smiling, carefree, but the boy's face is as sharp and alert as a raven's.

Tucked into a bottom corner of the envelope, I find a piece of tissue paper folded into a small square, taped securely. I peel back the tape and unfold the paper to find a ring. It looks like silver, two slim bands woven together, tiny stones—diamonds?—set throughout. I can't imagine who might've left it, but I'm not going to take it to the attic and let it tarnish in its tissue paper tomb. I slip it onto my finger. I'll ask Lucy about it later.

I'm torn about what to do with the photographs. It seems wrong to dump them; they're somebody's memories, and Lucy's got photos sprinkled throughout the house, of our family as well as bygone Stewarts. I draw a breath, considering, as a breeze moves past, stirring dust particles that dance and tumble in shafts of sunlight. A shiver creeps up my back as the awareness of being watched hits me hard. I glance behind me—nothing, nobody, of course—then shake the weirdness off.

Get it together, Callie.

I look again at the pictures of the boy and the girl. I can't relegate them to eternity in a landfill. I stuff them into the envelope, and the envelope into the box. I mark it STEWART PHOTOGRAPHS, then hoist it onto my hip and climb the narrow staircase to the attic.

The door sticks when I try to shoulder it open, and I have to throw my weight behind it to get it to budge, making my entrance less than graceful. I pause to catch my breath, tasting warm, stuffy air. I make my way to the far wall, pushing the box of photographs up against it before standing to look around.

There are windows up here, odd little hexagons that don't open, but the light flooding through them draws me forward, a moth winging its way to fire. Peering outside, I orient myself. I'm facing west; the vast ocean is all that's visible. I must be standing above the Gabriel, and another floor down, the bedroom I'm staying in. Stepping around a stack of crates, I move to the broken window I noticed when my dad pulled up to Stewart House the other day. The cracks are an intricate latticework. I raise a hand, laying my palm flush against the glass.

Beneath my touch, the smooth surface becomes suddenly warm.

The cracks begin to spread, trickling outward like rivulets of water.

Holy shit.

I snatch my hand away, horrified.

Shuffling back, I study my palm, flexing my fingers; my looted ring catches the light.

I look at the window.

My eyes are playing tricks on me—that has to be it. I didn't use enough pressure to do any more damage, and glass doesn't fracture spontaneously.

I reach out again. My hand trembles as I touch the window a second time.

It's cool. The cracks remain motionless, unchanged.

I drop my hand, shaking my head. I'm seriously losing it.

Through the window, I catch a fragmented glimpse of Tucker Morgan, almost obscured by a tangle of overgrown bushes. He's in shorts again, shirtless, yanking vines from sturdier trees, then cramming them into Lucy's yard-waste bin. His suntanned skin glistens with sweat, and the dark lines of an indecipherable tattoo mark his right bicep. That's unexpected. He's so golden, so seemingly charmed; the ink makes me curious about what else he's hiding.

He pauses, pulls off a work glove, and drags a hand through his hair. Then he looks in my direction.

I duck.

Damn it.

He couldn't have seen me. The windows are filthy, coated in disregard, and I'm three floors up. He definitely didn't see me.

Still, I crawl on my hands and knees, following the unpainted wall, traveling the perimeter of the attic until I reach another window. When

I stand, I find myself facing the side yard, a wall of trees stretching into the sky like overzealous fingers, far beyond the height at which I stand. I'm still spooked by the possibly expanding cracks, and residually embarrassed that Tucker may or may not have seen me watching him, so it's a second before I notice what's sitting on the window casing.

My hands fly to my mouth, muffling a gasp.

Goggles.

Chloe's swim goggles: Swedes with smoked lenses—her favorite.

Someone's messing with me.

Lucy's messing with me.

Except . . . What if she's not?

What if, somehow, this is a genuine attempt at contact?

The cap and the goggles are my sister's—there's not a doubt in my mind. And while Lucy *maybe* left them out for me, a misguided attempt at sparking conversation, she couldn't have orchestrated my falling phone or the bursts of cold or the mysteriously cracking window.

I pick up the goggles, running a finger reverently over the lenses, letting myself dare to hope. If there's a way to communicate with Chloe, my questions could be answered. The apology that's been trapped for nearly a year could be set free. Forgiveness could be granted.

I could, like my dad's always saying, get better.

I pocket my sister's goggles and head back down to the Gabriel, enlivened by the possibility—by *Chloe*.

11

Lucy comes home, and a while later, she calls me for lunch. Happy to leave the Gabriel, which is starting to feel like a crypt, I make a stop in my room to tuck the Swedes into my nightstand with Chloe's cap, then head for the kitchen. On my way, I chance a quick glance in a hall mirror. I look like the drudge I've become: shiny with sweat, hair a puff of frizz. There's a streak of dirt on my cheek.

Suppressing a groan as I turn the corner, I ram into Tucker, who's walking from the parlor to the foyer.

"Jesus, sorry," he says, steadying me with a hand on my shoulder. His expression is strange, probing, and a little hangdog. At least he's put on a T-shirt—a gray threadbare ringer that might be older than he is. It's screen-printed with the title of that old movie *The Goonies*, which Lucy made Chloe and me watch last summer because it's an eighties classic and, also, parts of it were filmed along the Oregon coast. My sister wasn't into it. "Too weird," she'd said before pointing out that if the Goonies had smart phones, their problems would've been easily solved. I found it bizarrely charming.

"Nice shirt," I tell Tucker, stepping back. I blow wisps of hair from my face. "What are you doing in here?"

"Bathroom. And then I—uh—got caught up looking at some of Lucy's pictures." He gestures into the parlor, where framed photos, old and new, sit amid the many books on the shelves.

"Oh. Why?"

"I . . . don't know." He sounds a little flustered, and he looks cagey, like I've caught him doing something wrong.

"What do you mean, you don't know?"

He shrugs, calling up that sun-drenched grin of his. "I was just checking them out. They're cool, yeah?"

I let his smile warm my face a moment, but then Lucy pokes her head into the foyer, drying her hands on a dish towel. "Hey, Tucker. Want to join us for lunch?"

He considers. "You don't mind?"

"Not at all."

We follow her into the kitchen and nearly have another collision attempting to step through the entryway at the same time. He backs up, letting me go first.

I scrub my hands at the sink and take my place at the table, watching as he lathers up, then pours a glass of water down his throat. He's been working as hard as I have, though he doesn't look so bad smeared with sweat and dust. He sits across from me. "Rough day, City Girl?"

I tuck a stray lock of hair into my ponytail. "Nope. You, Yard Boy?"

His grin humbles. "Making some progress in the garden."

Daisy meanders by, rarely far from the kitchen when there's food being served. I scoop her up and settle her on my lap, running a hand over her silky fur. She purrs, and I smile, just a little, scratching between her twitching ears.

My peaceful moment is interrupted when I notice Tucker watching me lavish attention on the cat. I flatten my smile and train my gaze down, uncomfortable under his study.

Fortunately, Lucy arrives with bowls of lettuce, topped with a rainbow of cut vegetables. She sits and says, "I can't wait to see how the garden looks when you've finished, Tuck. I bet it'll be stunning."

"I've almost got the path cleared," he tells her. "I think I'll be able to salvage most of the perennials if I trim them back. Next spring, they should be blooming."

"Amazing," Lucy says. "Thanks so much for taking the job on."

He shrugs, shooting her a lazy grin. "Can't think of anything I'd rather do this summer than pull weeds in the heat of the day while being eaten alive by mosquitoes."

She laughs.

I suppress a grumble, annoyed by the effortless way they make conversation—I used to be able to do that. I shovel a forkful of lettuce into my mouth and chew; the greens taste bitter.

Lucy and Tucker spend the rest of the meal chatting about the best flora to plant once he finishes cleaning up the garden. I choke down my salad, wondering whether either of them really has a clue as to what they're talking about. After, I clear the table while my aunt sets out a plate of lemon bars.

"Callie, let's go to town after dessert," she says. "There's a nursery on

Douglas. I want to check out their variety so we're ready to plant when the garden's cleared."

"You'll find a lot of stuff there," Tucker offers through a mouthful of lemon bar.

Lucy looks to me, eager. "What do you say?"

"I think I should keep working upstairs."

"The mess will be there when we get back, I assure you."

I wind my ponytail around my hand, stalling for an excuse that'll spare me an afternoon at a nursery with my aunt. "I'd have to shower first."

"Oh please," she says, lit up, apparently, by the idea of shopping for shrubs. "Who cares?"

"Seriously. I look—"

"Great. As usual."

Holy hell—we're related. She's obligated to say nice things. Flushing, I glance at Tucker to see if he considers Lucy's oblivious enthusiasm as silly as I do and find him peering at me from beneath his blond lashes. Our gazes lock, and I feel it: affinity. Perfunctory at best, but God, it's refreshing to share a connection with another human being.

"Fine," I mutter. "I'll go to the nursery."

Lucy stands, brushing her hands on her stonewashed jeans, pleased with herself. She bounds out of the kitchen, calling over her shoulder, "I'll meet you at the car in five!"

Tucker and I remain at the table with our lemon bars. After a couple of minutes of sticky silence, I summon the bravado to ask, "Do you actually know what you're talking about?"

He polishes off the last of his dessert, then raises a brow. "What do you mean?"

"Like, on a scale of one to total-bullshitter, how much do you really know about gardening?"

He smiles, sheepish. "Enough."

"Suuure," I say, drawing out the word, pleased to have found a chink in his armor of perfection, no matter how insignificant.

"Look. I know how to work hard. I know the difference between a flower and a weed. Your aunt wants the garden to look good—it's gonna look good."

"Uh-huh. What's a perennial?"

He laughs, rising from the table. He tosses his napkin into the trash, then heads toward the parlor. Just before he rounds the corner, he pauses to look back at me. "A perennial keeps coming back," he says, playful. "You might know as much if you got outside once in a while."

I take that in, lingering at the table until I hear him leave through the front door, wondering if he's as constant and reliable as the plants he goes on about.

As I hoist myself into the passenger seat of Lucy's Range Rover, she turns an irksome smile on me. "Thanks for tagging along, City Girl."

I'm dying to say something to her about Chloe's goggles. About Chloe's swim cap. Instead, I roll my eyes and clench my jaw, resolving to be the bigger person for the duration of this outing. I don't have the energy to argue, and besides, it's stupid to let her get to me.

After steering down the driveway, she reaches into the center console and pulls out a pack of cigarettes. She lowers the window and lights up before turning onto the paved road leading to Bell Cove. Hypocritical or not, I hate that she smokes, even occasionally. Chloe hated it, too. Last summer, we made a game of hiding her cigarettes: the freezer, the toilet's water tank, the bread box. Now, I give her my most judgmental glower.

"Didn't lung cancer kill Grandma?" I ask, fanning the air.

Lucy blows a slow curl of smoke. "Your sister drowned. Is that why you quit swimming?"

My mouth drops open, all thoughts of maturity, of *peace*, vanishing. "How about a little tact?" I sputter, my shock transforming into anger. "Not all of us can bury sadness in a remodel."

"Nobody said you should bury your sadness. I happen to think you should address it."

"Is that why you've been setting Chloe's things out for me to find?"

"I—what?"

"Her swim cap and goggles? You left them for me. Because you thought I'd come running, ready to pour my heart out?"

"I have no idea what you're talking about." She appears genuinely perplexed. And more than a little concerned. "You found her things in the house?"

Regret makes my face warm. I should've kept my mouth shut. "Never mind."

"No, I'm confused. Because I haven't seen any of her belongings since last summer."

"Then maybe I made a mistake. They must be someone else's."

Except, *no*. They're not.

Lucy turns onto Sitka, driving slower than necessary, glancing at me regularly. "Callie. We should figure this out. Talk about it."

"I don't want to."

"No, of course not. You only want to be miserable. What I can't understand is *why*."

I ball my hands into fists. “God, Aunt Lucy. Shut up.”

Her expression becomes a spiral of conviction and superiority, the ash at the end of her cigarette growing precariously long. “You’ve got to face this. Chloe’s not coming back. No matter how much you punish yourself. No matter how often you hope and wish. She’s *gone*.”

My desire for more time with my sister isn’t a hope or a wish.

It’s an affliction.

“Did you hear me?” Lucy says, as if she’s physically incapable of staying quiet, as if she’s *trying* to wreck me. “She’s gone. I don’t mean to be callous, but you’re living a fantasy if you think otherwise.”

I hate her.

I *hate* her.

My muscles twitch with the need to escape, to be as far from her as possible.

The second she brakes at a stop sign, I’m out of the car, slamming the door, dashing toward the hill that will take me back to Stewart House.

12

When I get back to the house, I dig out my little stash, fling a window open, and wallow.

The first time I smoked, I was with Isaac.

I should've been studying, but I couldn't sit still. My sister, conversely, had spent the evening stretched out on the sofa in the family room, watching Disney's version of *Hercules* with our dad. This was their routine: a Sunday night movie swap. Dad favored documentaries, almost always about Greece, and Chloe often chose something Greece-centric as well, but fun, like *Percy Jackson and the Olympians*, or *Clash of the Titans*.

I threw a wave as I walked past the two of them, calling, "Going for a walk," before escaping the confines of the house.

The night was balmy and clear. Isaac abandoned a mountain bike repair project to walk with me, a few blocks north to a greenbelt adjacent to Lake Union. The conversation swung my way, school and swimming and family, and he listened. Not like our dialogue was a transaction, not like he was racking up points to pay out later, but like he cared about what I was saying.

At the greenbelt, we found a bench tucked into a grove of trees. During the day, when sunshine streamed through gaps in the clouds, it was a perfect place to sit and watch seaplanes land on the lake. That night, it felt dark, private, safe.

From the pocket of his shorts, Isaac produced a small pipe, a lighter, and a canister with a clear cap. I'd never been around weed, but I wasn't so sheltered that I couldn't identify it. Marijuana's legal in Washington, though not so much for minors, and not in public parks.

Nerves kicked my pulse up.

"Stressed about finals?" Isaac guessed, packing the bowl.

I looked at my crossed legs; my foot bounced rhythmically. I gave a reedy laugh. "A little."

"I bet you'll do fine."

"I'd like to do better than fine," I told him, watching as he tucked the canister back into his pocket.

"You're a sophomore—you're good. Colleges care mostly about your junior-year grades."

"But my GPA. I need to maintain it."

He took a hit, using his thumb to flick the lighter. When he let the smoke go, he turned politely away. His breath was warmly herbal when he said, "You strike me as a high achiever."

There was no point in denying it.

He held the pipe out to me.

I shrugged off his offer. "Kind of want my lungs working at full capacity in the pool."

"Fair enough," he said, withdrawing his hand.

I didn't feel pressured; it wasn't like those antidrug campaigns with an asshole bully coercing an innocent lamb into shooting up. But I was curious. I glanced around to be sure no beat cops were lurking behind an evergreen's thick trunk, waiting to bust me. "You know—maybe I will try it."

Isaac showed me how to hold the lighter so my fingers wouldn't burn and suggested I take it easy at first. I did and coughed so hard my eyes streamed tears. Feeling intensely stupid, I passed the pipe back, bracing for laughter.

But all he said was, "It can be harsh the first time."

We spent a while sitting on that bench, talking about my approaching finals and his college application experience and how unnecessarily competitive high school can be. I tried a couple of more hits, and by the time we were on our way back from the greenbelt, I was this amazing blend of silly, slack, and sleepy.

Studying, school, swim team . . . *completely* manageable.

When Isaac reached for my hand a block from home, I twined my fingers through his and knew: In the space of an hour, in the shadows of the greenbelt, I'd changed.

At home, I had to sneak through the front door, past my dad and my sister and my mom, who'd curled up on the couch with a novel. Upstairs, I showered the smell of smoke away. When I left the bathroom in my robe, hair still damp, I found Chloe in my room, sitting at my desk.

"Where were you?" she asked.

"On a walk."

"With who?"

"Nobody."

It was the first time I'd ever outright lied to her.

It wouldn't be the last.

Around dinnertime, Lucy knocks on my bedroom door, ducks her head in, and tells me she's leaving for book club. I make no effort to hide my relief. She attempted a half-assed apology for what happened in the car earlier—after she got home from the nursery with a list of flowers and shrubs to pick up in a few weeks—but I'm still pissed.

As soon as she's gone, I make a peanut butter sandwich and take it to my room.

Daisy's curled up on the bed—the queen that continues to rattle me. She barely peeps an eye open when I sit beside her, but I reach out to scratch her head anyway. I appreciate her sixth sense when it comes to the strangeness of Stewart House. I stroke the length of her back while I nibble on my sandwich.

When I finish, I call home. Dad's happy to hear from me, but when I ask to talk to Mom, he tells me she's not up for it. I'm disappointed but not surprised. When Chloe and I were in Bell Cove last summer, my mom and I chatted almost every day, but I can count the number of conversations she and I've had during the last year on one hand.

I tell my dad I love him, then hang up and pull out my computer, content to poke around online until it's a reasonable hour for bedtime. I'm looking for an available outlet for the power cord when my skin tightens with goose bumps. The paralyzing certainty that I'm not alone swoops in, accompanied by a rush of alarm. I whirl around and sweep the room.

Empty.

Empty.

I stoop to shove the prongs of my computer's cord into the outlet behind my nightstand. I will *not* be afraid in this room. Daisy's sleeping peacefully on the bed, after all.

But when I glance in her direction, I find she's vanished through the cracked doorway.

Crouched in the corner, shivering, I give serious consideration to the idea that my overactive imagination isn't responsible for what I've been experiencing at Stewart House. The cold, the curtains, the sounds, the attic window, the eerie stillness. The terrifying sensation of invisible eyes skimming my body.

I'm seconds from ditching my room, the house, when a sudden calm washes over me.

I don't run.

Instead, I bury myself beneath the covers of the bed. I power on my laptop. I log on to Lucy's Wi-Fi. I pull up Google and type: *signs of a haunting.*

My finger hovers over the *return* key. I stare at what I've typed, letting its implications roll over me in alternating ripples of uncertainty and interest.

Am I admitting—even to myself—that I'm suspicious of a haunting at Stewart House?

I press *return.*

Google spits back more than a million results, and I sit up a little straighter, validated by these masses of hits.

I click on the first link, *Twenty Signs Your House Is Haunted.* The list is sort of predictable: strange noises, lights turning off and on, feelings of being watched or touched, strange animal behavior, unexplained sickness, cold and hot spots, disappearing and reappearing objects.

I let my mind turn unrestricted. Assuming hauntings are real and possible, it's conceivable that my sister is trying to connect with me. She died just south of Stewart House, and the circumstances leading up to her passing likely left her with business unfinished. But it makes sense to consider past Stewarts as potential haunters, too. They've got a century of history binding them to the property.

I clear my search and type: *Stewarts, Bell Cove.*

There are several articles about the earliest Stewarts and their move to the coast. I skim one detailing Joseph Stewart's contributions to the town, the money he donated, the plans he helped draft. There's another, more recent, that speaks of Clayton Stewart, the last to occupy the family home. The article mentions his death—heart attack—and the house's subsequent real estate listing by Dr. Hannah Stewart.

There are a few other Stewart-centric headlines, but one, from June 1999, grabs my attention. Filled with anticipation and foreboding, I click it, honing in on the paragraph that appears.

The disappearance of nineteen-year-old Annabel Tate has been declared a probable suicide by authorities. Bell Cove Police began to investigate Tate's disappearance after a sole witness claimed he had seen her jump from the cliff on the Stewart property last Saturday evening. Due to suspicious circumstances, police could not immediately rule out foul play. After interviewing Tate's family, friends, and the witness (who has been cleared of wrongdoing), it was determined that Tate was likely lost to suicide. Though Tate's body has not been recovered, a memorial service will be held Friday, 2:00 p.m., at Our Savior Lutheran in Bell Cove.

Annabel Tate. Not a Stewart, but connected to the family in some way. Nineteen. According to this article, she was claimed by the Pacific.

I envision her in silhouette, leaping from the cliff outside my windows, limbs extended, hair whipping wildly behind her.

My breath catches and, shuddering, I blink the image away.

I'm freezing, suddenly, and freaking disturbed. These sorts of intrusive thoughts barge into my consciousness sometimes, and once they exist, they're hard to banish. Usually they're linked to Chloe and her death, but Annabel Tate's possible suicide has supplied my brain with new and upsetting material to obsess over.

Hunkering beneath the covers, I twist the looted ring on my finger, trying to send my thoughts elsewhere. Except, I can't stop mulling over Annabel and her end. My sister and *her* end. Chloe's passing was an accident, while Annabel's might not have been, but their deaths are linked by proximity.

Both girls were so young, with whole lives ahead of them.

I keep asking myself: *Why?*

To clear my head, I abandon my Stewart research and pull up a series of videos featuring swim races, something like white noise or comfort food when despondency gets to be too much for me. I'm watching the first, fifteen-year-old Ye Shiwen kicking ass in the Women's 200 Meter IM at the 2011 World Championships, when the bedroom door hurls shut.

The room reverberates with a thunderous *bang*.

I startle, slapping my hands over my heart so it doesn't come crashing through my ribs.

When the door opens again, slowly, and with a *screeeech* that makes me shrink physically away, I pray my aunt will be standing on the other side.

She's not.

There's nothing there at all, save an invisible voice, softer than a whisper of wind. . . .

"Callie."

13

I hardly slept last night.

I kept hearing my name, *Callie*, cold and quiet.

Anguished.

Even after Lucy came home, I kept climbing out of bed to walk circles around my room. I spent the earliest dawn hours on the front porch, trying to make sense of who, and how, and *why*.

It was there, curled up in a rocking chair, the sky fading gradually from black to gray to blue, that I heard a different sound: tiny squeals—sad, little whimpers—emanating from the trees on the eastern side of the yard. They carried on constantly, persistently, until I went back inside, to my room, so I could pretend to have spent the night there.

After breakfast, Lucy invites me to Portland to shop for furniture. I pass. I'm over our fight, but I've got investigating to do. Those early-morning noises were different—corporeal, not spectral—and while I wasn't about to leave the porch before the sun had fully risen, I'm ready now.

From the parlor window, I watch my aunt climb into the Range Rover, turn the engine over, then pause to check her reflection in the visor mirror. She purses her lips and applies a shimmery lip gloss while I drum my fingers on the windowsill thinking, *Hurry up, hurry up, hurry up.*

Tucker's Wagoneer is parked haphazardly near where Lucy's SUV idles. Off in the western section of the yard, far from where the early-morning sounds originated, I spot him working.

I hope he stays put.

Finally, Lucy clicks her seat belt and cruises down the drive. As soon as she disappears down the hill, I'm out the front door. The sun sprays me with heat, its light too bright, and I'm sure—*sure*—I'm becoming a hermit as I hustle, shielding my eyes, squinting toward the tree line. I slow as the grass transforms into thicker underbrush, scratching at my ankles, making me itch. A wall of forest looms ahead, but I know: This is where the sounds came from.

Crouching down, I tilt my head and listen.

There they are again—a muted rustling . . . pitiful, little squeals.

Not scary.

Concerning.

I reach forward, nudging the weeds back, giving way to a bramble of flowering blackberry bushes. Carefully, I push a thorny branch out of the way. Beneath . . . kittens. Gray and white and black, wriggling, making that doleful, little mewing sound. Their eyes are open. They're tiny, dirty, and obviously underfed, but very cute.

I watch them for a few minutes, hungry and squirming in their little nest. Their helplessness, their longing for comfort, makes my chest ache. They're making enough noise to summon their mother. Between early this morning and now, she should've come running.

She must be lost or sick.

I think of my own mother, lost and sick.

How sad.

In the distance, a tree limb snaps.

Tucker.

I straighten, backing away from the kittens, out of the shade of the woods. I scan the yard until I find him, breaking dried branches, throwing them into a growing pile that'll probably become kindling this winter.

I call out to him.

He looks up. Even from a distance, I can tell he's surprised to see me outdoors.

I summon him with a wave, and he comes jogging over.

"What's up?" he asks, dragging a forearm across his sweaty forehead.

"Can I show you something?"

He quirks an eyebrow. "Yeah."

I walk back to the kittens, confident he'll follow. When I squat down next to the blackberry bushes, he matches my posture, his face full of questions. I push a barbed branch back, and he leans in to peer at the kittens.

"Whoa," he says. "How'd you find them?"

"I heard them early this morning."

"You were out here early this morning?"

I ignore this inquiry and think again of the mama cat. Lucy said she rescued Daisy from these woods months ago, and now a stray's been spooked away from her babies.

But why?

"Cal?" Tucker says. "What do you think we should do with them?"

I tear my gaze from the kittens to look at him. He called me Cal, like my dad sometimes does. Like Chloe almost always did. "I'm not sure."

"I don't think we should leave them out here. They'll starve." He gives me a teasing grin. "You don't want dead kittens on your conscience, do you?"

My expression must darken, because his smile disappears. He looks different without it, older, and even though his benign comment landed like a hammer to the chest, I miss his glow.

"I think we should help them," he says, his voice softer now.

I paddle out of an ocean of sadness—*be normal, Callie. For once, be normal.* "We could take them to a shelter."

The corner of his mouth lifts hesitantly. "There's one in town."

"Okay." I reach into the clearing to pick up a kitten.

Tucker takes hold of my wrist, his palm warm and a little rough. My cheeks catch fire. I pull in a sharp breath and look pointedly at where his tanned fingers wrap around my fair skin.

He lets go in a hurry.

"I don't want you to get scratched up," he says, chagrined, making a great effort to avoid looking at my scar. Because, what are a few scratches in comparison?

"I would've been fine."

"I know, but . . ."

I sigh and then, to spare us another awkward second, say, "Maybe you could you find a box or something?"

He rises to his full height. "Yeah. There're some old milk crates in the shed. I'll grab one."

"I'll get a towel from inside. So they're comfortable."

We rush off in different directions, and I'm relieved. Tucker Morgan is too beguiling, and I nearly had a moment. I can't do closeness, because closeness is the same as honesty. As vulnerability. I *especially* can't do closeness with Tucker, the one person who doesn't look at me with judgment or pity.

I find a plush bath towel in Lucy's linen closet. There's a hot water bottle, too, which I fill at the sink.

Tucker is waiting, sitting on top of an upturned crate. He stands and rights it when he sees me coming. I drop the hot water bottle in, then spread the towel over it, folding the edges to make a soft bed for the kittens.

"How about I reach in for them," Tucker says, "then pass them off to you."

The kittens resist rescue. Tucker's struggling, his arms quickly crosshatched with cuts thanks to the blackberry thorns, but when he at last manages to capture a kitten, he hands it off to me. I tuck it into the crate, fluffing the towel before turning to wait for its siblings.

Movement in the woods catches my attention.

A flash of white, a glint of golden light.

I stare into the trees, trying to track it, to make sense of it, but the disturbance is gone as quickly as it came.

14

We recover six scrawny kittens. One is particularly cute, the runt, mostly gray and barely mewing. I want to hold him, but before I have a chance, Tucker lifts the crate and carries it to the Wagoneer. He balances it on his hip, pulling his keys from his pocket.

"My aunt should be home soon," I say. "I'll tell her where you went."

"You're not coming?"

I have no desire to climb into his hippie wagon, much less spend an extended amount of alone time with him. I sense he's curious about what's going on with me, why I'm in Bell Cove, and why I'm so irritable all the time, and I already feel too exposed. "I'm sure you can make it to the shelter and back on your own."

"Yeah," he says, shifting the weight of the crate. "But it'd be cool if you could hold this. Otherwise, it's gonna go sliding around when I turn corners."

"Drive slowly."

"Oh, come on."

He's pushing.

I'm weakening.

"Tucker."

"Callie. The kittens need you." His tone, so earnest, sands the sharpness from my edges. He gives me a hopeful smile, and now I'm not sure I believe he wants me to tag along just to hold the crate steady.

Also, I can't believe we're bonding over stray kittens.

"All right," I say, giving in only because I don't want his smile to fall.

I climb into the passenger seat, relatively clean, save a few empty Jelly Belly packages strewn about the floor. After I buckle up, Tucker sets the kitten crate on my lap and heads around to get in.

"This is quite a ride you've got here," I say as he rotates the key in the ignition. The engine turns over with a roar.

"The Woody's older than you, so please, be respectful."

I tighten my grip on the crate as he descends the hill. "How far is the shelter?"

"Few miles. It's right behind Bell Cove Elementary."

"Your alma mater?"

He laughs. "Yeah, actually. I went to high school in Shell City, though. Bell Cove's not big enough for a high school of its own, so they bused us fifteen miles up shore."

"When did you graduate?"

"Last year."

Same as Isaac. The only commonality I've detected between them, though. Isaac is dry, serious, comfortable with quiet. His past and his family and his interests are all out in the open. Tucker is warm and charmingly self-deprecating, cheerful almost to a fault, but he hasn't given me anything personal.

"If it makes a difference," he says, "I sometimes bounce back to the maturity level of a guy in high school." He glances at me as we slow for Sitka Street traffic, raising his eyebrows in this exaggeratedly suggestive way that makes him look absolutely ridiculous.

A strange bubble, effervescent and irrepressible, rises in my chest. The stirring is so foreign, so long-dormant, it takes me a second to recognize it—it's *laughter*. It escapes, and I don't know who's more surprised—Tucker or me.

"Holy shit—City Girl laughs?"

"Rarely," I say, biting my lip. The lightness funnels away as quickly as it arrived, and my expression falls back into the sulk that fits like a favorite sweater.

Tucker lets me brood in silence a minute, until he brakes at another stop sign. "What about you? Still suffering through high school?"

"One more year."

"Then what?"

"Good question." Once upon a time, my future was planned in detail, the blueprint stamped with my parents' approval. Swimming scholarship, Pac-12 university, history degree, like my dad. It all went out the window when Chloe died and I quit swimming and let my grades fall to hell. Last summer haunts me, but the hours and weeks and years ahead are worse; I have to live them without my sister.

"What about you?" I ask. "Been tending gardens for the last year?"

His smoky voice takes a hint of playful arrogance. "I go to school in California."

"I thought Bell Cove was the shit?"

"So's Pepperdine, especially for collegiate water polo and, you know, getting a degree."

Holy hell—this new awareness that Tucker Morgan is likely miles out of my league is hard to swallow. Glancing furtively in his direction, I recognize the chlorine-bleached tips of his fair hair, the lean muscles of his forearms, and his broad shoulders for the sum total of what they are: a swimmer's physique.

How did I miss it?

I realize it's my turn to talk when he glances from the road to me, then back again. He's waiting for some kind of response to his Pepperdine announcement, probably.

The lamest question ever finds its way out of my mouth. "What's your major?"

"Interpersonal communication."

"Huh. Seems fitting."

"You think?" he says, grinning. "Since we're doing pretty okay with the communication thing today, if you ever want to ditch Lucy's for a while, you and I can go do something."

I grasp something significant. Mind-blowing, actually. In the few minutes that I've been talking to Tucker, the ball of tension that's remained knotted in my stomach for the last year has loosened. And so, briefly, I entertain the idea of taking him up on his offer. A new friend—a summer romance, even—might help me feel better. Feel *something.*

But using someone as decent as Tucker to my advantage would be incredibly egocentric.

The last time I thought purely of myself, my sister died.

Looking at the kittens, a mound of sleeping fur, I say, "I'm not sure that's a good idea."

He pushes a hand through his hair, focused on the road ahead. "Yeah. Okay."

He turns off Sitka, flies past the barren elementary school playground, and pulls into the lot of the Bell Cove Animal Shelter. He comes around to lift the crate from my lap, flashing me an affable smile, apparently unaffected by my rebuff. Inside the shelter, he greets a russet-haired man with REX embroidered on the front pocket of his shirt.

"Rex is the supervisor here," Tucker tells me. "He and my dad went to high school together. Rex, this is Callie, my—" he clears his throat, then settles on "—boss's niece."

He relays the story of our orphans to Rex, who appears enraptured. They lapse into small-town chitchat, and, to occupy myself, I lift the tiniest kitten from the crate. He's frail, mewing despondently as I try to warm him, gray fur silky against my neck. He nestles in and gives a tiny purr, and I have the sudden, absurd notion that I should take him home. I stroke his back, momentarily considering the idea.

Except, *no.*

I can't take care of a kitten.

I can barely take care of myself.

"Cal?"

I glance up to find Tucker and Rex looking at me. While I was lost in thought, one of them unloaded the kittens from the crate; they wriggle and whine on the stainless steel countertop. With a repentant smile, Tucker reaches for the kitten I hold.

Reluctantly, I pass him off.

"Far as I can tell, they're healthy," Rex says, giving the kittens a once-over. "Somewhere around six weeks. Of course, they'll need official check-ups and clean bills of health, but based on what I'm seeing, there's no reason they can't be adopted out."

Tucker beams, satisfied with the good deed we've done.

I wish I could feel so content.

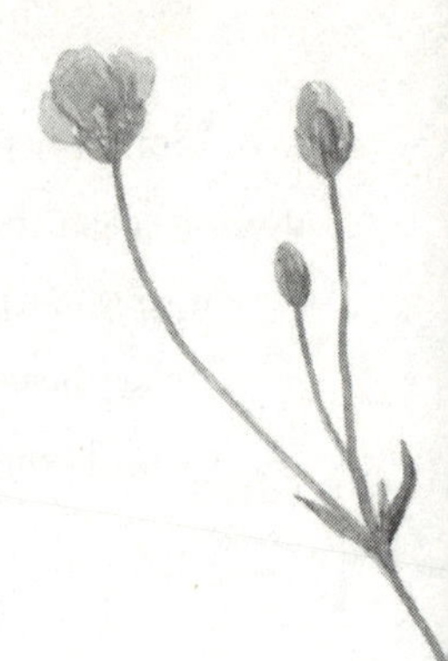

15

My first date with Isaac was on a drizzly Thursday morning, the week before finals. He intercepted me in our driveway before school and persuaded me to ditch first period for coffee with him. I took Chloe to North Seattle Prep first, listening to her complain about how Mom made her eat a banana alongside her peanut butter toast, going so far as to walk onto campus with her, only to circle back to the parking lot once she'd disappeared into the freshman wing. Sneakiness wasn't in my makeup back then, and I felt like a convict escaping the prison yard as I sped away from school—a little bit of fear and a whole lot of freedom.

Isaac beat me to the Starbucks on Dexter. He was waiting near the door, wearing dark jeans and a maroon sweatshirt, speckled with raindrops. The café was crowded.

"I was going to order," he said, "except I have no idea what you like."

"Chocolate," I told him. "Always chocolate."

He ended up with a mocha that matched mine, and we found a table offering scant privacy.

"I've got to get a green tea for my mom before we go," he said. "Don't let me forget."

I settled into my chair, pleased by the way he was slotting me into his world, making me part of his mundane morning duties.

"Did you tell your sister you're ditching?" he asked.

"God, no. She would've wanted to come."

"She seems cool."

"She is. I just . . ."

"Didn't want her crashing our first date?"

I arched an eyebrow. "Or whatever this is."

He smiled, tapping his paper coffee cup against mine. "First date, for sure."

His dimple, his laugh, his ease—being with him made me feel warm and melty and sweet, like a marshmallow toasting over a flame. I was starting to understand why a lot of my classmates did enough to get by, why many of my longtime swim friends had bailed on the sport upon starting high school—upon discovering romance.

Isaac dropped an open hand onto the table. I gave him mine. He tugged me forward, mindful of our steaming mochas, then inclined in my direction. I was brimming with anticipation, growing impatient with his leisurely journey forward.

When we met at the table's center, finally, he smiled, then touched his mouth to mine, tasting of chocolate and espresso, squeezing my hand within his.

It was a charming kiss, a Thursday morning kiss, a middle of Starbucks kiss, but it swept me up in its spontaneous magic and gave me a sense of reckless abandon where Isaac was concerned: Nothing he was part of could be wrong.

The time I spent with Tucker today—the blackberry brambles, the kittens, the ride, the animal shelter—left me with a different sort of feeling. One of tranquility and trust, despite its awkward pauses and stilted small talk and sidelong glances. Under Tucker's light, I could just *be*, and that makes me wonder if, in a parallel universe, Alternate Tucker and Alternate Callie might fall for each other.

Unfortunately, I live in *this* universe.

Lucy's not home by midafternoon. Tucker's been back in the yard for ages and I'm bored and stuck in my head, so I hole up in my bathroom to smoke. I feel shitty when I'm finished, regretful and jumpy, which is disconcerting.

I lie down to sleep it off and end up in the maze of a cemetery, wandering past headstones etched with strangers' names. I'm searching, searching, searching for Chloe, and then she's there. Her eyes shine, expectant, as I step forward. She moves beyond the tree line, summoning me forward. I follow, picking my way through shrubs and underbrush as the sunlight shimmers off her hair.

"Chloe, wait!"

She turns. Beckons me forward again.

I stumble, my toe catching a gnarled stump. I regain my footing, but when I look up, my sister's gone. I search, confused by all the green, moss dripping from branches, leaves rustling in the breeze, pine needles blanketing the forest floor.

"Chloe!" My voice bounces off the skyscraper trees. "Chloe! Please!"

The sound of her laughter propels me forward, and I burst into a small clearing. While the woods were cool and dim, here the air is warm, filled with light, honey-sweet. Red flowers with black centers stretch to meet the sun.

My sister steps out from behind a grove of trees, into the sunshine. Poppies lean in to brush her knees. She opens her mouth, murmuring something I can't make out. I strain to hear her.

When I do, I wish I hadn't.

"Callie, I've been waiting for you."

16

I sit up, groggy, my heart thrashing around in my chest.

Afternoon light filters in through the curtains, pulling me from the lingering threads of my dream, leaving me wide awake and confused and sadder than ever.

Chloe hasn't been waiting for me.

Chloe is gone.

I rub my eyes, swinging my legs around so my feet touch the floor. I need to get out of this room; I need to join the living. Because this—smoking, sleeping during the day, agonizing over my sister—is so *not* good for me.

I've almost motivated myself off the bed when I notice the poppies on my nightstand. Fresh. Woven into a wreath that encircles a small notebook with a marbled cover. A pink ballpoint pen sits atop it.

I recognize the items immediately: Chloe's training notebook, and the pen she used to record her swims, rides, and runs.

My nightstand was clear when I got home from the shelter.

I draw in a breath, pushing my hands through my tangled hair.

God, is it possible?

Gingerly, I move Chloe's pen aside. I pick up her notebook, flipping it open. Her entries cover pages, beginning eighteen months ago and spanning through the end of last June. She was meticulous, noting where she worked out, for how long, and with whom. She usually ran with a couple of her girlfriends. Toward the end, she biked with Isaac. Most of her swims were with me, though her growing enthusiasm for triathlon training drained her patience for formal practices. She still went, because our parents had invested a small fortune in the sport, and because the workouts our coaches drew up would help when it came time for the Seattle Summer Triathlon.

"Most of the athletes are probably swimming on their own, using whatever training programs they find online," Chloe told me one morning last year as I drove us to the pool for a crack-of-dawn Saturday practice. "Swimming with the team gives me an edge." And then she slumped down in her seat, scrubbing the sleep from her eyes, and groaned. "I just don't understand why it has to happen before the sun comes up."

In the pool, she rallied, powering through her sets with quiet determination.

After practice, I showered and dressed, tugging on black leggings and a chambray button-down. I wove my hair into a quick French braid, then left the locker room to wait for my sister, who, as usual, was taking her sweet time.

Isaac and I had made plans to spend the day together. I snagged the end of a bench and pulled out my phone to cement them. We'd been hanging out for a few weeks, but I hadn't mentioned him to my parents. They knew the Parks had moved in next door—my mom had taken over a plate of oatmeal raisin cookies—but they had no idea I was making out with Mr. and Mrs. Parks' son.

He returned my text quickly: *Movie? Hike? Ferry?*

All the above? I sent back.

Done.

I was grinning when Chloe came slamming through the locker room door. "My hair's turning into straw," she announced. She was dressed for a run: sneakers, T-shirt, and shorts.

"You know I'm supposed to drive you home, right? Dad doesn't like you running all that way alone."

"I'll take full responsibility," she said, gathering a ponytail. "I need the miles, Cal."

My phone buzzed with another text. I glanced at the screen. *Meet out front at eleven?*

"Dad checking in?" Chloe guessed.

I wanted to tell her about Isaac, and I would have if she hadn't spent the last week swooning over his niceness and his cuteness, glowing with the warmth of her first real crush.

I took a breath, ready to come clean.

And then: "I saw Isaac yesterday."

I blinked. "You—what?"

"Outside. He's kind of obsessive about those bikes of his." She peered into the glass-enclosed trophy case mounted to the wall, checking her ponytail in its slight reflection. "He doesn't know tons about road bikes, but he said he'd come over and take a look at mine. Make sure it's in the best possible shape."

Envy—my rawest, most instinctual response.

She beamed. "He's so great, Cal."

"I bet," I said as if I didn't know. As if I hadn't met up with him the night before, an hour spent under the stars. As if I didn't have plans to see him later.

"I wonder if he'll come over to look at my bike today. Meet Mom and Dad. They'll like him, don't you think?"

"I mean . . . probably."

She bent to tighten her shoelaces. "And don't worry—he's not even eighteen yet; his birthday's at the end of July." She glanced up, eyes bright. "So he's not *that* old."

She liked him.

More worrisome: She thought she had a chance.

She arched her back, stretching her arms over her head, limbering up for the run that was motivated, at least a little, by our dad's disapproval. That was Chloe: determined to make a point, to prove naysayers wrong, to chase what others said she couldn't have. Her resolve was one of her best qualities, the attribute I most often coveted, but that day, I found myself wishing she was the sort of girl who'd travel the path without branching off in search of adventure.

I still wish she hadn't strayed, but if I had it to do over, I'd step away from Isaac. I'd encourage my sister to go for him. I'd watch, heartened, as she sought the happiness she deserved.

I close her notebook and pick up her adorable pink pen.

I hold them close to my heart, daring to hope she left them with me in mind.

17

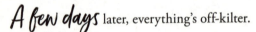

A few days later, everything's off-kilter.

I haven't come across any more of my sister's belongings. Despite talking to my dad regularly, I miss home. My aunt is still on my case to open up. And the run-ins I've had with Tucker have been too brief.

Also, he has today off.

Lucy and I've spent most of the afternoon stripping paint, peeling wallpaper, and moving dusty furniture. I've gotten pretty good at losing myself in the work around Stewart House; it's one of the few things that keep my mind off hauntings and the loneliness eating through me.

When the last of the wallpaper's been pulled from the Theodore, Lucy suggests we head into town. "I want you to see the bookstore. Meet my friend Shirley."

I snag a missed scrap from the nearby window casing. "But we're almost ready to start painting."

"Come on, Callie. It'll be fun to get out for a while."

I hate to admit it, but she might be right.

I head to my bathroom to get cleaned up. I dress in jeans and a faded black tank, then pull my hair back. I skip makeup; I haven't bothered with it in ages, and the local bookstore hardly feels formal enough to make an effort. I slip a pair of beat-up Converse onto my feet and check my phone, just in case my dad called while I was upstairs. He didn't, but I do have a missed call—from Isaac.

I haven't spoken to him since Christmas, when he was home from San Diego and I selfishly and very stupidly spent the night with him. My goal had been closure, or maybe distraction, but his had been reunification, which I inadvertently led him to believe was possible. I also terrorized my parents, who, in the dark of the night, were certain they'd lost me, too.

Why, why, *why* would he try to get in touch now?

I clear the missed call from my log, a sad list comprised almost entirely of Dad's number because my social life died with my sister, then head to the kitchen to find Lucy.

"Lucky you," she says. She pokes at her frizzy copper curls and scowls. "There's no way my hair will ever be wash-and-wear. Hey—that's a pretty ring."

I look at my finger, where the band has been since I found it packed away last week. I can't believe it's taken her so long to notice; she's so nosy about every other aspect of my life. "It's from a box in the Gabriel. I've been meaning to ask you what you want to do with it."

She takes my hand and brings it close to her face, inspecting the ring. "I think it's platinum—see how shiny it is? And those stones have to be diamonds. Cubic zirconia doesn't sparkle that way."

"You should try to sell it."

"It looks good on you. Finders keepers." She smiles and loops the strap of her crocheted bag over her shoulder. "Ready?"

It's a quiet drive into town. For the first time since I arrived, Bell Cove isn't capped by blue sky. Clouds have rolled in, low and fluffy, the color of ash. The sidewalks are deserted. Lucy parallel parks on the street in front of a building with A GOOD BOOK printed in white on a green awning. We hurry in as the first raindrops fall.

A Good Book is bigger than it looks from the street, a maze of shelves that stretch floor to ceiling. They're crammed with books, paperbacks intermingled with hardcovers, organized with little laminated index cards that display genres written in neat block letters. Oversize chairs are scattered throughout, faded and mismatched, and trailing plants crisscross like spiderwebs. The air is warm and smells of coffee and aged paper.

My aunt waves to the woman at the counter, then pulls me over by the hand.

"Nice to see you, Lucy," the woman says. She's grandmotherly, her skin a warm brown, her dark eyes gleaming beneath thick glasses.

"This is my niece, Callie," Lucy tells her.

The woman holds her hand out, and I take it. "Shirley," she says in the gentle, mournful tone I've grown accustomed to—Lucy told her about my sister, or she read about what happened in last year's news. "Your aunt talks about you nonstop," she says, all but confirming the former.

I flash a plastic smile. "Nice to meet you."

"I'm going to check out the cookbooks," Lucy says to me. "Go explore. We can meet at the counter in a half hour or so."

I wander off to browse, passing by history, sci-fi, romance, and picture books. It's not long before I find myself facing a small alcove devoted to books on the mystic, supernatural, and occult—like an invisible force has drawn me to this particular nook. I scan the books; they're not so different from those my grandma used to have on her living room bookshelf.

One title sticks out, embossed in gothic letters on a thick, burnished gold spine: *Help for the Haunted.* Checking first to be sure Lucy isn't close by, I pull it from the shelf and crack it open. It smells musty, and its pages are tissue-thin, yellowing around the edges. I turn them carefully until I find an introduction printed in faded ink.

Some people feel a powerful need to communicate with the dead. Sometimes, this desire stems from a longing to contact a lost loved one, particularly if that loved one died in a tragic or untimely manner. Others are curious about the existence of unknown spirits in their homes or places of business and wish to learn more about their presence. Help for the Haunted *hopes to assist individuals with methods for communing with the dead.*

I skim the paragraph again, zeroing in on one line: . . . *a longing to contact a lost loved one, particularly if that loved one died in a tragic or untimely manner.*

My situation, categorically. The hairs on the back of my neck stand up as I read on.

Some ghosts hope for companionship. Some linger because they have a message to share. Still others remain because their dealings are unresolved; these ghosts may be released, or pass from our plane to the next, when their business has been finished.

Though there is no need to be afraid in the presence of a spirit, alarm is not uncommon. Ghosts occupy a place many of us fear—the mystifying realm of death. We must defy our apprehension in the face of the paranormal. Fear will only hinder our understanding of the spirits with whom we hope to communicate.

I twist an escaped lock of hair around my finger, turning the antiquated words over.

Is this what I want? To communicate with a ghost?

To communicate with Chloe?

Yes.

I page through a few more sections of the book. Even though I'm trying to keep an open mind—I'm *not* a skeptic—it reads more as lore than as a true guide. Occasionally, it comes off as trite. I wonder if it's actually *helped* anyone.

And then I turn to a chapter full of directives that might actually be worthwhile.

To establish contact with a spirit, position yourself in the quietest part of your dwelling. Relaxation is crucial. Distractions should be eliminated. Lights should be dimmed. Work to empty your mind. Slacken your muscles and allow your eyes to defocus. Notice the fragments of your visual field that are usually ignored. Watch for movement, light, or color.

If you are unsuccessful in fostering a clear and tranquil state of mind, try viewing artwork or listening to soothing music. These activities can help achieve a more far-reaching sense of awareness. Practice until you advance to images. The images you encounter might be brief, though with practice, your endurance will increase.

An aisle away, a book falls to the floor with a thud. Through the stacks, I spy Lucy bending to pick it up, tucking it back onto the shelf among dozens of others.

If she catches me studying a book on hauntings, she'll sit me down for another of her come-to-Jesus conversations. Or she'll call my dad.

I slip my phone from my pocket and snap a quick photo of *Help for the Haunted*'s advice on communing with ghosts. Then I shove the book back onto the shelf and duck out of the alcove, dodging Lucy and a certain inquisition.

I hide out in a section of the store reserved for local authors: books about the history of Oregon, the microhistory of Bell Cove, seafood cookbooks, and children's books with starfish and hermit crabs as protagonists. I slide *Bell Cove: A History* from the array because it seems perfectly bland, a safe departure from the occult.

Curling up in an overstuffed chair, I read, marveling at how little Bell Cove has changed in more than a hundred years. I happen on a section detailing the city's population growth: census data and blurbs about Bell Cove's slow increase of residents, along with their apparent predisposition for depression and, in a few cases, suicide. According to *Bell Cove: A History*, the town's long, rainy winters and lopsided elderly population factor in to its inflated number of mood disorders.

I think of the article I found online, Annabel Tate and her likely death. I find it hard to believe crappy weather could drive a nineteen-year-old girl to suicide.

The bell affixed to A Good Book's door tinkles, and incoming laughter pulls me from my reading. A few voices travel through the stacks, but Tucker Morgan's stands out. I straighten in my chair as he says, "Hey, Lucy. What's up?"

They must be a shelf or two away, because I can't see them, but I hear the pleased surprise in Lucy's voice. "Tucker!"

"These are my buddies," he says. "Drew Taupo and Brynn Stevens. This is my boss."

Lucy greets Drew and Brynn, who respond with polite hellos.

"I'll catch up with you guys in a minute," Tucker says, apparently dismissing his friends. And then, "Shopping for cookbooks?" There's a smile in his voice, I can tell, and I bet his eyes are crinkled at the corners.

It's quiet. What is Lucy showing him?

"Ahh." Tucker's voice is softer, less jovial. I lean forward, peeking through shelves for a glimpse of them. Nothing. "What'd you need those for?"

"Well," Lucy says, "after everything that's happened over the last few years, I'm working on getting my life back together."

Shit. What kind of books does she have? *The Lonely Woman's Guide to Redecorating a Victorian*? *How to Drive Your Depressed Niece Crazy with Questions*? Poor Tucker—I doubt he's interested in playing concerned with my aunt when he's supposed to be enjoying a day off with his friends. But he surprises me when he says, "Anything I can do?"

"All the work you're taking care of outside . . . You have no idea how big a help you are."

"Yeah, but that's my job."

"Thanks, Tuck, but I won't bore you with the details of my heartache."

He gives a sympathetic laugh, and now I feel like I've undersold him, pegging him as this good-looking guy who's handy with a hedge trimmer. Yet here he is, thoughtful, a comfort to my aunt without being flippant or snotty—without trivializing her feelings as I've done.

His voice filters through the stacks. "Is Callie with you?"

"Yep," Lucy says. "She's around here somewhere. You should go find her."

18

My stomach comes alive with butterflies, unexpected and unwelcome. I flip the book on my lap open and pretend to be absorbed. When Tucker rounds the corner, I glance up, eyes wide, like I had no idea he was in the store.

He looks different in jeans, more put together than he does in gardening clothes. His gray T-shirt is dotted with raindrops, and his hair's stylishly disheveled. He probably spent all of ten seconds getting ready this morning, yet he could have just stepped out of a J.Crew ad.

"What're you reading?" he asks, standing over my chair.

I glance at the cover of the book I'm holding, my mind inconveniently blank. "Oh. *Bell Cove: A History.*"

"Nice choice," he says, smiling. "It's good to see you out. I was starting to think you'd grown roots to that old house."

"I get out."

"Yeah? Where's the last place you went?"

I frown sheepishly and mumble, "The animal shelter."

His laughter is low and knowing. "Speaking of the kittens, Rex called to tell me that all but one have been adopted. They haven't found a home for the littlest yet."

I don't know why this bothers me, the idea of the runt kitten left behind, deemed undesirable by Bell Cove's cat-seeking population. "Is something wrong with him?"

"Nah. He's just taking longer to place."

"Do you think Rex will be able to find him a home?"

Tucker shrugs like it doesn't matter, but he's looking at me inquisitively. "Guess so. He was cute, yeah?"

"Yeah, he was."

He shuffles a little, looking around the shop, at the books and the weird spiderweb plants—anywhere but at me. I get the impression he's got something on his mind, something he's working up the courage to say, but he doesn't get a chance, because a guy in an OSU T-shirt rounds the shelf that's been shielding us. He's built like a football player, muscular and thick-torso-ed. His skin is ocher, his black hair cut short; he looks like he could have a Polynesian background.

"Dude. I've been looking for you," he says, slapping Tucker on the shoulder with an enormous hand.

Tucker whacks him back before gesturing at me. "Callie, my friend Drew."

Drew smirks like he's got a secret, lifting an eyebrow at Tucker. He offers me his hand. I rise from my chair to take it.

He pumps my arm up and down, grip strong, his gaze skimming my face. "How long you in town for?"

I falter, rusty when it comes to meeting new people, and especially rusty when it comes to appreciative attention.

Tucker gives Drew a shove. "Leave her alone, asshole."

He chortles affably. "Brynnie," he bellows. "I found Tuck!"

She appears, brown-sugar hair bobbed short and angular, gray eyes huge and extraordinarily bright. Her jeans are dark and fitted, and she's left the top button of her cardigan unfastened. Her arms are laden with magazines, and she's smiling, open and carefree, not an insecure bone in her cute, little body.

"Tuck!" she says as cheerful and buoyant as a bunch of colorful balloons. "We've been here all of five minutes, and you've already made a friend?"

"This is Callie," he says. There's a meaningful bite to his tone.

Brynn and Drew share a glance. "Callie," she says. "Lucy's niece, right? Tucker talks about you all the time."

"He does?"

Tucker clears his throat. "Not all the time."

She laughs. "*Yes*, all the time. But your aunt's been keeping him so busy. We've hardly seen him this summer, much less had a chance to hang out with you."

"Oh, um, sorry?"

"Ignore her," Tucker says. His hand finds the small of my back. Heat seeps through my T-shirt and soaks into my skin. I quash the urge to step closer.

Brynn huffs. "Ignore me? You're the one who's been hogging the new girl. Did it ever occur to you that maybe I'd like some female company after hanging out with the two of you for so long?"

Tucker rolls his eyes, and she laughs, a light, confident sound that makes me feel like a schlep among sophistication. The jeans and tank I threw on earlier hang like rags. Would it have killed me to put on a little mascara?

And then my head crowds with conjecture: What if Brynn likes Tucker? What if he likes her? What if they're *together*?

"We'll let you two finish up," Brynn says, linking her arm through Drew's. "It was nice to meet you, Callie. Maybe someday Tucker will learn to share."

"Oh—okay." I hope the smile I've managed doesn't appear as forged as it feels.

"See ya," Drew sings as they walk away, his laughter rumbling through the store.

"Sorry," Tucker says. "My friends can be . . . a lot."

"Brynn seems okay," I say, fishing for clues as to the nature of their relationship.

He doesn't take the bait. "Drew is, too. Sometimes not in an observable way, though."

"I'll take your word on that."

He smiles faintly, sweetly, and my cheeks warm under the intimacy of his gaze. It's been a long time since a boy sent my heart spinning this way, and, honestly, I'm terrified. When I was with Isaac, I surrendered bits of myself. Not because he asked me to, but because trading parts of me for pieces of him felt right. Symbiotic.

It wasn't.

"Anyway," Tucker says. "I should catch up with them, but when you're ready to explore, you know I'm game."

I wonder what Chloe would say if she knew how often I think about this boy. How I look forward to seeing him out in Lucy's yard and catching up with him at lunch. How he makes me feel like, someday, the cloud of gloom I live under might start to dissipate.

I hug *Bell Cove: A History* to my chest and gaze up at him. "Thanks. I'll keep that in mind."

Later, after Lucy's paid for two cookbooks, we walk outside to her SUV.

The clouds have cleared. The sun is shining.

The first time I betrayed my sister, I was hanging out with Isaac on his home's third-story patio. It overlooked Seattle, aglow in the overcast night, and was furnished in wicker and linen. It was, conveniently, on the side of the house opposite mine, so there was no risk of my parents or my sister catching me with a pipe, a lighter, and a glazed expression.

"Chloe has a crush on you," I blurted out.

I regretted the words instantly, but Isaac smiled, impassive. "I kind of figured. She's come around a few times to talk about biking. She's cute. Kinda flirty."

"She's barely fifteen," I said, suddenly cross. "She doesn't know how to flirt."

After exhaling a billow of smoke, he gave me a pointed look and said, "You're sixteen, and you flirt just fine."

I ignored his attempt at humor. "I don't want her to like you."

"Well, apologies. I'm very likable."

"You know what I mean. Chloe and I don't do competition. When she wants something, I let her have it. Like, a few years ago, she had her heart set on swimming fly, which used to be my stroke. But to see her work so hard at dropping her time . . . I started to focus on freestyle so I wouldn't be the person standing in her way."

Isaac passed me the pipe. "What about when you want something. Does she clear out?"

I thought on his question, feeling more capable with the lighter, and pretty freaking comfortable with inhaling, too. "I guess I've never wanted anything bad enough to test her."

He'd given me a charged look then, daring me to prioritize my feelings. It was an uncomfortable notion, putting myself before Chloe, but for the first time in as long as I could remember, I didn't want to step out of her way.

Quietly, I qualified my statement. "Until now."

Isaac smiled.

I'd met his parents earlier, over the steaks and asparagus they grilled. He'd been right about Mr. and Mrs. Park; they were relaxed and darkly funny, a lot like their son. When they left to have drinks with a few of Mr. Park's coworkers, Isaac and I baked cookies from premade dough we found in the fridge. We took them up to the patio, where we'd been since.

"Your parents don't care that you smoke up here?" I asked, finishing off a cookie.

"I haven't asked their permission."

"Where do you get it?"

"My gall?"

I sank into my chair, muscles as loose as my tongue, and stage-whispered, "Your *cannabis*."

He laughed. "In San Diego, I had a friend whose brother owned a dispensary. He hooked me up with someone here."

"Interesting," I said languorously.

"I can give you his info."

"But I don't need it. I have you."

He grinned, dimpled and gratified, summoning me with a wave of his hand. I left my chair for his, giggling as he pulled me down to sit on his lap. His fingertips made a slow trip up my spine, and I shivered.

"Chloe doesn't know I come over here," I told him, breathing in the scent of his shirt: detergent and earth and smoke. "She doesn't know you and I are . . ."

"A thing?" he supplied.

"A thing," I repeated. "I shouldn't have told you. About her crush. That was shitty of me."

"I'm glad I know," he murmured against my ear. "I don't want to encourage her."

I sighed, nestling closer. "I think you already have."

19

A few days later, I'm back in the Gabriel, sorting junk. After two hours and a dozen boxes, I've found nothing valuable or even interesting. Sweaty and dispirited, I open one more box, vowing to break for fresh air after I've sifted through it.

There are novels inside—*A Separate Peace*, *The Adventures of Huckleberry Finn*, *The Count of Monte Cristo*—and a big pile of *Runner's World* magazines from the late nineties. I'll dump the periodicals, but Lucy will be all over the classics. Right between *Frankenstein* and *Moby-Dick*, I find a journal, wrapped in leather. Front and center on its cover is an ornately inscribed *S*. For Stewart, I suppose.

The first page is blank, lily white, but I flip on. With each turn of thick paper, my frustration swells. Except, what did I expect? A cordial letter from the ghost who's haunting me?

I toss the journal aside, ready for my break. As it skids across the floor and bumps against an old steamer trunk, though, a few pieces of loose paper come untucked. I snatch it back up and pluck the pages from it.

Letters, unaddressed, written on pink stationery, in beautiful, swirling script.

I read the first, holding my breath.

I know you saw me on Sitka this afternoon. You can't ignore me forever. Bell Cove is too small for avoidance. I broke what we had—I know that—but it was special. Too special to throw away. I never would have thought we'd go months without talking, even after everything that's happened. Won't you give me another chance?

~A

It takes a minute for the enormity of this discovery—this *initial*—to sink in.

A . . . Annabel?

The synchronicity makes my hands shake.

The next letter sounds more desperate:

Last summer feels like ages ago. With every passing minute, I regret my time with him more. Every day I doubt my decision to stick it out, to commit to him, to do the right thing. What is the "right thing" anyway? What my parents want? What this tiny town thinks is best? Is the right thing sacrificing it all to be with the person I love?

Or, is it right to follow my heart?
I know I've made mistakes. I carry my
biggest mistake with me, every day.
~A

The romantic in me hopes the recipient of this letter went to the sender, wrapped her in his arms, and laid the kiss of all kisses on her. That's stupid, though, because A speaks of mistakes and betrayal. If *A* really does stand for Annabel, her story didn't end in grand declarations and deep kisses. It ended in hopelessness and, very possibly, a flying leap from a sheer cliff.

Her next letter is brief:

Meet me. Let me apologize in person. I owe you that
much. I'll be in the poppy meadow tonight.
Please—don't tell anyone.
~A

My stomach twists; she's toying with him, whoever he is.

I'm starting to feel like Lucy: unquenchably nosy. I flip to the final letter.

It was good to see you. I feel better now that we've talked,
but still . . . I miss you. Despite all the ways I screwed up,
despite my permanent tie to him, it's always been you.

I've hurt you, and now I'm hurting him. He's a good person—you know he is—and it's not fair, the way I keep thinking of you. I'm not sure I can stay with him, trapped in a weak imitation of love. I have to make a choice, but first I need to know if you can forgive me. I need to know if we can reclaim what we lost.

~A

"Callie?"

I startle; A's letters flutter to the floor.

Lucy. She's just down the hall in the Theodore, but her voice sounds far away, stifled. Or maybe I'm just consumed by my reading. A's appeals bring a wash of empathy that makes me dizzy. She was unhappy, remorseful, selfish. It sounds like she desperately wanted something she shouldn't rightfully have.

I feel a weird and very unsettling sense of kinship.

What's more—the words she used to describe the way she was feeling—*hurt*, *regret*, *trapped*—might, if intense enough, lead a nineteen-year-old to suicide. Suicide at Stewart House, where these letters have been stored for years and years.

I sit back on my heels, wondering: Am I so eager for something new to dwell on, something different to obsess over, I'm jamming pieces from various puzzles—mine, Annabel's, A's—into the same stubborn frame?

"How's the progress in there?" Lucy calls.

"Good. Fine. Everything's fine."

"Do me a favor and haul what we're keeping up to the attic?"

I grumble an assent, stuff A's letters into the pocket of my shorts, and drag a carton marked SILVER to the third floor.

Ten minutes later, I've stacked a tower of boxes against the attic's north wall. I blot the sweat from my face and go about checking the window casings for relics of my sister. At the east-facing window, a hexagon of white light, I peer out onto the yard. Tucker's progress in the garden is observable—it's actually starting to resemble a garden—but he's nowhere to be seen.

It's a problem, the way I look forward to talking with him now. I shouldn't add tinder to the spark of affection I feel, but I can't get the kind way he spoke to my aunt at A Good Book out of my head. I keep thinking about the heat of his hand on my back.

Everything's so muddled.

When I peek out the west-facing window and spot him standing at the cliff, I want to stand beside him.

Before I can convince myself that it's a bad idea, I trot down two flights of stairs, avoiding Lucy on the second floor, and fill a glass with ice and lemonade.

I'm being friendly. It's warm today, and he's been working hard.

I leave through the back door and walk barefoot across the grass.

20

I've only been to the fringes of the yard, where grass gives way to scraggly weeds and gravel fades to dust, once before. That memory holds more angst than I have the energy to unpack, so, as usual, I push away the residual shock and hurt and anger and guilt. I grip the glass of lemonade and focus on Tucker, who's still watching the waves.

"Hey," I call when I near him.

He spins quickly around, like I've startled him.

"Break time?"

"Something like that, yeah." His eyes travel once more to the ocean, dropping momentarily to the frothy water below. I chase his gaze as a wave races in, crashing against the craggy rocks, sending up a shower of mist.

This is where Annabel Tate spent her final moments.

I put myself in her place, absorbing the sun's heat, letting the breeze tousle my hair. I contemplate suffering another day. I close my eyes . . .

lean forward . . . consider how easy it'd be. How quick. And then I think of my parents, and Lucy, and how much they all *care.* I imagine their absolute devastation were something to happen to me.

"So," Tucker says, sounding as cheerless as I suddenly feel. "What's up?"

I open my eyes and take a step back, away from the cliff and an irrevocable fall.

I pass him the lemonade. "I thought you might be thirsty."

"Yeah, I am, actually. Thanks." His fingertips brush mine as he takes the glass, but I ignore the tingles that skitter up my arm because he isn't himself. My mixed signals have probably thrown him. *No, Tucker, hanging out together isn't a good idea, but here, have some lemonade.*

"Where's your drink?" he asks.

It would've made sense to bring two glasses, but I can't say I was thinking all that clearly before I went outside. "I wasn't thirsty," I tell him. "You just looked so hot out here."

He quirks an eyebrow, his mouth coiling into a smirk. "Yeah?"

I frown and prop a hand on my hip. "Tucker—"

"Hey, you said it."

I'm so out of practice, it's hard to tell if he's flirting or mocking or teasing as a friend might, but all at once, this trip to the cliff feels like a bad idea. I make a move for the house, tossing, "Anyway, enjoy," over my shoulder.

"You know," he calls after me. "Part of bringing a guy lemonade is hanging out with him while he drinks it. You're not supposed to just go."

I pause, turning to look back at him. "Who came up with that rule?"

"I did, obviously. What if I choke or something?" He moves forward a few paces, until the lawn is emerald green and thriving, then sits down facing the Victorian. "You gonna join me, or do you have something against grass, City Girl?"

I give in, sinking down beside him.

"My friends had a lot to say after meeting you," he says after a swig of lemonade.

"God. Do I want to know?"

"Brace yourself. Brynn wants your life story. She needs to get you out for some girl time—her words, not mine."

"You two are close?"

He shrugs. "I've known her and Drew most of my life. The three of us have been tight since Bell Cove Elementary."

"Did you guys ever go out?"

As if his romantic history is my concern. My face is on fire.

"Drew and me? He's not my really my type, Cal."

I attempt chagrin, but it's hard to keep a straight face.

"Oh! You mean Brynn and me? Nah." His tone is casual, but my curiosity must flatter him, because he's smiling. "Drew thinks you're hot, by the way. He wants to know if you're single. If you are, he wants me to pass his number to you."

"Oh—uh . . ." The sun beats down on my forehead, my shoulders, the backs of my hands. I'm in a broiler, and I'm overcooked by anyone's standard.

"It's cool," Tucker says. "I'll make something up, if you want. Tell him you're not interested in getting to know anyone." His eyes go round and inquiring, jumping to the ring on my finger before landing on my face. "'Cause you're not, right?"

I'm supposed to say something. *No,* would work splendidly, but the word sits idle on my tongue.

"Anyway," he says, letting me off the hook. I can tell he's disappointed. I am, too, because maybe—*maybe*—I am interested in getting to know someone. "What've you been up to today?"

"Organizing. Lucy's got rooms full of junk that need sorting."

"I bet there's, like, a century of leftover shit in that house."

"There is. The Stewarts were total pack rats. They saved all of their bank statements and every *National Geographic* ever published."

"Those are the magazines with the naked people, yeah?"

"Yep. They're so brittle the pages disintegrate when I turn them—not that I'm trying to look at naked people," I add hastily.

He laughs. "Found anything cool?"

A's letters are searing a hole in the pocket of my shorts. I kind of want to keep them to myself, but Tucker's a lifelong Bell Cove resident. He might be able to say with certainty who A is. Or was. I pull out the stationery. Unfolding the letters, I hand them over. "I came across these. I'm not sure who A is, or when they were written, but they seem sort of scandalous."

Tucker skims the elegant script of each letter, his brow furrowed. He checks out the back of each page, the pink papers fluttering as his hands, usually unfaltering, waver. When he's done, he looks at me, his face clouded over. "So?"

"So . . . I found them in a journal with an *S* on its cover—*S* for Stewart, right? But who's A? And who's this other person who's apparently keeping them apart?"

Tucker hands the letters back to me. "Who cares?"

"I do, kind of. Do you know anything about the Stewarts?"

"Not really."

"Bell Cove's the shit and all, so I thought maybe—"

"Callie, those letters must be crazy old," he says, his expression wiped clean now. "Those people probably ditched Bell Cove the first chance they got."

"But aren't you curious about how it all played out?"

"Not even a little bit."

I fold the pages and push them back into my pocket, embarrassed by what he must be thinking. I can hardly maintain my half of a conversation, but I'm fixated on a few letters penned by an unnamed stranger?

"Well," I say. "That's the highlight of what I've seen up in the Gabriel. Unless you're into silverware and teacups and classic novels."

He smiles, not so serious anymore. "What're you gonna do with it all?"

"Toss the old magazines and paperwork. Move anything remotely valuable to the attic for Lucy to look over later."

"Did you know she's gonna let me paint the exterior of this place when I finish the yard?"

I look up at Stewart House in all its dilapidated glory. "I kind of like the chipped paint. Gives it character."

"Yeah, but if it's gonna open as a B&B, it's gotta look its best."

"I guess . . ." My attention drifts to the west-facing attic window. There's a funny glare, the sun, probably, but it creates a shape in the hexagon frame, washed-out and still. I blink, trying to discern its details.

Tucker offers me his glass. "Thirsty yet?"

I take it, fixated on the attic window as I sip lemonade. The glare's still there, and then it flashes, becoming a pale, featureless face. It ducks away in a glint of light.

I choke.

Coughing, sputtering, I lean forward, gaping at the window. "Did you *see* that?"

"What?" Tucker asks, thumping my back.

I point at the third floor. "That window. There was . . . something."

He squints; the window's dark. "Probably the sun."

"No. It moved." It's possible I've lost it completely—I'm *so* certain about what I just saw, yet bursting with doubt, too. It's one thing to indulge this contradictory nonsense privately—*silently*—but to invite Tucker in is a whole new level of foolish.

"Lucy, maybe?"

"Lucy doesn't hang out in the attic."

Tucker thinks on that, then says, "You know, some people think Stewart House is haunted."

I keep my face composed as a tickle of foreboding lifts the tiny hairs on the back of my neck. "Haunted? Like, how?"

"I don't know. Weird shit's happened, supposedly."

"What do you mean? Like, ghosts?"

"I guess. At least a few people must've died here over the last century, right?"

I know of one off the top of my head, and another who passed down shore.

Not for the first time, I wonder if Tucker's heard about Chloe.

"Take the kittens," he says. "Have you seen evidence of the mother cat since we took them to the shelter?"

"No."

"Me neither, and I'm out in the yard all the time. What would make her bail on her babies? And there's other stuff, too."

"Like what?" I ask, breathy and eager.

He gives me a long, analytical look. "You know what? Never mind."

"No, tell me."

"You have to sleep here—I don't want to freak you out."

"Tucker." I drop my hand onto his arm, brazenness that comes out of nowhere. I feel kind of bad, attempting to manipulate him, but if he has information about this house and hypothetical paranormal activity, I need it. "Please, tell me."

He deliberates. "Is your aunt gonna fire me for giving you nightmares?"

I give his arm a squeeze before moving my hand. "She'll never know we talked about this."

He clears his throat, bemused, before saying, "When I was in high school, the year before Lucy moved in, a bunch of people from my class used to drive down from Shell City to hang out on the property—Brynn and Drew, pretty much everybody."

"You?"

"Not really my scene. But the house was abandoned and secluded, and they could get away with a lot."

I nod, trying to appear vaguely interested, not ravenous for more.

"Sometimes they'd see weird stuff. Blinking lights. Shadows behind a window, kind of like you. They'd hear—I don't know—*unnatural* sounds. All that stupid shit from ghost stories nobody believes. I mean, why would a ghost hang out here, fucking with teenagers by whistling and flashing lights?"

Why would a ghost scare a lonely girl late at night?

"It doesn't make sense," I say, because it doesn't. The stretch of time Tucker's talking about was before Chloe died. Either his friends have imaginations more active than mine, or the ghost that haunted them wasn't my sister.

My heart sinks. Does this mean the ghost that's haunting *me* isn't Chloe?

I open my mouth to tell him what's been happening—the poppies, the sounds, the chills, the dreams, my sister's cap and goggles and notebook—but I quickly change my mind.

I don't want him to think differently of me.

"What?" he asks, all rasp and suspicion.

I shake my head. "I need to get back to work."

21

After turkey meatloaf and benign dinner conversation with Lucy, I search for Bell Cove Public Library's address online. My ghost hasn't needled me since the attic window, but A's letters and their possible connection to Annabel Tate won't let me be. Despite Tucker's lack of interest, I want to know more about this person who wrote of her *biggest mistake*.

After borrowing a bike from Lucy's shed, diligently ignoring the lone wet suit draped over an old sawhorse, I take off toward town. The wind tosses my hair and makes my eyes water, but the ride is rejuvenating. I haven't gotten any real exercise since the day I ditched Lucy's Range Rover and sprinted up the hill, and I'm flying high when I park in front of the library.

It's a brick building, its interior bright but sparse. Aside from the librarian behind the circulation desk—she gives me a friendly wave—the place is empty. I browse for a few minutes, walking the perimeter, past novels and reference books and magazines that've seen better days, before finding myself in a section of gardening books. The shelves are packed with hardcovers detailing trees, flowers, shrubs, seasons, and the pH balance of soil. I recognize a few titles from my mom's collection—though, she hasn't done anything garden-related in a year. Toward the bottom of the shelf, one book catches my eye, facing out among the many spines: *Common Flowers and Their Symbolisms.*

I lift it and open to the index, surveying the entries until . . . *Poppies.*

I find the entry, photographs of colorful flowers splattered across the page. I read standing in the aisle, beginning with a Greek legend I've heard before: the kidnapping of Persephone by Hades, who claimed her as his bride and whisked her away to the underworld. Persephone's mother, Demeter, was distraught by her disappearance and searched the world for her, neglecting her duties as the goddess of harvest. A piece of the myth I've never heard, though, according to *Common Flowers and Their Symbolisms*, is this: Too distressed to sleep while searching for her daughter, Demeter created the poppy flower to get some rest. The entry ends with a list of the many things poppies have historically symbolized—beauty, eternal life, loyalty, slumber, death.

I wonder: If the poppies I've found really were left by a spirit, what message were they meant to communicate?

I pull my hoodie tighter around me, warding off a draft, then prop *Common Flowers and Their Symbolisms* back on its shelf and get down to business.

It's a half hour to closing when I approach the circulation desk. The librarian looks like she's in her midtwenties, brunette and pretty. I suspect she's a Bell Cove lifer.

"What can I help you with?" she asks.

"I'm looking for yearbooks," I tell her. "From the high school in Shell City."

"We have them all the way back to the fifties, when the school opened. We keep them behind the desk, though, because they have a tendency to become defaced. Kids these days." She smiles, rolling her eyes. "What year are you looking for? I'll hunt it down."

I do some quick math. If Annabel was nineteen when she died in 1999, she likely graduated that year, or the year before. "I'm not sure," I say. "Late nineties. Can I look at a few?"

"Sure. You can't check them out, but if you need photocopies, I'm happy to run them."

She disappears into the back. I wait, trying to recall what happened to my junior yearbook—did I even pick it up during the last week of school? I know I ordered one; I distinctly remember my dad writing a check last fall, insisting we try to carry on, promising I'd be thankful for the memories one day.

Doubtful, I think as my phone starts to ring. I pull it from my pocket to silence it, expecting my dad, or maybe Lucy.

But—no.

Isaac.

My heart stutters as I stare at his name on the screen, as I hurtle back to the first time I saw him with my sister, a warm afternoon last June. I'd just pulled into the driveway after an intense swim practice and an epic finals study session, frazzled, sure my family would be gathered around the table, Mom tapping an impatient toe as dinner grew cold.

I'd almost missed him, sitting on his house's front porch swing.

With my sister.

I abandoned my things and made my way over. Isaac was wearing jeans, a Padres T-shirt, and a sheepish smile. Chloe was in spandex shorts, a fitted workout tank, and her favorite sneakers, which kicked the planks as she kept the swing moving. She'd let her hair free of its usual ponytail; it was dampened with sweat along her hairline.

"Hey, Cal," she called as I stepped up onto the porch.

"What's up? Good run?"

"Always."

I glanced at Isaac as I leaned against the porch railing. There was a foot of space between the pair of them, but all I could see was him, next to her. I felt dizzy and terribly left out.

"Enjoying your summer break?" I asked. It was weird, pretending he and I were casual acquaintances.

"Couldn't be better," he said, eyes flashing surreptitiously.

"I can't wait for summer," Chloe said. "Three more days until school's out!"

"Can't come soon enough," I agreed, wondering if my irritation translated at the same potent level with which it coursed through my veins. Mostly, I hoped not. It was silly to be jealous of my sister. Ridiculous to doubt Isaac. It was senseless, speculating about the two of them, but a small, petty part of me wanted them—*him*—to realize how awful I felt.

Chloe raised a hand to push her hair from her face. Her top drifted up.

I stared at Isaac, silently daring him to look.

His eyes stayed glued to mine.

I smiled.

He was a good guy.

"Mom's going to want us home for dinner any minute," Chloe said, a hint that we should both be on our way.

"And Dad's going to kill you for running around the city in those clothes," I countered.

She hopped up, leaving Isaac to swing alone. She launched into a twirl, showing off the attire that would likely send our dad into cardiac arrest. Her arms came up and her stomach peeked out and her hair haloed around her. She was two parts angelic, one part vixen, and in that moment, I loathed her.

"See you at the house," she said. She blew me a kiss, then scampered down the porch steps, legs disproportionately long, sunset hair swishing against her back, provoking a startling shift in my perception.

She wasn't a coquette; she was an awkward kid with big dreams and questionable focus.

Chloe was my sister, not a threat.

Green was hideous on me.

"Callie," Isaac called as I'd twisted around to trail after her.

"I'll talk to you another time," I'd said, too ashamed to turn back.

I can't talk to him today, either. Not after so long. Not after the reckless night we spent together last winter. And not while whatever went on between him and Chloe—the *truth* of it—remains an empty void. I can't ask him about my sister, the two of them, because I don't trust that he'll be honest. And I definitely can't ask Chloe.

Which means I live, every day, with questions, with doubts, with irrepressible guilt regarding the part I played.

I leave the call unanswered.

As I'm shoving my phone back into my pocket, the librarian comes out of the back room, arms laden with a stack of yearbooks.

"1996 through 1999," she says, dumping them on the counter. "If you don't find what you're looking for, let me know and I'll pull some others for you."

Forget about him, forget about him, forget about him.

"Thanks so much," I tell her, pushing my shoulders back, deleting all thoughts of Isaac from my head.

I heave the stack of yearbooks off the counter and carry them to a table well away from the circulation desk, in need of space, room to breathe. I get started searching the 1999 yearbook, but it's empty of Annabel's name and photo. I grab the 1998 edition, thumbing to the senior class, and then to the students with last names that begin with *T.*

And . . . top, left corner . . . *Annabel Tate.*

Her face is framed in a rectangle, and she's smiling at me like we're old friends. She's beautiful and healthy and *alive*, dirty-blond and bright-eyed, the kind of girl who sweeps homecoming selections and gets cast in skin-care commercials. She looks like fun, like someone who makes her friends laugh, who makes boys take a second look, who makes the people around her strive to be better versions of themselves.

She reminds me of Chloe.

22

All night I lie in bed, in that weird in-between state of sleep and awareness. Every time I start to drift off for real, I hear the phantom trill of Isaac's call and end up thinking about Chloe and my regrets. Annabel and her regrets. I've been up more than once, opening my nightstand drawer to look over its contents: my sister's swim cap, goggles, notebook, and pen. A's letters.

She was caught between two boys.

Chloe and I battled for the same boy.

The link makes my stomach jittery. My hands clammy. Sends my mind spinning.

I want to smoke, but I'm running low. I've got no one to buy from here in Bell Cove, and it seems prudent to maintain a reserve for emergencies.

I flip onto my back and stare at the ceiling, considering a different anxiety fix, the activity that used to calm me the way smoking has over the last year.

When dawn colors the sky, I climb out of bed and, without allowing myself to think too hard about what I'm about to do, dig the single swimsuit I packed from the bottom of a pile of clothing in the wardrobe. I pull it on, the black Lycra hugging my body, then slip sweats and a sweatshirt over top. I retrieve my backpack and double-check the front pocket for my swim cap and goggles, nearly identical to Chloe's. With a few quick keystrokes on my laptop, I locate the local pool and jot directions onto a scrap of paper.

Last summer, when we visited Bell Cove, Chloe was in serious training mode. She convinced me that the ocean was where we needed to swim; she'd benefit from the added challenge of waves and currents. Lucy was hesitant about our going to the beach at first—the water is *cold*—but it didn't take much in the way of cajoling to get her to drive us to Portland for a pair of wet suits. Chloe loved swimming in the Pacific; she'd run at the waves screaming "Freedom!" with such exuberance, flocks of seagulls were scared into the sky.

I prefer pools—treated water and measured laps and safety—but I'd follow Chloe anywhere.

Silent as a shadow, I tiptoe into the hallway to the closet where Lucy keeps beach towels and add one to my backpack.

I peek into her room before I go. She's sleeping, curled into a corner of her California king, wild hair fanned out across her pillow. The lamp on her nightstand is still on, a copy of *Anna Karenina* facedown on the mattress beside her. When she lets out a deep sigh, I fight the urge to wake her, to tell her everything, to confess to the weed and the shame and the ghost, Tucker and my opposed feelings, and how, maybe, I'm not so okay at all.

The urge slips away as quickly as it arrived, and then all I want is to be in the water.

The sun isn't entirely up, but the sky is gorgeous, like someone blended pink and tangerine and violet chalk across the heavens. I wheel a bike out of the garden shed, hoist my backpack onto my back, and take off down the hill. Once I'm on the outskirts of town, I pull the directions from my pocket. The pool is part of a larger park, out on Pine Street. I follow Bell Cove's empty roads to the address, apprehension building with every rotation of the bike's pedals.

When I see the chain-link fence, a rectangle of turquoise water sparkling beyond, my heart ramps into high gear. Parking the bike, I heave countless memories of swimming with my sister out of my head.

A groundskeeper walks the deck, sweeping the pool for debris. "Morning."

I give a curt wave, too high-strung to play at friendly.

"Don't see many people out this early," he says, rounding the pool. "New to town?"

"Visiting."

He nods. "I'm done here, but I'll be around the park if you need anything."

I wait for him to duck into the storage shed before kicking off my flip-flops and peeling my sweats away. After unearthing my cap and goggles from my backpack, I leave it and my clothes on a lounge chair, then walk across the smooth concrete to the edge of the water. It's a lap pool, twenty-five yards, with floating lane lines stretched across its surface. The water's clear, reflecting the deepening colors of sunrise. It washes gently over the grated gutters, inviting.

I sit, dangling my legs. My last swim was with Chloe, in the ocean, two months before the triathlon she never got to compete in. I close my eyes, releasing a breath with thoughts of my sister and the many, many dreams she never had a chance to see through. Then I stretch my cap on, twisting my hair so it fits beneath. Goggles come next, tiny windows that remind me of what life used to be: simple, happy, privileged.

I ease into the water. It's cool, but not so cold I lose my breath. Sinking to the bottom, I release a stream of bubbles and look around. I could be in the Caribbean. I could be in the Arctic. It's so quiet, just me and the water, the weight of it pressing against me, holding me together.

With a burst of exhilaration, I push off the bottom, long and streamlined. A torpedo. I surface almost halfway down the lane, kicking hard, propelling myself forward with alternating pulls of the water in my cupped hands.

I swim freestyle to the far end of the pool, then roll into a flip turn. When my feet hit the wall, I shove off, stretching my arms over my head, shooting through the water as unbound and graceful as a dolphin. And then I'm kicking again, crawling through the water with long, powerful strokes, energized by the freedom of it.

Holy hell, I've missed this.

I'm only about five hundred yards into my workout when there's a splash in the lane next to mine, down near the wall I'm swimming toward. I slow, watching through my goggles as a million silver bubbles form around the person who's interrupted my solitude.

He sinks, reaching his arms over his head, bowing his back in a way that makes me do a double take. His shape is familiar: tall, muscles cut across his abdomen, expansive shoulders. But it's his hair, shining in the warm morning light, that's unmistakable.

Tucker waves, eyes invisible through dark goggles. I wave back, then continue my swim. He stays in the lane next to mine, powering through his sets, kicking past me more times than I can count. He must rack up eight or nine thousand yards by the time the sun's fully risen.

When I hoist myself out of the pool to sit on the gutter, my legs are Jell-O, and my arms are about as useless. Breathing hard, I remove my goggles and strip the cap from my head. Shaking out my damp hair, I stare unabashedly as Tucker glides to the wall. Placing his hands flat on the grate, he lifts out of the water, twisting around to sit next to me. He flings his goggles onto one of the chairs behind us.

"Hey," I say, weirdly shy about my suit, my wet hair, and my skin, pink with exertion. "Don't you get enough exercise pulling weeds all day?"

"Pulling weeds isn't gonna do me much good when water polo picks up in the fall." He runs a hand through his dripping hair. My eyes follow tiny water droplets that streak down his cheeks, his neck, his chest. Lower. He's wearing a black training suit, jammers that cover his thighs but sit perilously low on his hips.

I shake my head in a futile effort to clear it. "I didn't expect to run into you here."

"I could say the same." His expression is drawn, wounded. "You didn't tell me you swim."

"I don't. This morning was a one-time thing."

"Huh. 'Cause it looks like something you've been doing your whole life."

"I haven't been in a pool in ages. More than a year."

"How come?"

I splash water over my legs. "I needed a break."

"Why?"

"God, Tucker. I don't know. I just did, okay?"

He draws back. "Yeah. Okay."

He hops up and walks to the chairs circling the pool. Grabbing a towel from his bag, he rubs himself dry, then scrubs the terry cloth through his hair. He doesn't say anything else, doesn't even look at me.

I sit on the grate, dumbfounded and sort of annoyed, the same emotions I experienced the first time I upset Isaac. I'd dropped the news about my trip to Bell Cove on him like it was no big deal, like I up and left boyfriends regularly, and he'd said, dismayed, "The *whole* summer?"

"It's a couple of months," I replied, as if he'd blink and I'd return.

"But . . . why?"

"Because my aunt just moved to Oregon and she needs help fixing up this house she bought. She's cool, and Chloe's going, too, and it's going to be a chance for us to all bond."

"When are you coming back?"

"Middle of August."

He gaped at me. "I leave for San Diego at the end of August. That gives us, what? A couple of weeks?"

I'd been looking forward to my Oregon trip, but seeing how stricken he was had me second-guessing my plans. We hadn't been together long—what if we didn't survive a summer apart?

Following on the heels of vacillation, though, was irritation. Did I really owe him an explanation?

"I have to go," I said, though actually, I *wanted* to go.

"You don't even seem bummed."

"I am. But I'm excited about seeing my aunt and hanging out with Chloe."

We'd been holding hands, and that was when he let mine go. "Aren't you going to miss me?"

"Of course. I'll be busy, though. And so will you."

He tilted his head, considering me with his dark eyes. "What if I come down for a visit?"

That seemed a reasonable compromise. Anything to get him to stop looking at me like I'd taken a mallet to his pride. "Yeah," I said, reclaiming his hand. "That could be fun."

He smiled then, showing off the dimple that never failed to charm me.

Shaking the memory off, I leave the gutter to retrieve my towel, wrapping it like a toga. To appear impervious, I pull a paddle brush from my backpack and go about detangling my hair while Tucker winds his own towel around his waist, then digs into his bag. He's being all huffy, shoving clothes and an extra towel out of the way until he unearths a pair of board shorts.

I can't stand the quiet or his obvious aggravation. "Are you seriously mad?"

"No," he says, still not looking at me.

"Are you sure?"

"Callie, I don't know enough to be mad."

I have no idea how to respond to that—if I even should. He strips his suit from beneath his towel, tosses it onto the chair, then pulls the board shorts on. He zips the fly before yanking the towel away. He reveals nothing.

Impressive.

I zone in on the art embellishing his bicep, constricting with his movements. It's a circle containing three undulating lines, beneath three curling waves, done in neat black strokes. I try to picture him in a tattoo parlor, clenching his jaw as a brawny, heavily inked man marks his tanned flesh. It's a difficult image to conjure.

My voice is a striking contrast to the quiet when I ask, "What's with the tattoo?"

He glances at it, then pulls on a T-shirt, letting its short sleeve cover the art. "Nothing."

"I like it."

He's in the midst of stuffing gear into his bag, but he pauses to tell me, "I had it done when I got to Pepperdine."

"You're into the water. It's cool."

"I guess." He shrugs, zipping his bag, preoccupied, and it occurs to me, suddenly and startlingly, that he's keeping something from me.

He straightens, hoisting his bag onto his shoulder, then looks toward the gate leading to the parking lot. It's clear he's hurt by my swimming omission, and if only I could tell him why I didn't mention it, why it was so hard for me to come here this morning, why I feel hollowed out by the awareness that, for the first time in a year, I swam.

Without Chloe.

And then, with certainty that alarms me, I realize I *want* to tell him these things.

More than that, I want him to stop looking at me like I've betrayed him.

"Do you come here every morning?" I ask.

"Pretty much."

"Maybe I'll see you again."

"I thought swimming was a one-time thing?"

"I don't know. Maybe not. It felt good to be back in the water."

"Yeah?"

"Yeah. I didn't realize how much I've missed it."

"Funny how that happens," he says, smiling at last. "What're you up to now? Lucy cooking you a four-course breakfast?"

I shrug. "Not that I know of."

He drops his gaze, toeing the deck a second, like he's collecting courage. When his eyes find mine again, they reflect the clear green-blue of the pool water; he looks so eager, so hopeful. "If you're not eating with her, maybe you and I can grab something. There's this place down by the beach. . . . It's kind of a local secret."

I've sidestepped this moment, the one where Tucker gets direct and asks me out, a few times. But this morning my choices are clear: the honest but risky: *Yes, Tucker, I'd like to have breakfast, you and me,* or the deceitful yet safe: *No thanks, Tucker, I'm not interested in you.*

He makes me happy is the simple truth of it. He makes me forget, and right now nothing in the world sounds better than breakfast on the beach with him.

23

Chloe and I used to go for strawberry-smothered waffles at a hole-in-the-wall Seattle diner to pig out after early weekend practices. It was our tradition. I'd give her my whipped cream; she'd give me her bacon. I try not to dwell on this as Tucker promises to load my bike into the back of the Woody while I change.

I swap my suit for dry clothes in the small locker room, then brave my appearance in the cloudy mirror. Wet ponytail, bare face, sweats. I never would've gone out looking so unpolished before. But Tucker must not mind—he's the one who suggested breakfast.

It's hard to keep that in mind when I climb into his car. He looks like Poseidon. Self-consciously, I fluff my ponytail.

We drive north through Bell Cove, past the Green Apple Grocery, A Good Book, a zillion shops selling kites and paintings and shirts. The streets are quiet, misted by the light fog that has rolled in off the ocean.

When we pass the turnoff to the animal shelter, I can't help but think of the tiny gray kitten, alone and unwanted.

It's not long before Tucker parks in front of a café on the northern edge of town. Sun-bleached paint on rustic driftwood labels it The Sandbar Bistro. We follow a hostess in a denim skirt through the beach-themed interior and out to the patio. She seats us inches from the sand. Tucker has to shoo a seagull from his chair before he falls into it. When the waitress arrives, I suggest he order for both of us. He does: blueberry-stuffed crepes, sausage, and orange juice.

"Breakfast of champions," he tells me when she places our plates in front of us shortly after.

"Are you working today?" I ask after a bite of spicy sausage.

"Later. I'm helping my dad this morning."

It's strange to imagine him at home with his parents. Possibly siblings. He's such a bright individual force, it almost seems like there wouldn't be room enough in a house for anyone but him. "What are you guys doing?"

He grimaces. "Painting the fence."

"Sounds kind of like what you do at Lucy's."

"Yeah, but I get paid to help your aunt." He busies himself smoothing whipped cream over his crepes. His voice is low when he says, "Plus, you're always at Lucy's."

I flush. This isn't the playful Tucker teasing I'm growing accustomed to. It's tentative. Sincere. "What's your dad like?" I ask him.

His eyes become guarded, the doors to his world swinging shut. "He's okay."

"Your mom?"

"Out of the picture."

I narrow my eyes. "What does that mean?"

"It means that it's always been my dad and me. He's a loner, basically. His parents live in Fort Lauderdale now, and his sister and her family moved to Malibu—part of why I chose to go to school there. I know pretty much nothing about my mother. Her parents died when I was in middle school, within a year of each other. That's the extent of my family tree."

A weight settles on my chest. Sometimes it's easy to forget that others suffer hardships. My grief is so ardent, so concentrated; it's hard to fathom that any one person could feel the anguish I experience daily.

Maybe Tucker has to some extent.

I rest my fork on my plate, feeling unmoored. The drifting girl.

He must realize, because he reaches across the table to touch my arm. I wonder, for the millionth time, if he caught wind of Chloe's story last year on the news or through the grapevine. He must have heard; the tragic death of a teenage girl has to be a big deal in a town as small as Bell Cove.

Still, even if he knows Chloe's story, he probably doesn't realize it's *my* story.

The warmth of his hand is bleeding into my skin, and I want to cry. More than that, I want him to comfort me. But it's easier to breathe through the bloom of emotion, to wait in awkward silence while seagulls swoop through the billowy clouds, until the hurt withers enough to become manageable.

Tucker pulls his hand away. "You okay?"

I nod, unnerved by how much I miss his touch. "I'm good."

It's clear he believes otherwise, but to his credit, he lets it go. He smiles, and the morning fog dissipates. Rays of sunshine heat my back, drying my pool hair.

It's a relief when he fills the quiet. "My dad's been married and divorced three times since my mother disappeared, all before I turned ten. He's been single since my last stepmother got the hell out of Dodge, and now all he does is sleep, work, and watch ESPN. How's that for dysfunctional?"

"All families have weirdness, though. I bet he does the best he can."

"When he's present, that's probably true." He shrugs. "How's your breakfast?"

I take a bite of crepe; the blueberries taste summery sweet. "Really good."

"What about your parents? Are you gonna tell me about them?"

I shrug, chewing, trying to summon a safe answer to his loaded question. "They're cool," is the best I can come up with. I tack on another nugget of truth. "It's pretty quiet around my house, too."

Tucker and I have more in common than I expected. Loss. Isolation. The whole swimming thing, which is kind of huge. Maybe that's why it's so easy with him, why I feel more comfortable with him than I have with any other person since Chloe died.

"I bet your dad's lonely when you're in California," I say.

"He's lonely for sure, but not because I'm away." The fall of his smile tells me there's more to the story. I hate this new veil of secrecy surrounding him, clouds blotting out an otherwise brilliant sunrise.

I take a sip of orange juice and steer us to a safer topic. "Tell me about water polo."

"You've never played?"

"Nope."

"I can teach you."

"No, thanks. I swim because it's solitary. Besides, water polo looks borderline violent."

He flares back to life. "It's *totally* violent. It's crazy what goes on underwater, where the refs can't see. That's part of the fun."

"I find that hard to believe."

He laughs, and somehow, I'm grinning, too. "Do you really think you'll come back to the pool?" he asks while we wait for the check.

I look into the vastness of his eyes and say, "I think so."

"Where've you been?" Lucy asks when I walk through the front door midmorning. She's in tattered jeans and an oversize plaid button-down that's seen better days. She's piled her hair into a messy ponytail, and her cheeks burn crimson.

"I went for a swim. I left you a note."

She follows me down the hall to the kitchen, tugging on the hem of her shirt. "Yeah, I found it hours ago. You've been at the pool all this time?"

"No, but—"

"Your parents trust me to take care of you, Callie. To keep you safe. You can't disappear for the better part of the morning, especially if you leave your phone sitting on your nightstand."

"Sorry," I say, glib, dumping my backpack in the laundry room. "I didn't think to take it to the pool, and I didn't think you'd care if I got something to eat after my workout."

"I care a hell of a lot. In fact, I can't think of anything worse than discovering my niece has gone missing."

Chloe.

I turn to face her, and, God, she looks agonized. "I'm sorry," I say with sincerity now. "Next time, I'll check in."

She blows out a big breath, as if she's been holding it in all morning. "Thank you. I'd appreciate that." And then: "You went to breakfast?"

"With Tucker. I ran into him at the pool."

"Oh. How was it?"

"Okay. I'm out of shape, but swimming felt good."

"No, breakfast. Was it a date?"

How is she able to swing so effortlessly from concern for my safety to an attempt at creating a girlfriend moment? "It was a meal."

"Are you going to see him again?"

"Uh, yeah. Later today, when he comes to work in the yard."

"Oh, Callie," she says, like she can't believe how dense I am. "I think Tucker—"

"Please don't say he's pining for me while he pulls weeds."

"I don't think he's pining. But I've noticed the way he looks at you. What if whatever's going on between you two turns into more? Are you ready for that?"

She's talking around Isaac—around what happened last summer with Isaac. And truthfully, no, I'm not sure I'm ready for more. I'm not even sure I deserve more. But I think I *want* more.

"We're just friends, Aunt Lucy."

"Okay," she says, but she doesn't sound convinced. "I hope you had a good breakfast, because I need your help moving furniture in the Victoria. And I'll love you forever if you'll assist with wallpaper removal after."

"Can't wait," I say, traipsing up the stairs behind her.

The Victoria overlooks the garden, and I get an occasional peek at Tucker as he places paving stones along a meandering path. I linger near the window, holding the steamer to dreadful wallpaper, paying little attention to what I'm supposed to be doing.

"That ought to do it," Lucy says, nudging me aside to tackle the wet paper with her scraper. She peels back a long strip with little effort. "Well. Soaking the paper with steam for *over an hour* sure makes the removal process easy." She glances out the window, spots Tucker, and turns an I-told-you-so look on me. "Enjoying the view?"

I wave the steam wand in her face. "Perfecting my technique."

We both look out the window again, but the garden's empty.

The front door slams, and Tucker's voice echoes up the stairway. "Hello?"

"Up here," Lucy calls, waggling her eyebrows.

His footsteps thud up the stairs, and before I've had a chance to tame my hair or wipe the sweat from my forehead, he's in the doorway. I glance down at my grubby clothes, the very sweats I wore this morning to the pool. To breakfast. Damn it. Why didn't I take ten minutes to shower and change before joining Lucy?

Tucker grins, oblivious to my vanity. "Making progress?"

"Oh yeah," Lucy says, waving toward the bare wall we've uncovered. "Callie's perfecting her technique."

I shoot a glare at her before turning my back to resume steaming, as if this is a job for which I'm salaried. Hopefully my ass isn't covered in dust and tacky wallpaper.

"I'm gonna take a break," Tucker announces. "If that's cool."

"Go for it," Lucy says.

"Mind if I grab a bottle of water from the kitchen?"

"Help yourself."

There's a beat of quiet, but I know he's still in the room because I feel his presence the same way I've felt the sun's heat. The steamer hisses, spitting beads of water onto my arm. I try to blot it dry on the front of my shirt, but I drop the wand in the process. I bend to pick it up and knock my head on the windowsill as I straighten.

Holy hell.

"Cal?" Tucker says. "You up for a walk?"

I spin around, rubbing my head. "Um . . ."

Lucy nudges me.

I pass her the steam wand. "Yeah. Okay."

We swing by the kitchen to grab waters before heading outside. The morning clouds have burned off and the weather's beautiful—perfectly summer, I decide as we cross the lawn.

"Thanks for rescuing me," I say, pulling my hair off my neck and into a twist. "Where are we headed?"

"There're some trails that weave through the woods, around the hilltop. Sound okay?"

I nod as we step under the canopy of trees, shoes padding over moss and pine needles. The temperature drops about ten degrees. Everywhere I look, there's green—underfoot, shielding the sky, dripping from tree bark—and I'm reminded of the last dream I had, following Chloe through the forest.

Tucker finds a trail, winding through shrubs that reach out to snag on our clothes. He makes a left, and we ascend a steep hill.

Isaac would surrender a limb to mountain bike out here.

"How do you know these trails?" I ask Tucker.

"I used to come up here when I was a kid, especially during the summer, when I wanted to get out of the house. The trails were trampled by a lot of Stewart kids, I guess. We'll stop soon, but if you kept going, you'd find this, like, meadow. There're flowers this time of year—poppies, I think."

Poppies: beauty, eternal life, loyalty, slumber, death.

A shiver scurries down my spine.

The incline evens out, and we come to a clearing where a huddle of flattened boulders waits. Winded, I sit on the largest, the stone cool and smooth. Tucker plants himself beside me, closer than a friend would probably sit, but I don't mind.

He bumps me with his elbow. "Nice, yeah?"

"Yeah. Bring a lot of girls out here?"

He grins, and I find myself envious of the way he glows from within, like his soul is a 100-watt lightbulb. "Nah. I haven't been out here in a long time."

"How come?"

"When my dad figured out this was where I was spending my time, he told me I wasn't allowed to come anymore."

"He was worried you'd get lost?"

"He didn't want me near the Stewart property. Not then, not now."

"But you work on the Stewart property—what used to be the Stewart property, anyway."

"Yeah, he doesn't know that."

"Seriously? What does he think you do all day?"

He pulls at a long blade of grass. "Yard work for a lady who's new to town. I'm not lying, and he's not exactly involved, so it's no big deal."

"What's he got against the Stewarts?"

Tucker splits the grass at its seam. "The Stewarts always had a shitty reputation in Bell Cove. They were drinkers and shady businessmen, not afraid to knock around their wives, supposedly. My dad's never wanted me mixed up in it."

"But Lucy owns the house now. He'd really be mad if he found out you work for her?"

"He won't find out."

I spend a moment musing this new layer of the mystery that is becoming the Morgan family, then ask, "Your dad grew up in Bell Cove, like you?"

"My mother, too." He touches my knee, lightly, only for a second, but I feel the contact down to my toes. "Sorry about being a downer at breakfast—my family and everything. I didn't ruin our first date, did I?"

"Who said this morning was a date?"

His eyes go wide with feigned offense. "It wasn't? Because I wouldn't've picked up the check if I'd realized."

A giggle billows out of me. The urge to tamp it down isn't immediate, which is strange and disconcerting but not entirely terrible, because Tucker seems pleased.

"Tell me why you came to Bell Cove this summer," he says. "Not just to help Lucy, right?"

I can't figure out if he's trawling for information or if he wants me to validate what he's already heard. I hesitate, running a hand over the moss covering the lower part of our rock before realizing I can give him this. I can tell him what instigated my trip to Lucy's without discussing the whole sordid story. "Okay, no, I'm not just here to help Lucy." I inhale a woodsy breath, sifting for words that'll explain my wrecked home life. "My parents . . . They're going through a hard time. And my dad—well, he caught me doing something I probably shouldn't have been doing, and he threatened to send me to this, um . . . summer camp. Lucy's was the alternative."

"Wow," Tucker says. "I have so many questions."

"I figured you would."

He takes that as an invitation. "What'd your dad catch you doing?"

"Smoking out in my bathroom."

His laughter is a surprise. "Really? You?"

"Yes, *me*."

"You know, every time I think I've got you pegged, you end up doing or saying something totally unexpected."

"Glad I amuse you. I'm actually running low. Do you know anyone I can buy from?"

"Probably, but—" He studies me a moment, brow crinkled. A breeze rustles the branches overhead. I listen for the sound of distant ocean waves as my face becomes insufferably warm.

"Tucker," I say when I can't stand his silent scrutiny another second. "What?"

"It's just . . . You don't really want to buy more."

"How do you know?"

He shrugs. "I just know. You don't need it."

I want to be irritated by his assumption, by his certainty, by the way he thinks he knows me *so well* after a couple of weeks. I want to argue. *Yes, Tucker, I* do *want to buy more, and thanks for minding your own business,* but I can't, because he may not be wrong. This morning, when I needed an escape, I swam. That worked out okay.

Still, I'm not ready to make a grand declaration about how I've taken my last hit.

"So . . . ," I say, nervous out of nowhere.

Tucker smiles, teasing. "So, no, I won't give you my dealer's number."

I roll my eyes and move to swat his leg, but he captures my hand and folds it between both of his. Instinct tells me to pull away. He's the only person who can coax laughter out of me, and hand-holding—*hand-holding!*—blurs all kinds of lines. If this doesn't work . . . If something goes wrong and I lose the friendship we're building, it'll be so hard to bounce back.

But then he weaves his fingers through mine, all slow and sweet. His skin is warm, his palm feels nice against mine, and the way he's looking at me . . . It's not the way a boy looks at a friend.

It's the way a boy looks at someone he wants: eyes searching, lips parted . . . longing.

He squeezes my hand. "Is this all right?"

I nod because I don't trust my voice to remain steady. But it is all right. Better than all right.

"So, Lucy's," he says, "superior to summer camp?"

"Maybe."

His grin is steeped in arrogance. "Because of me?"

He's not far from the truth. On good days my mood is unpredictable, and on bad days, well, I've let my inner bitch shine. But Tucker's been patient. He's been constant.

The sun is moving west, stretching shadows across the forest floor, and it's probably time to get back to work. As that thought cements itself, Tucker stands, pulling me up, too, then leads me to the trail home.

My hand remains in his all the way back to Stewart House.

25

I can't sleep, again, but not because I'm scared or tense or sad. I feel almost *good*, and that's as unsettling an emotion as any other.

What right do I have?

When I'm sure Lucy's out for the night, I treat myself to a modest smoke, considering Tucker and his optimistic but naive belief that I don't need weed. The motion is therapeutic and the herbal aroma is faintly sedative, but my heart's not in it.

I keep seeing that pale face in the attic window. And wondering about Chloe's belongings. And hearing my grandma's sage advice: *Why not keep a mind open to possibility?* I pull up the photo I snapped of *Help for the Haunted*'s recommendations for establishing contact with the paranormal. *Relaxation is crucial. Distractions should be eliminated. Work to empty your mind. Slacken your muscles and allow your eyes to defocus.*

I could try.

Inspired, I dip into my nightstand. Grabbing Chloe's things, as well as my phone, I sneak out to the porch with a blanket and a fierce longing for my sister.

I sit in the rocking chair farthest from Lucy's bedroom window, opposite where I sat when Tucker and I first met. The sky's clear, and the night is very quiet, save the waves beating the rocks below the cliff. The air is warmer than usual, so I put the blanket aside, then spend a minute arranging Chloe's things on my lap—cap, goggles, notebook, pen.

I'm reasonably relaxed, my mind as empty as can be expected. I let my muscles loose, melting into the chair, and then, gazing into the dark yard, I let my vision go blurry.

I spend a long time watching for light, for color, for movement.

I see nothing.

Discouraged, I study *Help for the Haunted*'s directives again. Viewing artwork and listening to soothing music to establish *a clear and tranquil state of mind* seems pointless, especially considering I just smoked a substance known for magnifying thoughts and perceptions, not to mention amping dopamine levels.

I can do this; I *need* this.

If communication is possible, if it really is Chloe's spirit that lingers, there's no reason we can't make a connection tonight.

I have to be patient. I have to practice.

I'm not sure how long I sit on the porch, thinking about my sister, staring into the yard, stretching my awareness to its farthest reaches, but I don't notice how cold it's become until I'm forced to clench my jaw to keep my teeth from chattering.

I reach for the blanket, not ready to give up. Settling back into my chair, I let my vision go hazy again. And then I see it—a gently lit figure moving through the yard.

Chloe, in her yellow dress.

My eyes flood with tears.

She glides toward the porch, toward me, ethereal and beautiful. Nostalgia surges through me, robbing my breath.

And then comes an onslaught of questions. . . . Does she see me? Will she be able to speak to me? Will she *want* to speak to me?

Does she miss me as much as I miss her, every single day?

"Cal," she says, her voice like gossamer.

I've been desperate to talk to her for months and months, and now she's here, and I'm struck speechless as she stands over me.

"It's been a long time," she says.

"I've missed you," she says.

"Are you okay?" she says.

She looks lovely, like herself but softer, airbrushed by a meticulous hand. There's an eerie radiance about her, like death made her phosphorescent.

Help for the Haunted spoke of fear, but I'm not afraid.

Joy—that's what I feel.

"It was you all along," I whisper, blotting my tears. I want to hug her *so* tightly, smell her hair and feel her warmth and confirm that she's real, *here*, looking at me through darkened eyes, speaking to me in a wispy voice. But she's keeping her distance and I'm not sure why, so I stay in my chair, hands in my lap, clutching her little notebook.

"Took you long enough to figure it out," she says, and I'm so happy her sarcasm has sustained the last year I could cry all over again.

"Took *you* long enough to make an appearance."

"I've been nearby since you came back."

"You left the poppies? And all this?" I ask, waving a hand over her belongings.

"I wanted you to know it was me. I didn't want you to be scared."

"I'm not."

I expect her to grin, but her expression has sobered. "You were."

"God. Obviously. You're freaking—"

I snap my mouth shut, horrified.

Does she realize?

"Dead," she supplies tonelessly. "You can say it."

No, I can't. Instead, I whisper the apology I've spent the last year wishing to convey—the only words that matter. "Chloe, I'm so sorry. It was my fault, all of it. I shouldn't have . . ." I trail off, because she's looking at me like she hasn't a clue what I'm talking about. Emphatically, I say, "What I did. The things I said."

"I don't remember," she says, shaking her head. And then she clarifies. "I remember home. Mom and Daddy. I remember school, and summer break, and coming here. I remember being with Aunt Lucy and you. I remember our promise to come back—I *knew* you would. I remember running. And biking. And swimming."

"In the ocean."

She nods, lighting up. "Aunt Lucy didn't want us to."

"But you insisted."

"And you loved it."

"No," I say. "*You* loved it."

She absorbs this. "Have you been since you came back?"

I maintain a carefully neutral expression because *she really doesn't remember*, and I'm not sure, yet, what that means. I stall, searching for the right answer, one that won't alarm her, finally settling on, "Not to the ocean."

"Why not?"

"It's . . . dangerous."

"You sound like Aunt Lucy. Like Dad."

I peer up at her, panic churning in my stomach. She knows she *died*, but she doesn't know how or why. She's glad to reconnect because she doesn't remember how ugly I was at the end. This must be why she hasn't left Bell Cove: There are loose threads. Empty swaths of memory.

I'm her business unfinished.

My head hurts, suddenly and intensely.

"I swam this morning," I tell her. "First time I've gone in a long time."

She gives me a sad smile. "I miss the water."

"I miss *you*."

"You don't have to. Not anymore."

I nod, rubbing my forehead, trying to contain shivers that lurk beneath my skin.

"You're feeling bad?"

I pull the blanket tighter around my shoulders. "I'm just cold."

"Then you should go inside. Get some sleep. You don't do that enough."

I want to remind her that I'm the big sister. I want to tell her she's wrong, I'm fine, and I'll endure a blizzard if that's what's required to spend time with her, but she's drifting away.

"Chloe, please don't go."

She smiles. "I'll be back."

"When?"

"Tomorrow night. You'll meet me?"

"You know I will."

She blows me a kiss before fading into the darkness.

26

When my alarm goes off early the next morning, I'm drained and a little loopy.

All night, my dreams were fevered, crowded with Chloe, broken up by a lingering headache. Now that I'm awake, barely, our reunion returns in fragments, glimmers that dim as quickly as they surface. I can just barely call up the basics of her image: yellow dress, rose gold hair, luminous as she stood before me.

I roll out of bed and, bleary-eyed, stuff my swim gear into my backpack.

Physically, I feel like shit, but mentally, I'm blissed out.

Last night, I reunited with my sister.

Tucker's beaten me to the pool. He's swimming slow warm-up laps in a middle lane as I dump my bag on a chair and strip out of my sweats. He doesn't stop when I slip into the lane next to his, and I'm relieved.

I'm becoming pretty damn fond of his amiable presence, but I need a while to just be.

After a few hundred yards, the rush of water begins to dull the thudding in my head. I swim on, pushing myself, working through last night's conversation. My recollection is choppy, but one detail clings, urgent and upsetting: Chloe doesn't remember the day she died—what she did or what I said.

The anniversary of her death is tomorrow; I've spent almost a year trapped in an endless loop of those awful hours. It's unfathomable that she could forget.

I roll into flip turn after flip turn, apprehensive, now, thinking about how I'll observe the one day I'm desperate to forget. I swim hard until my breath comes short and my face goes hot, until I'm light-headed. I'm about to pull up at the wall when I catch a glimpse of Tucker crossing beneath the lane line to join me.

I slow my pace, catching my breath, cooling down, ready to think about something else for a while. Tucker follows for a few leisurely laps, and by the time he reaches out to grab playfully at my ankle, I'm craving his attention.

"Morning," he says, tugging his goggles off, revealing his sea-glass eyes, all alight. "I brought you a surprise."

He hoists himself up and out of the water, dripping all over the deck as he crosses it. His muscles flex and relax, flex and relax; he's built like a Grecian sculpture, one my father showed me a picture of a few years ago, the *Discobolus*: a man preparing to hurl a discus. He pulls a yellow ball from his bag, roughly the size of a volleyball, and, I swear to God, twists his abdomen exactly like the *Discobolus*, winding up to pitch the ball into the water.

"Tucker," I say, freezing him in his prethrow pose. "I said I didn't play water polo."

"Why not start?" He straightens and spins the ball on his palm—show-off. "You can tread water, yeah?"

"Yes, I can tread water," I say, indignant.

"And we know you can swim. You're gonna be a natural." He tosses the ball into the middle of the pool, then launches off the deck in a dive after it.

I leave my goggles on the grate and push off the wall. After last night, I feel like I might be capable of anything. And, anyway, if I don't at least try, I'll never hear the end of it.

We spend the next half hour going over the basics. What Tucker calls dribbling, swimming freestyle with my head above water, the ball riding the wake between my arms—a skill I suck at. Passing is equally draining. Tucker considerately blames my struggles on the fact that his ball is men's regulation. "Women's are a little smaller," he explains. "I'll try to find you one. It'll fit better in your hand."

He shows me how to maximize my tread, demonstrating first, then asking me to sit on the wall and physically moving my legs in the egg-beater motion that will apparently keep me afloat for hours. His hands are gentle, swirling my feet around and around. I try to do it right, though his proximity is kind of distracting.

But when I swim into deeper water and attempt treading on my own, he nods his approval. "You're getting it."

I throw my hands up and sink to the bottom, my legs wobbly with the exertion of my workout. When I open my eyes, immersed, the world's a blur. Without goggles, the chlorine stings, but it's reassuring. I'd forgotten how good for the soul regular time in the pool can be.

I plant my feet on the concrete and push toward the wall. When I surface, I find Tucker sitting on the gutter. "I was starting to think I was gonna have to come in after you."

I pull myself up to sit next to him, splashing water over my legs.

"You love being in the pool," he says.

"So do you," I return.

I don't miss the way his gaze jumps from my eyes to my mouth. He's been so sweet, and in my most honest moments, I can admit that I like him—a lot. But there's comfort in the simplicity of his friendship, and I'm not sure if I'm ready to risk it.

He doesn't lean in, as I thought he might. Instead, he takes my hand, stretching my arm across his lap. So slowly, he draws a finger along my palm, across my wrist, higher. I close my eyes as he traces the length of my scar like he's scrawling a line through sand. Nobody's ever touched it—nobody's ever wanted to—and the sensation is bizarre. The tissue isn't entirely healed, and the nerve endings are ultrasensitive, giving me the tingly sensation of being touched everywhere, yet nowhere at all.

"Broken wing," he murmurs, dragging his finger lightly down my arm.

I don't know why, but his comment makes me smile. "It's healing."

"Tell me about it?"

I shake my head, falling helplessly into his gaze. I've hated my scar for as long as I've had it, the remnant of a battle lost but somehow survived.

"Someday?" Tucker asks.

I nod because I do want to tell him, when I can relay the story without worrying that my revelation will change things between us.

I reach out with my free hand. Tentatively, I trace the lines of his tattoo. His breath hitches, and I look up to see him watching me. His skin is slippery, still wet, as I outline the curling waves, then follow the infinite circle that encloses them.

"It's meant to be the ocean," he says.

I catch a bead of water on my finger before it drips down his arm. "Not a pool?"

"No. My mother loved the ocean—one of the few things I know about her."

Chloe loved the ocean, too.

Loved. Past tense.

I wonder when Tucker gave up on his mom, stopped thinking of her as a part of his life, as a possibility. I'm hoping he'll go on, but he stays quiet. There's so much happening behind his gaze, though. I watch indecision and conviction and need tangle around one another, and I realize he's deciding whether to give me a secret. I can relate; I'm torn about opening up to him, too.

Finally, he twines our fingers and says, "The beach—Bell Cove—is where I feel most like me. I hated it here when I was a kid. I bailed as soon as I graduated, spent most of last summer in Malibu with my aunt and uncle and cousin, but it didn't take me long to miss Bell Cove. My tattoo's a reminder of home, of everything home's supposed to be. I feel my mother when I'm here, and I feel her when I look at it." He gives a quiet laugh. "Does that sound crazy?"

"Not at all," I tell him, envious of the closure he seems to have found.

He opens our linked hands, measuring his palm against mine. "So? Do you still think it's cool?"

I look at his tattoo again, the ocean, *home*, a reminder of his mother and their untested connection. "Maybe not cool, so much. But I like it."

He smiles as if my answer is exactly what he wanted to hear.

I decline Tucker's offer of a ride home. I like the bike, the winding down of my thoughts as I pedal, fresh air blowing my damp hair dry. It's not until I hit the hill, my legs burning with the challenge of the incline, that my headache creeps back in. It's subtle, an annoying tickle of pain, but it wipes out the endorphins I earned swimming.

Lucy's in the kitchen when I come through the door, her hair a blur of auburn. "How was your workout?"

"Good," I say, shedding my sweatshirt. My neck is clammy, too warm.

"How's Tucker?"

I consider telling her the truth: Tucker is kind of amazing. When he holds my hand, I feel comforted. When he smiles, it's easy to smile back. When he tells me his secrets, I want to tell him mine.

"Fine," I say.

She pushes her lower lip out in a pout. "You're stingy with the good stuff." She places a plate of scrambled eggs and buttered toast in front of me, flipping her frown into a grin. "But I'll still feed you."

I nibble in the name of decorum, trying to stifle unrelenting yawns as Lucy devours her food, telling me about her plan to install bead board in the Victoria before we paint the walls lilac.

I push my plate away. "Is that something we should let Tucker handle? Or, like, a carpenter?"

She flexes her nonexistent biceps. "We can manage bead board. I bought a nail gun!"

I know she's waiting for me to laugh or protest or agree wholeheartedly with her can-do declaration, *something*, but all I can muster is a listless nod.

She touches my arm. "You okay?"

"Yeah. Just a headache."

"Allergies. The pollen count's been high. I'm feeling it, too. I'll get you some Motrin." She leaves her chair to root around in a cabinet while I massage my temples, trying to relieve the pressure. Daisy orbits the legs of my chair, her meows insistent and severe.

Lucy brings me pills and a glass of water, then returns to her breakfast. It's almost as if she's shouting directly into my ear when she asks, "Did your head hurt while you were swimming?"

"Not really," I say, modeling a softer tone. "I started to feel bad as I was riding home."

"I wonder if you overdid it."

"Maybe. Tucker's teaching me how to play water polo."

"Well, tell him to take it easy next time."

"He only showed me a few of the basics," I say, inclined to defend him.

"Maybe you should skip home improvement. Go nap instead."

That sounds wonderful, actually, but the work keeps my mind from my parents, from tomorrow's unwelcome anniversary, from smoking. And, hopefully, from the brain-bending fact that last night I had a conversation with my dead sister. "The Motrin's kicking in," I lie.

Lucy's skeptical.

I stand, using the table to steady myself, hoping she doesn't notice. "Come on. Show me this new nail gun."

Up in the Victoria, I try to keep up. My struggle must be obvious, though, because all Lucy will let me do is sit on the floor and hold the bead board panels while she tacks them to the wall. Although I learn to anticipate the sharp *pops*, I jump every time she pulls the trigger, blasting nails into the wood.

By the time we've gotten the bead board in place and adjusted the panels that hang crooked, an army of tiny men with nail guns of their own has moved into my skull. My aunt's busy winding up an orange extension cord, so I lean against the wall and close my eyes, warding off the afternoon glare streaming in through the windows.

Lucy's voice floats over from across the room. "Still not feeling well?"

I swallow around the swell of nausea inching up my throat. "Not really."

"We're done for now. Go get cleaned up. You've earned a break."

"Aunt Lucy—"

"You look awful, Callie. Seriously. Go lie down."

I do.

She comes into my room a few minutes after I've climbed into bed. She spreads another blanket on top of the ones I'm already beneath and covers my forehead with a wet washcloth, something my mom used to do for Chloe and me when we weren't feeling well.

"Get some sleep," she says. "Your dad'll have my ass if I let you catch pneumonia."

I try for a courteous laugh because I'm touched by her concern, but it comes out low and lethargic. The last thing I hear before drifting off is the quiet click of the shutting door.

I spend what's left of the afternoon in bed, alternately napping and sipping the tea Lucy brings. I'd almost forgotten what it's like to be mothered, and I can't bring myself to discourage the attention she's showering on me.

She comes in early evening with yet another mug of tea. "How're we feeling?"

"So much better."

She sits down on my bed. I catch traces of nicotine under her lavender body oil as she plucks the lone paperback from my nightstand. She holds it out, admiring its cover. "*Little House in the Big Woods*. I've always loved this book."

"I found it in the parlor." And then, warily, "Chloe loved it, too."

Lucy hesitates, then says, "Do you remember that Christmas—?"

I nod, panic bubbling up inside me. Of course I remember; I think about it all the time, especially since I've been here, the last place Chloe and I were together. But I don't want to talk about Christmas, or *Little House in the Big Woods*, or my sister. It doesn't matter that I spent time with her last night. She was different—not flesh and blood, not altogether *my* Chloe—and her absence from the corporeal world will always be crushing.

I need Lucy to let it go.

My headache, combined with mention of my sister, must have been enough for today because, thank God, she changes the subject. "Tucker asked about you. He was bummed when I told him you were sick. I swear, if that kid had a tail, it would've been tucked between his legs."

I sip hot, honey-sweetened tea. "I'm sure you didn't downplay my headache."

"No, but I'm glad you've got some color back. I thought you were going to keel over earlier." She grins and pats my knee. "I went out while you were sleeping and got the red paint you liked for the Abigail, a sage green for the Theodore, and the lilac. I hope we can start painting tomorrow, if you're up for it."

"I will be," I say with a decisive nod.

"Will you please skip the pool in the morning? I want you fully recovered before you go pushing yourself again."

I agree, but I'm bummed. I'd been looking forward to my workout, but more than that, Tucker has tomorrow off, which means I won't see him again for something like thirty-six hours.

Why does that strike me as an unbearably long time?

"You're thinking about him, aren't you?" Lucy says.

"No." Though I blush, giving myself away.

"He's here."

"What?"

"In the parlor."

"But he should've left by now."

"He did. He came back. He has something for you."

I comb my fingers through my hair, anxious out of nowhere. "Why didn't you tell me?"

"I'm telling you now. Better get freshened up." She winks before rising from the bed. Just before stepping into the hallway, she stops, turns, and looks at me. Something poignant and maternal softens her expression, tugging at my heart.

"Thanks for taking care of me," I say.

She smiles. "You're welcome."

After washing my face and swiping a brush through my hair, I pad down the hallway to the parlor. I'm feeling a little self-conscious about the sloppiness that is my appearance, but the second I peek into the parlor, all that's forgotten.

Tucker's sitting on the settee with a sleeping kitten in his lap.

My hand flies to my mouth. "Is that . . . ?"

His face splits into a grin. "The kitten you liked? Yeah."

"Why do you—? What are you—?"

He slides over, patting the empty space next to him. "First, how're you feeling?"

"Better." I step into the parlor and sit beside him. I take a deep breath and concentrate on the formation of a complete sentence. "Tucker. Why do you have a kitten?"

"For a nominal fee, Rex let me adopt him." His response is without fanfare, though he's obviously dampening his excitement.

"But . . . *Why*?"

"Because he needed a home." The kitten doesn't stir as Tucker cups its face in his palm. Its whiskers are miles long. "Look at him, Cal. How could I resist?"

I reach out to brush my fingers over the kitten's fur.

"Here's the thing, though," Tucker continues. "My dad's not exactly a pet guy, so I thought maybe . . ."

It dawns on me so suddenly—what he did, why he brought the kitten here—I have to blink back tears before I can look up at him. My voice is hushed when I say, "You thought the kitten could stay with me?"

"Yeah. If that's cool."

Tucker Morgan bought me a cat. Because he knew I liked it, because I was sick, because he cares about me enough to do something spontaneously wonderful. I'm not even sure what to do with this information, but my heart's skipping around in my chest, and Tucker's passing me the kitten, and I'm accepting it like I'm prepared, like people gift me living, breathing creatures all the time. The kitten's little body is warm and delicate, and I snuggle him against me, a mixture of gratitude and confusion and elation making soup of my thoughts.

The kitten lets out the tiniest purr, filling the parlor with the sound of contentment.

"He likes you," Tucker says.

I want to reply with something gracious, something as heartfelt and profound as what he's done. There are so many things I want to say, a million sentiments I need to express, but words fail me.

Finally, I come up with an earnest, "Thank you."

I can tell by the way his eyes smile . . . It's enough.

28

Later, I call home. I miss my parents, but I'm not raring to return to Seattle anymore. Avoiding Isaac's parents, sneaking into Chloe's shrine of a bedroom, slapping on a charlatan happy face for my dad. I don't like that version of myself.

Besides, Chloe is here, in Bell Cove.

When Mom answers the phone, she slurs. She's sloshed. Still, I tell her about my new kitten and the redecorating that's been keeping me busy. It's trivial stuff, but she doesn't seem to care; she *mmhmms* in almost all the right places and even laughs a little when I go into a detailed description of Lucy's latest outfit. When she passes the phone off to Dad, I repeat my stories for him, then mention that I've been to the pool.

"I'm happy to hear that," he says. "Chloe would be, too."

I blink, taken aback; he hardly ever speaks my sister's name. He misses her a lot: their Sunday night movies, her running shoes dumped in the front hall, her heedless resolve. Dad and Chloe butted heads sometimes, but there was so much love between them.

He goes on: "You know, it's okay to talk about her, Callie. I want you to feel comfortable coming to me. About anything, but especially about your sister. Your aunt said—"

"Wait. Lucy put you up to this?"

"No, but she's worried about you. She said you're keeping your feelings inside."

I sit up, disturbing my sleeping kitten. "God, Dad, you do the same thing."

He sighs. "That doesn't mean it's the best way to cope. Tomorrow will be a year since she left us, and I'm starting to realize that's too long to keep quiet. I think about her all the time, and I want to talk about her—even if it hurts. I want us to be more open. About Chloe, about what happened last summer—anything you want. When you're ready, I'll be ready."

A year.

It's so surreal: Chloe could have died yesterday or a century ago.

I try to imagine what it'd be like to sit my dad down and tell him about the ocean swims she and I made last summer. Her determination when it came to triathlon training. Her feelings for Isaac, and how I brushed them off right up until it was too late. What would he say if I told him that Chloe and I fought the night she died? If he knew what I said to her before she left for the beach, the last words she likely heard? How would he feel if I told him that I want to get better but can't—not while I lack my sister's forgiveness.

"Do you and Mom talk about Chloe?"

Softly, he says, "Mom and I don't talk about a lot these days. She's not as strong as you."

I'm not strong—not like I used to be. But there are moments when I sense my strength attempting a comeback. When Lucy makes me laugh, or when I'm a few thousand yards into a workout. Pretty much any time I'm with Tucker.

"I should go, Dad. But I love you. Mom, too."

After we hang up, I lie in bed for a long time, thinking about strength and its many, many shapes.

Very late, I prepare.

I smoke as scantly as last night. I dress in leggings and a sweatshirt. I wrap up in a blanket. I'm not sure how much they matter, but I gather my sister's things. And then I resume my post on the porch, stretching my awareness to the far reaches of the yard.

It's easier this time, connecting with her.

She appears, again, in her yellow dress, something she never would have picked for herself. My mom bought it two days after she died, a tear-soaked journey to Nordstrom to shop for Chloe's final ensemble. Both my dad and Lucy volunteered for the task, but Mom insisted, and I went along. Honestly, I was scared she wouldn't make it back to the house on her own.

"You look pretty in that dress," I tell my sister now, because she does, and Mom would want me to pass along the compliment.

She wrinkles her nose. "You guys should've buried me in my running shorts."

I smile.

"I'm serious," she says, hovering before me. "That could've been my final act of defiance where Daddy's concerned."

"He misses you," I tell her, solemn now. "Mom, too. So much."

We're quiet a moment, watching each other. I imagine my expression matches hers: love spun with wonder and disbelief, because holy hell, this is incredible.

It's also unnerving. The version of Chloe standing before me is different: so still, so much more introspective. In life, she was always in motion, always speaking before thinking. I'm not sure if the change has to do with death or how she spent the last 364 days.

I ask the question that's been on my mind since we said goodbye last night. "What's it like?"

"This?" she asks, sweeping a hand through the air. Her movements are different, too: slower, more graceful. She used to remind me of a fawn, but now she's all doe: fluid, elegant, and sure.

"Yeah. Do you feel . . . ?"

"Dead?"

"I was going to say *different*."

She rolls her eyes, so quintessentially Chloe my throat swells with wistfulness. "I don't know. I hardly remember what it's like to be anything *but* dead. Like, the basics are there: I was a daughter and a sister and an average student and an athlete. I liked to watch movies with Dad and help Mom with her garden and, more than anything, I wanted to be like you. But *life*? How it *felt* to be alive?" She shrugs. "Time passes differently now—I have no real sense of it. I mean, I exist. I watch Lucy and the waves. I wander the beach and the town and the woods. But it's all peripheral, like I'm observing a girl who looks like me. I don't even know how long it's been—days or weeks or months."

It's like pressing hard into a bruise, hearing her talk like this. I'm not sure whether to give her the truth, even about something as inconsequential-seeming as the time line.

But then, the last time I lied, something terrible happened.

"It's been a year," I say. "A year tomorrow."

She nods once.

"It doesn't feel like that long?"

"It feels like it doesn't matter. I'm here, and I'm not going anywhere."

"You know that for sure?"

She spends a minute in quiet thought. I wonder if she's formulating a genuine response or trying to figure out how to avoid freaking me out. "If there's a heaven," she finally says, "I missed it. Because it can't be this—roaming Bell Cove, alone and lonely, for eternity. But I can't imagine that this existence is hell, either. I don't remember how I died, or why, but I couldn't have done something so horrendous I earned eternal damnation."

The uncertainty in her voice shreds me. "Chloe. You didn't."

Her shoulders rise, then fall. "I'm . . . stuck. Here. Probably forever."

"Maybe not. Maybe you're here because you have business to finish."

Remember, I think. *Please, Chloe. I need you to remember.*

"I mean, yeah, I have business to finish," she says, scornful. "I was going to compete in a triathlon. I was going to graduate high school. I was going to fall in love. How am I supposed to know which of the thousands of missed opportunities sentenced me to purgatory?"

My arms prickle with goose bumps, reassurances and justifications gathering on my tongue.

What I don't say is this: People die young all the time, before they chase their dreams and meet their goals. Before they find true love. I can't imagine that each and every one of them is like my sister: trapped.

Chloe lingers because of what happened the night she died.

She has unfinished business with *me.*

Somewhere, locked in her head or her heart or her soul, she has information we both need. Information about Isaac and what happened between the two of them. Information that will clear him of culpability or confirm the suspicions I've carried for the last year. If I can help her recall that day, that *night*, the questions that have tormented me for the last year will earn answers. If she remembers, I can apologize for the part I played. I can beg for her forgiveness.

I wrap my arms around my middle, folding in on myself, the weight of our impossible situation crushing.

"Are you cold again?" Chloe asks.

I look up and see an angel in a yellow dress.

I'd trade places with her if I could.

"I'm okay. This is just . . ."

"Hard. I know."

I nod, blinking back tears.

Her melancholy quickly becomes amusement. "God, Cal, don't you dare cry. You're supposed to be the brave sister."

"No. That was always you."

She accepts my admiration in stride, forever Chloe. "Tell me about the last year. I want to hear about Mom and Dad and swim team and all the boys you've been out with."

Up until recently, my life was a shit show, but I'm not about to admit as much. "Mom and Dad are okay. I'm taking a break from swim team. And boys . . . There's not a lot to tell."

"Liar," Chloe says. "I've seen the hottie Aunt Lucy's got working on the yard."

"That's Tucker." My face betrays me, warming despite the chill that comes with being near my sister. I try to play it off like, *oh, Tucker, he's no one,* because discussing boys with Chloe is cruel, like rubbing her nose in a mess she doesn't realize exists. "He's cool, I guess."

"Uh-huh," she says, raising her eyebrows in the same absurd way Lucy does when Tucker comes up.

I'm trying to figure out how to explain him and *us* when pain flares behind my eyes. Another headache, though this one has come out of nowhere and feels a hell of a lot more severe than any that have come before it. Allergies, Lucy said, which I'm probably exacerbating, hanging out outside at all hours of the day and night. I squeeze my eyes shut and bargain with the discomfort: Give me ten more minutes, and tomorrow I'll practice some self-care.

"You're feeling bad," Chloe says.

"I'm fine."

Her expression asserts, *Don't bullshit me.*

"It's the pollen," I concede. "Lucy said it gives her headaches, too."

"Then you should go inside. We can talk again tomorrow."

I close my eyes again, just briefly, trying to beat back the pain because the last thing I want is to go inside. If I'm going to survive tomorrow, I need this time with my sister.

But when I open my eyes, she's gone.

29

My dad calls after breakfast, wanting to know if I'm okay.

I tell him I am.

I'm not sure what else to say.

In truth, I'm having a hard time getting a handle on my emotions; they're bright and dim, soft and hard, glad and sad. Last night I spent time with Chloe—what a privilege. Her capricious spirit is infinitely better than the permanency of death, and I won't take our connection for granted.

Yet it's not the same.

It can *never* be the same.

After a few minutes of conversation, Dad passes on my mom's love, and we hang up.

I can't imagine what they'll do today.

All morning, Lucy does her best to keep me busy. She chatters nonstop as we roll a couple of coats of crimson paint onto the walls of the Abigail. Duran Duran and the Cure provide the sound track. The work feels good and Lucy's an okay distraction, but my mind keeps drifting.

Over and over, I think, *It's been a year—a whole year.*

Am I heartbroken, because I endured 365 days without my sister, or heartened, for the very same reason?

We finish painting just before noon and stand back to admire our work. Even without basics like the bed and dresser in place, the room looks rich and cozy. Finished, it'll be gorgeous.

After a quick cheese-and-crackers lunch, Lucy promises to look after my kitten, tucks several twenties into my hand—"for all your hard work," she says—and insists I take the afternoon off. When I object—what am I supposed to do with an afternoon alone in Bell Cove?—she shoves me out of the kitchen and down the hall to my room. "The possibilities are endless!" she says. "Find some fun!"

I shower, then wield my hair dryer and a round brush, followed by my long-neglected flatiron. When I'm done, for the first time in months, my hair lies straight and glossy down my back. In my room, I dress in jeans and an airy black tank, then go about applying makeup.

I'm stalling. I'm not sure how to *find some fun*, as my aunt suggested.

I'm putting tubes and brushes and little pots back into my makeup bag when a compact of bronzer slips from my fingers. It lands on the hardwood with a clatter, falls open, and tosses powder everywhere. With a groan, I bend to survey the mess. Dust particles stick to the damp rug and fan out across the floor. Damn it.

Using a wad of wet toilet paper, I crouch down and clean the hardwood, then fold the edges of the rug in toward its center. Beneath it, the floor is stained, but not with makeup. The slats of wood are discolored by a maroon, bubble-shaped splotch, almost as big as the bath mat. The blemish piques my interest in the most dread-filled way.

It's blood. Old blood, but . . . *blood.*

I think first of Clayton Stewart, but, no. I read online that he died of a heart attack. Then my mind leaps to Annabel Tate, but she was last seen in the backyard. Far as I know, she never bled in this bathroom.

Somebody did.

In the bedroom, my phone begins to ring. I jump up and hurry to answer it, expecting my mom because today of all days, she should make an effort. But it's not Mom—it's Isaac.

"I didn't think you'd answer," he says.

I wouldn't have had I looked at the caller ID.

I collapse on my bed. It's been months since I last heard his voice, and I expect to feel something. A sliver of the affection I used to have for him, maybe. Rage, for sure. But there's nothing—nothing but speculation about why he's been trying to get in touch.

"I'm in Seattle," he tells me.

"I'm not."

"I know. I talked to your dad."

I silently curse my father for neglecting to tell me. "What do you want, Isaac?"

"To know how you are."

"Alive." I know I sound like an asshole, but that's the stripped-down truth.

"I've been thinking about you. Today especially. Are you okay?"

"I'm fine."

"Are you really?"

"I'm trying to be."

A long silence passes before he whispers, "Callie. I miss you."

"Please, don't. I can't. Not today."

"I know. God, *I know.* I'm selfish—a dick. It's just, the way things ended. I'm not over it."

Lucy's singing filters in from down the hall; porcelain clanks and clatters as she loads the dishwasher. If she hears me, if she figures out who I'm talking to, she'll be pissed. As far as she's concerned, Isaac is a monster, capable only of chaos.

"I have to go," I tell him.

"Don't hang up," he pleads. "I want to know how you've been. How you're spending your summer. How you're spending today."

"You lost the right to know anything about me."

"Callie, if you'd just hear me out—"

"We're done."

I end the call.

I don't mention Isaac's call to Lucy, but I do ask about the stain in my bathroom.

"I have no idea what caused it." She touches paint-speckled fingers to her chin. "It was sanded down as much as possible, but the crew would've had to put a hole through the hardwood to erase it completely. That's why I bought the rug."

I tell her I'm headed out. I need to talk, but not with her, and not with my dad, and definitely not with Isaac. I need a fresh perspective from someone who won't bullshit me.

Tucker Morgan has yet to bullshit me.

I swing my leg over the seat of my claimed bike and pedal furiously toward town. I'm on autopilot when I stop at a dilapidated phone booth outside Bell Cove's only gas station, kicking myself for never once thinking to exchange phone numbers with him. There's not an actual phone in the booth anymore, but there's a years-old phone book tethered to a little shelf. I flip to *M* and quickly scan for *Morgan*. There's only one, Benjamin Morgan, who's got to be Tucker's father. I memorize the address, then ride to Beech Street.

The neighborhood is quiet. There's pride in the well-maintained sidewalks and neatly trimmed lawns. There's peace in the screen doors and potted plants. The Morgans' house is small, clean, and tidy like the houses adjacent to it. It's painted a fresh, crisp white. The front door and shutters are black, and ivy grows up and around two columns that frame the porch. There's an enormous lilac tree in the front yard, sprigs of purple flowers weeping from its branches. I catch their powdery fragrance as I lean my bike against the low fence surrounding the yard. Pushing my shoulders back in a plaintive display of feigned confidence, I approach the porch, then knock on the door.

Please be home, please be home, I think as the seconds tick by.

When the front door swings open, I know I'm looking at Tucker's dad. His eyes are soft green, his hair sandy blond. The most notable difference between father and son is that Mr. Morgan does not smile.

"Hi," I say, flustered. "Um, is Tucker home?"

Without a greeting, he shouts, "Tuck!"

Then he walks away, leaving me to stand alone on the porch.

When Tucker rounds the corner and sees me outside, his expression falls somewhere between incredulity and bewilderment. He rests a hand on the doorframe, casual in khaki shorts and a navy T-shirt with PEPPERDINE scrawled in orange across its front. His gaze floats over my styled hair and my made-up face and my not-sweats-for-once apparel. "Hey, Cal. What's up?"

"I was hoping I could talk to you." I'm not sure why showing up here, uninvited, seemed like a reasonable idea ten minutes ago, but it feels absolutely unreasonable now. "Do you think we could . . . ?"

"Go somewhere?"

I nod.

"Yeah. Come in while I find some shoes."

I follow him into the house, a bachelor pad if ever there was one: eat-in kitchen, small living room, a couple of closed doors off a short hallway. The furniture is various shades of beige. There's no art on the walls, no fresh flowers on the small dining table, no curtains hanging over the slatted wooden blinds.

Mr. Morgan sits in a recliner, feet propped up, beer bottle in hand. There's a baseball game on the very large television. "Dad," Tucker says, resting a hand low on my back. "This is Callie."

He barely glances up from the game. "Hello."

Tucker rolls his eyes. "My father."

"It's so nice to meet you," I say, laying it on thick. "Tucker talks about you a lot."

Mr. Morgan looks up, mildly surprised. "Nice to meet you, too—Callie, is it?"

I nod, breaking into a wide smile. Once upon a time, I was good with parents.

"Have a seat," Tucker says, nudging me into the room. "I'll be right back."

I perch on the edge of the well-worn sofa and assess Mr. Morgan. He seems drained, as if he's just worked a full day or never gets enough sleep. He's got that look about him, the one that says, *You've got to earn my trust.*

Hoping Tucker will hurry with his shoes, I check out the living room. It's barren, with the exception of a silver-framed black-and-white photograph propped on an end table, the only personal item I've noticed. The picture, taken on a beach, is of a tow-haired baby, brand new and bobble-headed, propped on the shoulder of a woman with windblown hair. Her back is to the photographer, and the baby's tiny and wrinkled, and the whole image is sort of blurred and ethereal. It's stunning.

"Tucker and his mother," Mr. Morgan says.

"Oh—I . . ."

He takes a swig of beer and refocuses on the baseball game. Absently, he says, "It's okay. Go on and look."

I do, for longer than is probably warranted. Tucker was, predictably, an adorable baby. "Where was this taken, Mr. Morgan?"

"Down on the beach, a few blocks from here." He clears his throat. "Right around this time of year, actually."

"It's beautiful."

"Yeah," he says plaintively. "I know."

Tucker's leather flip-flops come slapping down the hallway. "Sorry, Cal. You ready?"

I hop up. "It was nice to talk to you, Mr. Morgan."

"Benjamin," Tucker and his father correct at the same time. I smile as Benjamin adds, "Nice to talk to you, too, Callie."

30

I follow Tucker out to the garage, where his car sits next to a beat-up pickup truck with a bed full of construction equipment. He lifts the garage door and loads my bike into the Woody. We're quiet as we climb in and buckle up. It's not until he backs down the driveway that he says, "So? How weird is my dad?"

"Not weird at all."

He gives a dry laugh. "Come on. A little chilly, don't you think?"

Maybe, but the disappearance of the woman he loved and the subsequent raising of his son, alone, has got to contribute. "He was fine," I say truthfully.

Tucker snorts. "That's generous."

I'm tempted to delve into this, to take a stab at defending Benjamin, but it's none of my business. Besides, I appreciate the way Tucker refrains from pushing me for information, so I'll grant him the same courtesy. "Where are we going?" I ask as he pulls off Sitka, onto a side street.

"Coffee shop. Cool?"

I nod, and a few minutes later he parks in front of a little nook called The Coffee Cove. A blast of espresso-scented air hits me as we walk in. The walls are paneled in sheets of dull, textured metal. Empty burlap coffee bags hang from them like fine art.

"Another local secret?" I ask, following Tucker to the counter.

"Obviously. What do you want to drink?"

Mochas used to be my usual, but I don't have a taste for them anymore. It's been forever since I've visited a coffee shop—I don't even know what to ask for. "Something iced," I say. "I trust you."

He smiles. "Want to find a table?"

I pull cash from my pocket, one of the twenties Lucy gave me, and slide it onto the counter in front of him. "Will you get us something to eat, too?"

He pushes the money back.

"Tucker." His name comes out on a sigh.

He folds the bill into my hand. Stooping, he meets my eyes. "Go find us somewhere to sit. I'll bring food."

I nod, nervous, now that we're about to sit down to coffee and conversation.

I claim a table in the back corner, and Tucker joins me a few minutes later, two iced coffees and a scone in hand. "Caramel," he says, passing me my drink, and then, gesturing to the pastry, "Vanilla bean."

"Thank you, and you're sharing with me."

"Twist my arm," he says, sinking into his chair. "How's your kitten?"

"Really good. I named him Buddy." I shrug and break off a piece of scone. "I might be lacking in the imagination department. Namewise, anyway."

"Buddy. I like it." Then he becomes serious, leaning in to ask, "So, what's up?"

My throat is desert dry. I need to talk—my sanity demands it. I trust Tucker, maybe more than anyone, but there are so many secrets between us: my messy history with Isaac, my sister's death, my sister's *ghost*. Plus, there's the matter of the bloodstain in my bathroom, which I'm hoping he might have some insight on, being local and all.

He's staring expectantly, chewing through a bite of scone.

I square my shoulders. "I want to run something by you, something that might sound sort of nuts. Remember that day we talked by the cliff?"

His eyebrows go up as he rests his forearms on the tabletop. "Yeah."

"You mentioned that some people think Stewart House is haunted."

"Yeah."

I look down at our scone, then back to him. "I think those people are right."

A muscle in his jaw ticks. "Why's that?"

"I've had some experiences. At first, I thought I was seeing things, like that day I thought there was someone in the attic window? But unexplainable stuff kept happening. And then—" I'm about to mention Chloe, *proof*, but I falter. Chloe is personal. Chloe is mine. I rummage through my head for a way to clarify, grappling for an anecdote to substantiate my claim, one that won't drag my sister into the conversation.

Tucker reaches across the table to rest his palm on my arm, exactly as I did to him that day by the cliff, when I wanted *him* to divulge. "And then *what*?"

"And then today . . . I found blood."

He blanches.

"Old blood," I say. "A stain on the floor of my bathroom, one my aunt's been covering with a rug."

He's shaking his head, taking a breath like he's got plans to interrupt, but I barrel on, worried if I stop, I won't be able to start again.

"Something terrible must've happened," I say. "I can't even imagine. And there's other stuff, too. Daisy acts weird sometimes. I've heard sounds at night, and it gets really cold—like, wildly cold—and one day, the cracks in the attic window *grew*—" I stop, letting my head fall into my hands. I sound frenzied. Deranged. "You must think I've lost my mind," I mumble. I look up, meet his gaze, fall into it. "But it's true. There's a ghost haunting my aunt's property."

"Cal," Tucker says gently, skeptically, *piteously*. "You know ghosts aren't real, right?"

Chloe.

"I swear, my ghost is."

"Callie . . ."

He's not buying it, and I can't even blame him. It's hard to believe such a sensational story has fallen out of my mouth. Embarrassment makes me defensive.

"Who's to say it isn't possible?" I demand.

He takes a gulp of his coffee and then, ignoring my question, says, "So you've been . . . what? Communicating with this ghost?"

"Yes," I whisper, because I'm in too deep to backtrack now.

He pulls his hand from my arm, probably afraid my crazy is contagious. "I'm not sure what to say."

His doubt is so blatant; it hurts like a blow to the middle. I've made myself too vulnerable, opened my doors too wide. Thank God I didn't tell him about my sister.

"You're judging me," I say quietly.

"Damn, Cal. I'm not. I just think there's another explanation." He reaches for me again, but I pull away before he makes contact. Wincing, he folds his hands on the tabletop. "It's an old house," he says, burying my confession beneath his good sense. "There're gonna be drafts and weird sounds."

I can't breathe in this stupid coffee shop. It's too warm, and I'm mortified, and I feel a headache coming on.

I shove my chair back and stand. "I need to get out of here."

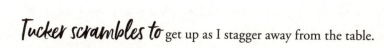

31

Tucker scrambles to get up as I stagger away from the table.

"Callie!"

Deep down, I know I'm being insufferable—storming away when I'm the one who initiated this outing—but I'm too upset to care.

I march through the door, outside, to where the air is fresh, free of judgment.

Tucker follows me down the quiet side street and onto crowded, sunny Sitka.

"I can't believe you're walking away," he says, sidling up next to me.

I don't slow as we weave through the throng of tourists.

"Cal, this isn't going to work."

My footsteps fall in cadence with the thudding in my head.

"I'm not gonna let you storm off. I'm not Lucy."

I walk on, but his words are splitting faults in my obstinacy. He's so composed, so reasonable, and I'm stomping down the sidewalk like a toddler in the midst of a tantrum. For the first time since I learned of it, I'm truly conscious of our age difference.

"Callie, please," he says, taking hold of my wrist.

His touch would've been enough to make me pause, but that *please*, that desperate, suppliant *please*—it stops me. Cements my feet right to the sidewalk.

"What, Tucker? What else could you possibly have to say?"

He sighs, strong fingers encircling my wrist. "I don't know. . . . I just can't stand to watch you walk away."

"What did you expect? I thought I could confide in you. I thought I could trust you. There's *so much*, and I thought you'd listen. I was wrong."

"You weren't. I just—I don't know what I was thinking. I *can* listen."

People are watching us. Families headed to the beach, paused on the sidewalk to gape. Couples sharing saltwater taffy, gawking. Elderly residents who've suspended their strolls to observe Tucker and me. Their stares make me wish I could sink into the pavement.

"I can listen, Cal," he says again. His hand slides from my wrist to wrap around my palm. "Let's go to the beach. Walk for a while."

The beach is the last place I want to be, today of all days, but I can't drop his hand, and I can't turn away.

I want him in my corner too much.

We head for the sand and walk a long time, weaving around families building sandcastles, whacking beach balls, flying kites. It's a while before I can manage breathing without reminding myself to inhale and exhale, and even longer before I've loosened my viselike hold on Tucker's hand.

I've reviled the ocean for a year; it's a daunting notion, forgiving an entity so powerful and destructive.

Finally, we find a quiet spot and sit side by side on the sun-toasted sand. I pull my knees up, digging my toes deep to find the damp, cool grains beneath. It's quiet here, but for the rhythmic cresting of waves. Tucker and I are still at odds, which is wrong, like snowflakes in July. I've grown so accustomed to him radiating light; the solemnity of his mood, of this afternoon, turns the blunt twinge of my headache into the pounding of a bass drum.

I'm tired, deep in my bones and head and heart.

"I'm sorry," he says, cutting into the silence. "I should've heard you out. Shit, Cal. I want you to trust me. You *can* trust me."

I shrug, like none of this is a big deal. And, God, maybe it isn't—not all arguments have to end in catastrophe.

"I shouldn't have stormed off," I admit. "That's kind of a bad habit of mine."

He cracks a smile. "I kind of noticed."

I'm not so pissed anymore—Tucker's proved himself impossible to stay mad at—but my head's killing me. I drop my forehead onto my knees, letting my hair curtain around me. I see white spots on the backs of my lids. I draw figure eights in the sand to remain upright, while my skull pulses in sync to the blood pumping through my veins.

"You okay?" Tucker asks over the ocean wind.

I nod without lifting my head.

"Another headache?"

I nod, again.

"What's up with that?"

I straighten to look at him, wisps of blond streaking across my face.

He brushes my hair back, and his touch makes me more alert than I want to be. The shift between us feels profound, a change in the salty air that makes what's growing between us weightier.

Better.

The somber tone of our afternoon passes when his mouth lifts into a genuine smile, one that makes me smile, too. The longing in his eyes says he wants to kiss me. Right here on the beach. After everything that's happened.

I want to kiss him, too. I want to taste him and touch him and know the softness of his hair, the fullness of his lips, the caress of his breath on my skin. I want to savor the sensation of my hands on his face, his neck, his back.

He inches closer.

My emotions spin circles, discouraging me, mocking me, cheering me on.

"Let's see what we can do about your head." He slides back and over, behind me, and the moment passes. I can't decide if I'm relieved or disappointed.

Not *entirely* disappointed, I decide as he stretches a long leg out on either side of mine and moves forward so we're touching, his warm mingling with my cool. He grips my shoulders, draws me back, then slowly, so slowly, passes his hands beneath my hair. His splayed fingers run the length of my scalp, from the base of my neck to my crown. He does it again, and the pressure is amazing. I turn to beeswax, softening under the heat of his fingers, melting into the fine sand. Seagulls fly overhead, unaware. The sun dips lower, casting the sky in peaches and plums, and for the first time in eons, I'm swimming in a welcome pool of peace.

The serenity evaporates the second I acknowledge it. This happiness, on this beach, with this boy—I don't have a right to it. But then Tucker's arms come around me, pulling me back until I'm against his chest. Reason tells me to move away, but something unreasonable keeps me still.

"How's your head?" he asks.

"Better."

"I'm not so bad to have around, then?"

"Tucker, I never thought you were."

"Yeah, you did. In the beginning. A little while ago, even."

"Well, not anymore."

I bring my hands up to rest on his forearms, hyperaware of his scent, spice and cedar, the solid feel of his chest against my back, and his even breaths. His skin is as soft as suede and covered in hairs as blond as those on his mop-top head.

"I really am sorry about earlier," he murmurs.

I shake my head. "I know how it sounds. Outrageous."

"No."

"Yes."

"Okay . . . maybe a little. I mean, a haunted house? A ghost?" He pauses, and I can almost hear the tinkering of wheels rotating in his head. "What if you tell me more? Why's it so easy for you to believe in this ghost?"

Because she's my sister. Because I've spoken to her. Because I need her.

"It's not easy; I've doubted my sanity a thousand times since I've been back in Bell Cove. It's the sounds and the cold and the things I've found. I can sense a presence, like when you're racing in the pool and you're out in front, but you know the swimmer in the next lane's gaining on you without ever turning to look? It's like that—another soul existing in your space. And then . . ."

So badly, I want to give him my truth.

"And then . . . ?" Tucker prompts.

I shake my head. "Nothing."

He drops his chin onto my shoulder. "Callie? Why don't you ever talk to me?"

"I do. I just did."

"Yeah, but there's other stuff. You could tell me, but you don't. How come?"

Because I'm a mess. I can't talk about things that matter without tears, and tears would snuff out your sunshine. Because you might turn away.

These are the things I should say. Instead, I ask, "What do you want to know?"

"Uh, everything?"

I giggle, a silly girl who has no idea how to direct this conversation somewhere safe.

"What's your favorite color?" he asks.

"Are you trying to warm me up?"

"Something like that. I bet it's black."

I glance down at my black tank and grimace. "It's green."

"Favorite food?"

"Breakfast."

He smiles. "Can you be more specific?"

"Not really. Most important meal of the day and all."

"Okay. How many boyfriends have you had?"

"One. How many girlfriends have you had?"

"None, really. I mean, there've been girls. There was one a few months ago, at school . . ." He clears his throat, sounding suddenly uncomfortable. "It was a one-time thing."

"Huh."

"Yeah. Kind of forgettable. What happened with the boyfriend?"

"It ended."

"Oh?"

"Badly."

He digests that bonus tidbit. "Did he give you that ring you're always wearing?"

I look at my hand, diamonds and plaited platinum encircling my finger. "No."

He lets me go, scoots back, and drapes his arms across his bent knees. I give my filched ring a twist as the blissful aftereffects of his massage drift away on a breeze. With a palm on my cheek, he urges my attention up. His expression is excruciatingly gloomy. "How about I tell you what I know? Then you can add something new, if you want."

"Okay," I say, only because I'm desperately curious as to what he thinks he knows.

"I know you were in Bell Cove for a while last summer."

My stomach sinks into the sand.

"I know about your sister." He finds my hand and holds it in both of his. "I know you're sad because she died."

I sit very still, staring at him while a tornado of anger coils through me. "Lucy told you?"

He shakes his head. "I heard right after it happened, just before I left for Malibu. It was in the news, but there wasn't a lot of information, since she was a minor. People talked, but it was mostly hearsay. When I started working for your aunt, when I met you . . . I put it all together. I asked Lucy about it last night, when I brought your kitten."

I don't even know what to say. He introduced me to his dad and bought me a scone and chided me for believing in ghosts, all the while knowing about Chloe.

I slip my hand from his.

"Cal?" he says imploringly.

"It was a year ago today." But that's all I can get out because my eyes are threatening to spill over with tears. I try to blink them back, like talking about my sister—*thinking* about my sister—doesn't open my chest and batter my heart. But they come, the damn traitorous tears I've so successfully kept at bay. They come with a vengeance.

Tucker's expression twists with distress; he's seen me a lot of ways, but never this way.

It's clear he wants to hear more, but not because he's interested in the gritty details. He's willing to take on part of my burden. I know, because he doesn't ask. He sits next to me, waiting, warm against my side, his patience constant and enduring.

I take a shaky breath, and then the words are buzzing over one another, teeming in the air like a locust swarm. "We came to help Lucy. It was supposed to be the three of us, taking on all these projects. It was supposed to be fun. It *was* fun, sometimes. But Chloe and I had a lot going on—sister stuff. One night was particularly shitty. She did something she shouldn't have, and I said terrible, terrible things. Things I'll never be able to take back." Tucker's face has gone ashy, his mouth pressed into a grim line. Hot tears sear my cool cheeks as my dam of silence comes crashing down. "She went down to the beach—she liked to swim in the ocean—but she shouldn't have gone in the dark. She shouldn't have gone by herself. If I'd known, I would've followed. But I didn't know, and I didn't follow, and she didn't come back."

He cradles my face in his hands, whispers, "It couldn't have been your fault."

"I should have been with her."

"She shouldn't have gone into the ocean alone—you just said so."

"If I hadn't been so mad at her." I'm choking on sobs, short of breath, trying to draw air and speak at the same time. "She was my little sister. I should've been looking out for her."

"Callie, if you'd been with her . . . Those currents are crazy strong. You wouldn't have been able to help."

"But at least she wouldn't have been by herself."

He folds me into his arms and holds me while I cry, tracing warm circles over my back, laying his cheek to the top of my head. His silence feels like commiseration, like empathy, like he *knows*, and when I'm able to gather my misery and stuff it back into the darkness it escaped from, I unwrap myself from him, surprised to see it's officially dusk.

He presses his hands to my cheeks, looking me over. My face is hot, and my eyes feel swollen, raw. Embarrassment rushes in. "I'm so sorry," I say. "That never happens."

"Jesus. Don't apologize. Do you feel any better?"

"A little." Lighter, somehow.

He smiles, tentative. "See? I told you I'm an okay listener." He presses a kiss to my forehead, tender and innocent, then pulls back to gaze at me. "You know, you're beautiful even with your eyes all red and puffy."

I laugh, the sound still foreign and wrong-sounding, but it feeds Tucker's smile. Thank God his sunlight managed to outshine my tears. "You're so full of shit."

He stands, brushes sand from his shorts, and pulls me up. "Let's go get some dinner."

32

Tucker pulls onto Stewart House's gravel drive after dinner at Bell Cove's only fast-food restaurant, a small, old-fashioned drive-through called The Beach Bum. While the name was kind of a turnoff, the food was greasy and delicious; we stuffed ourselves with burgers and malts. It's dark now, but rays of light stream from the windows of the house, like Lucy's trying to make the place visible from space.

"What the hell is she doing in there?" Tucker asks, coaxing the Woody into park.

"Refinishing the hardwood on the floor while jamming to her beloved eighties music, probably. She's bananas."

"Says the girl who hangs out with ghosts."

I give him a teasing *watch it* look because joking with him is a thousand times better than bickering with him, and he's trying. "*A* ghost," I clarify.

He stretches an arm across the back of the bench, making the barest contact with my shoulders. He's being suave about making a move or I'm reading too much into what's going on between us, but either way, my head's in a tailspin. And just how experienced is he anyway? *There've been girls,* he said earlier. I'd be willing to bet he's got more going for him than the one night I spent with Isaac, that ill-conceived attempt at feeling *something.*

I'm still searching, but I've stumbled on a sliver of contentment, one that has everything to do with Tucker Morgan.

He grins, bathing the dark interior in the light that seems to burn within him. "So. We should do this again sometime, yeah?"

"Yeah."

"Really?"

"Yes, really." I flash him a smile, one that comes effortlessly. It feels good to be this girl again, capable of flirting and fun, willing to say *yes.* It feels so good I refuse to think of all the reasons I *shouldn't* be this girl.

He runs his hand over my hair, lazily twisting the strands around his fingers. My eyelids flutter. I have half a mind to stretch out across the seat and request another massage.

"I should go in," I say, though my voice is seriously lacking in conviction.

He leans forward, drawing me closer with a hand on the back of my neck. "I'm gonna see you at the pool tomorrow, right?"

"If you're lucky."

His mouth curls into a lopsided smile. "Oh, that's how it is?"

I'm about to reply, *Yes, Yard Boy, that's exactly how it is,* when he cuts me off with the press of his mouth against mine. It's tantalizingly drawn out, and it comes with the mind-blowing, *holy hell!* realization that Tucker

Morgan is kissing me—kissing me as I've *never* been kissed before. When he pulls away, I'm breathless and giddy, a new kind of high.

With an expression part awestruck, part triumphant, he climbs out of the car and unloads my bike from the back while I look on, wishing I could kiss the smirk off his face. But before I can summon the courage, my bike is safely inside the shed and he's walking me to the porch.

"Tomorrow morning?"

"Sure," I say, still a little dazed.

He waits a second, then: "I thought you had to go inside?"

I set off to look for my aunt.

I can't find Lucy, which is odd because with every light in the house on, there aren't a lot of places to hide. The kitchen's a mess, the counters cluttered with stainless steel bowls, a hand mixer, and various baking ingredients. A bitter, burnt odor hangs in the air, and a heap of charred cookies lies in the sink. Daisy and Buddy play beneath the kitchen table, batting around a bit of wadded-up paper towel. It's not until I step into my room and glance through the wide windows that I spot my aunt in the backyard.

She's standing near the cliff, facing the black emptiness of the ocean. She's wearing a sundress, pale pink, rippling gently in the wind. Her copper hair is bigger and frizzier than usual.

She's smoking.

I hurry through the backdoor, traipsing across the grass toward her. As I get closer, I spot cigarette butts speckling the ground around her shoes. "Aunt Lucy?"

She whips around, hand to her heart. "Callie!"

"Hey. Are you okay?"

She draws a stream of smoke and flashes a smile that doesn't touch her eyes. "Sure," she says, nodding like she's trying to convince herself. "How was your afternoon?"

"Okay."

Her flitting eyes settle on my face. "I'm glad. Did you see Tucker?"

"Yeah, we just finished dinner." Honestly, I was ready to lay into her for talking to him about Chloe, but it's easy to set my anger aside. Something's not right, the way she's chain-smoking, fluttering around so close to the cliff's edge. She talks a big game about opening up and sharing, but in truth, she buries her feelings almost as deep as I do. "Aunt Lucy, are you sure you're all right?"

She glances toward Stewart House, looming over us, lit windows like gaping eyes. "I was making cookies," she says, "and it hit me all at once. Today—how hard it must be for your parents. For *you*."

"For you, too."

She shakes her head, eyes bright with tears. "I keep thinking about that night. The beach."

We went down together, my aunt and me. After I sent Isaac away. After I told Lucy what I'd witnessed. As soon as we realized that Chloe was missing and that she'd taken her wet suit. We'd gone in the Range Rover, me in the passenger seat, seething with anger, Lucy flying down the roads like she was leading a high-speed chase. I thought she was being melodramatic; we'd arrive at the beach, see the bike Chloe favored parked near the dunes, where she and I'd left our bikes every time we'd gone together. Lucy and I would spot her bag and her towel, and then we'd see her, in the distance, navigating the waves.

The moon had been nearly full. The sand glowed under its white light, and the water glittered. As I predicted, we found Chloe's bike. We found her bag. We found her towel.

We didn't find her.

"I know," I say now. "I've been thinking about her all day. All the time."

"I keep going over it," Lucy says. She's crying—*weeping*. I'm so shocked, so panicked by her uncharacteristic display of heartache, I'm frozen where I stand. She didn't cry last year, not that night or the day after, not the afternoon of the wake. Except, maybe she did, in private. Maybe she put on a show of strength for me. For my parents. She says, "I keep wondering what I could've done differently. How I could have stopped her from leaving. Saved her before it was too late."

"You couldn't have," I tell her.

It was me who should have stopped her. Despite Tucker's reassurances, *I* might've been able to save my sister. But Lucy . . . Lucy is blameless.

"If only—" she starts.

I raise a hand to cut her off. "Aunt Lucy, please. I can't relive it. I can't what-if. Not tonight."

She drops the butt of her cigarette, snuffing it out with the toe of her ballet flat. "God, I didn't want to be like this—not in front of you. My plan was to have warm cookies waiting when you got home." She shrugs sheepishly. "I burned them."

"I saw them in the sink."

She wipes away her tears and gives me a cautious smile. "How are you? I mean, really. This summer . . . Has it been okay?"

She deserves an honest answer, taking me in, tolerating my moods, letting me claim a piece of her remodel, attempting to bake me cookies on this, the *hardest* day. "Yeah. Parts of it have been better than okay."

"Tucker?"

"And swimming. And working on the house with you."

Sometimes I feel like I'm starting to move, snail-like, through this journey called grief, inching toward the end of the road, toward elusive acceptance. But then I stall out, like when I'm talking to my sister, or condemning Isaac, or tangling myself in Annabel Tate's story.

Is that how it's supposed to go: two steps forward, followed by a giant backward leap?

"Sometimes I hear you," Lucy says. "Late at night. Moving around in your room, in the parlor, on the porch. I worry you're not sleeping. That you're not content." Her voice drops to a whisper. "I worry I could lose you, too."

I've grossly underestimated her level of perception.

I could tell her about how scared I was, at first. The sounds, the cold, the poppies. How I tried to explain away my experiences with baseless theories. I could tell her that she's right—I'm not sleeping much. I'm *not* content, because I'm communing with my sister, experiencing a phenomenon that's wonderful and terrifying equally.

I'm about to—I swear to God I am—but then, over her shoulder, I see Chloe's vague shape circling the house.

I'm stunned. I haven't smoked; I wasn't trying to reach her.

She must know I need her.

Or maybe she needs me.

I want to go to her. I want to end this night with her.

"Aunt Lucy," I say, reaching out to squeeze her hand. "You're not going to lose me."

33

I tell my aunt that I need some time by myself.

Reluctantly, she goes inside.

I wait near the cliff, watching her through the kitchen windows. She moves swiftly, returning flour and sugar to the pantry, scrubbing the sink, wiping down countertops. It's not long before she flips off the lights. When her silhouette retreats to the master bedroom, I go in search of my sister.

She's near the shed, sitting cross-legged in the grass, her dress billowed out around her.

She looks like a daffodil, golden and proud.

"Aunt Lucy's upset," she says.

I sit across from her. It's not yet midnight, but the grass is cool, damp with dew. "Today's been hard."

"Because of me."

"Because of what happened."

Her expression goes blank; she's as still and placid as a summer pond. "Doesn't seem like you're suffering all that much."

My eyes stretch wide. "Chloe. How can you say that?"

"I saw you earlier. In that stupid car. With the guy who mows Lucy's grass."

"He doesn't just mow the grass," I say, like it matters.

Her eyes roll skyward. "Sorry. He pulls weeds, too, right?"

Yeah, he does, and he plays water polo and goes to a good school and his eyes are supernovas when he grins. She's right—I was happy tonight, pretending to gag when Tucker dipped french fries into his malt, smiling at his stories of childhood mischief with Drew and Brynn. I feel his phantom touch now, a warm palm on my cheek, fingers combing gently through my hair. "He's a good guy, Chloe."

She gazes down at the blades of grass that stand tall around her, running a hand over their green tips. They don't even rustle. Softly, she says, "There was another guy, wasn't there?"

My pulse skids to a halt. I stare at her, increasingly light-headed, until my heart takes off like a shot, leaving my mind racing to catch up. I want her to remember—I do. I want to know, once and for all, what happened last year. I want, more than anything, to tell her how much I regret the part I played.

Except, I'm still not sure what the consequences of closure are.

"Do you remember?" I ask cautiously.

"I'm starting to. Little things. About him. Dark hair. Tall." She looks at me for confirmation. "Is that right?"

"Yes."

"He doesn't live in Bell Cove."

"No."

"You like him?"

"I liked him."

"What's his name?"

I hesitate.

"Cal. Tell me."

"Isaac."

Recognition sparks in her eyes; at the same time, a headache consumes the space behind mine. I reach up to rub my temples.

"You've moved on?" she guesses.

I nod.

"Because of Tucker."

"I moved on before I met Tucker. Before I came back to Bell Cove."

"Why?"

"Because . . . The feelings went away."

She studies me while I struggle to keep my face carefully composed, afraid that if I let on how badly my head hurts, she'll disappear, like last night. When she's gathered all she can from my expression, she says, "You're keeping something from me."

"I'm keeping a lot of things from you."

"You never used to."

That's the truth—at least, it was until I met Isaac. "Things are different now," I tell her.

"That's not fair."

I shrug, a lift of my shoulders that sends pings of pain through my neck. "Nothing about this situation is fair. Why can't you remember on your own? Will you ever? What happens if I help you?" My eyes fill with tears, blurring my sister and her halo of light, and I'm *pissed*; I've cried enough for one day. I wipe roughly at my eyes and ask the only question that matters. "*Why* did you have to go away?"

Her expression goes slack with sympathy, the first genuine feeling she's revealed since we've reunited, and I'm sure—*sure*—she gets it. But then, a shade swings over her face, shuttering her emotions away. "I don't know. That's what I'm trying to learn from you. But you're too busy to help—you've got boys to kiss."

Her obstinacy shuttles a militia of jackhammers into my head. I pinch the bridge of my nose, squeezing my eyes shut, trying to dull the pounding. The irony of her anger, her accusation, is bleakly laughable. Chloe and I have clashed a hundred times, but only once over a boy.

Tonight, she saw me kiss Tucker.

A year ago, she saw me kiss Isaac.

"I'm sorry," I tell her, because I have no idea what else to say.

"You're going to keep seeing him?"

"Not if you don't want me to."

"I'm not going to tell you what to do, Cal."

"But you kind of are."

She's watching the shimmering grass again, pensive. This version of her is so unsettling, and not just her new restraint and lovely grace. These moments of desolation scare me.

"You're moving on," she says quietly.

"Chloe, I've been a wreck this last year. Sad to the point of dysfunction—that's the truth of it. But lately, I've been almost myself. It's being here with Lucy and my return to the pool and hanging out with Tucker, but mostly it's reconnecting with you. I'm learning to cope, maybe, but I'll never move on from you."

Her eyes find mine. They were once as blue as sapphires, but they've darkened with defeat—with death. Her voice is cold when she says, "Prove it."

My heart hurts the same way my head aches.

An intense pounding.

A slow splintering.

I wish Lucy would wake up. I wish she'd come outside and rescue me. But I'm alone.

No—I'm not alone. I'm with my sister.

Except . . . I hardly know this girl.

"I'm not feeling well," I say weakly.

"Then you should go."

For the first time in all the years we've been sisters, I walk away first.

34

Early the next morning, I bike to the pool. My headache has dimmed, but I'm strung tight with tension and worry.

Prove it, Chloe said.

I don't know how to prove loyalty and love. When it comes to my sister, my allegiance is unwavering. The fact that we've connected a year after she *died* should be proof enough.

Last night she acted like I'm the villain in our story—the story with a plot she can't remember—and she's not entirely wrong. I screwed up epically. But she's not innocent. If Isaac personifies blame and I embody guilt, Chloe falls somewhere in between.

Except, the scene I interrupted last summer was at its crescendo. I have no idea what led up to it, aside from what Isaac swore to me, his voice spiked with desperation.

He can't be trusted.

I park my bike at the fence and see Tucker in the water.

Already I feel looser, freer, calmer.

I can't wait to join him, to swim thoughts of last night's conversation away.

I hurry through the gate, dump my bag in a chair, and ditch my sweats. I grab my cap and goggles, watching Tucker travel the length of the pool. There's no urgency in his movements, no real effort. Just the pull of strong arms, the steady kick of powerful legs.

If his easy strokes are any indication, he's been a swimmer his whole life. Somehow, though, I can't imagine Benjamin cheering him on at meets and water polo matches. Swimming isn't an easy sport, a fact I'm all too aware of after years of two-a-day practices, chlorine-dried skin, and a meager social life. If not for the encouragement of my parents and the companionship of my sister, I might've given it up a decade ago.

I sink down onto a deck chair and watch him roll into a flip turn, his splash cresting into the gutter. He pushes off the wall, long and lean, exuding athleticism. If ever I've envied another person, it's Tucker now. He's indomitable.

On his way back down the lane, he slows and pulls up at the wall. He smiles when he sees me. "You coming in?"

I nod, an unquashable grin tugging on my mouth. I want to feel this way all the time: exhilarated by a life full of possibility.

He lifts his goggles as I sit down at the head of his lane, dipping my legs in the cool water. His raised brows get lost beneath his dripping hair. "Joining me today?"

I twist my own hair behind my head and pull my cap over it. "Is that okay?"

He nods, his eyes the same shimmering green as the water that laps against his chest. He looks like he has something momentous to say—something momentous to *do*, and I panic, recalling last night's kiss. Recalling my sister's reaction. I fiddle with the rubber strap of my goggles, flustered, reluctant to put them on.

Should I back away and pretend we're still just friends?

Should I lean in, because we'll never be just friends again?

I push Chloe's dissuasions and Tucker's expectations out of my head, honoring my own emotions for a change.

I set my goggles aside and send him a smile. He reads it as encouragement, placing his palms on the grate and lifting out of the water. I slip a hand around the back of his neck, drawing him in. He lays the gentlest of kisses on me, then he whispers, "Morning, beautiful girl," without a trace of cheesiness.

My heart beats, steady, filled, alive.

He falls backward into the water with a splash. "Let's swim."

When I get back from the pool, Lucy's at the kitchen table with *Anna Karenina* and a mug of milky coffee.

"Morning," she says cheerfully.

Her neon clothing is present and accounted for, last night's charred cookies apparently forgotten. I pull a box of cereal from the pantry and fill a bowl. Skipping milk, I make my way to the table, scooping tiny, mewing Buddy from beneath my feet. I sit and settle him on my lap before snagging a piece of cereal.

"Sleep well?" Lucy asks.

"Always."

I don't love lying to her, but I can't tell her the truth: Last night, I barely slept. I couldn't calm my nerves after leaving Chloe.

It's occurred to me that tonight, I could stay inside. But I can't do that to my sister, lonesome in her in-between place.

"Did you swim with Tucker?"

I crunch through another piece of cereal, scratching my kitten behind his ears. "Yep."

"What's going on with you two?"

"Nothing."

"He adopted a cat. For *you*."

"So?"

She takes a sip of coffee, eyeing me over the top of her mug. "He makes you smile."

"You noticed?"

"Of course I noticed."

Her haughtiness is getting on my nerves. She and I may be growing tentatively closer, but that doesn't mean she knows everything about me or what's best for me. That doesn't mean she gets to meddle. I whittle my gaze to a sharp point. "Then why'd you talk to him about Chloe?"

The smug grin slips from her face. "He mentioned her?"

"Of course he mentioned her. What did you think was going to happen?"

She brushes a speck of dust from the tabletop. "He knew. I just filled in a few blanks."

"It's not your story to share."

"She was my niece."

I place Buddy on the floor and rise from my chair, dumping what's left of my cereal into the trash can. "I think I'll work in the Gabriel today. Alone."

I'm a few hours into the infinite mound of boxes when I make an attic run, hauling a few cartons up to slide against the west wall. After moving a crate of antique sports equipment into place, I pause to blot the sweat from my brow.

Two floors down, a deep voice shouts, "Cal?"

I call back, "Up here," because if Tucker and I are going to talk, I'd like to do it away from my aunt's prying ears.

His footsteps ascend the stairs. He pokes his head into the musty attic. "What're you up to?"

"Working."

"Uh-huh. Avoiding your aunt?"

"How'd you guess?"

He moves farther into the attic. He pauses to lift the flap of a random box, peeking in on its contents. Rifling through the paperwork stacked inside, he says, "Because she told me you yelled at her."

"I didn't yell at her. And don't worry; she'll be over it in an hour. She's moody like that."

"*She's* moody?"

"What are you implying, Tucker Morgan?"

"Oh, you know," he says, looking up with an impish grin. He abandons the box and its paperwork and sinks down onto a trunk, one I've stuck with a piece of masking tape labeled WEDDING GOWNS. "So, anyway, I wanted to see what you're up to tomorrow night."

"Um. I don't know."

"It's the Fourth."

I stare blankly.

"Of July? Independence Day? I'm assuming you've heard of it."

"Oh!" God, what an idiot I am. Since Chloe's death, I've forgotten so many special occasions. Thanksgiving, Christmas, Valentine's Day, and Easter passed virtually uncelebrated, along with, shamefully, both of my parents' birthdays. They acknowledged mine, back in October, with a cake and a few gifts I was too baked to properly appreciate.

Tucker gives me a lopsided smile, one that reeks of sympathy. "Do you have plans?"

I pretend to scroll through my mental date book, the one that's been wide open for a year. "I think I'm free."

"Then will you come to town with me? Bell Cove puts on a fireworks display every year, and attendance is obligatory for tourists, which, technically, you are." He lifts a folder from a stack on the floor and flips it open. He shuffles through its documents as he continues. "After, some of my friends are having a bonfire on the beach. Brynn and Drew will be there."

I suspect he shared that bit to sway me, but it has the reverse effect. Brynn and her flawlessness are intimidating, and Drew seems like kind of an ass. Plus, gatherings consisting of more than three people give me wicked anxiety. But when Tucker glances up from the folder, he looks excited, eager to show me Bell Cove's version of a good time. And he'll be with me all evening, spouting merriment every which way.

"Okay," I say. "I guess that sounds like fun."

"Yeah? Cool. I'm off tomorrow, but I'll come pick you up in time for fireworks."

"I'll be ready," I say, infusing my voice with the enthusiasm I know he's expecting.

He stands, presses a kiss to the top of my head, and then he's gone.

35

I spent an hour on the porch last night, waiting for Chloe.

She never came.

I spent another hour awake in bed, cataloging possible reasons why: I didn't smoke, I didn't have her cap and goggles and notebook and pen, I didn't relax enough, or focus sufficiently. Except, the night before we connected with hardly any effort, which leaves me with just one plausible explanation: She stayed away because she wanted to.

I spend the better part of Independence Day with Lucy, painting the Theodore a sage green. She tells me that the color's called Stonewashed and that she chose it specifically for its nod to eighties fashion. The silliness of her selection criteria evaporates what's left of my irritation.

When we finish, she gives me orders to shower, then meet her in her bathroom.

Half an hour later, I do, wrapped in a bathrobe. She's armed, hair dryer in one hand, round brush in the other. "Have a seat," she says, pointing to the stool at the vanity counter.

She sections off my hair. Pulling it taut with the bristly brush, she begins what appears to be a professional blowout.

"How'd you get so good at this?" I ask her over the drone of the dryer.

She pauses to flip a curl off her forehead. "Beauty school. Your grandma made me go."

"Why?"

"Because I didn't want to go to college. I was more interested in moving to Los Angeles and going to casting calls. She wouldn't support me until I had an education. Beauty school it was."

"Did you ever work in a salon?"

"Nope. I needed my days for auditions. I did my friends' hair, though."

That night last summer, when my sister and I huddled in Lucy's bed to watch movies and drink Mountain Dew, she spent forever weaving our hair into braided crowns. We looked like royalty, gilded, even in our pajamas.

I wish Chloe was here now.

"So you didn't want to go to college," I say, "and my dad doesn't want to leave college."

Lucy starts on another section of damp hair. "Funny how that worked out, isn't it? He and I are different in a lot of ways, but he's a good big brother. A pretty great dad, too."

Well. I wasn't a fan of his parenting style all those months ago when he insisted I try therapy, and I thought he was the absolute worst when he decided I couldn't spend this summer in Seattle. But what he said about my needing a change of pace . . . He might've been on to something.

"He has the right idea working at a university," Lucy goes on. "He's teaching what he loves, and his students keep him young. Relatively, anyway." In the mirror, her eyes find mine, and she winks. "Have you thought about where you're going to apply come fall?"

I wrinkle my nose. "Not even a little bit."

"But college is in your plan?"

What plan?

Except lately, surprisingly, the idea of college has been flitting around the fringes of my consciousness. I'm not considering where I want to go, but *if* I want to go, and what my transcripts will look like as part of an application packet.

I veer us in another direction. "Did you know Tucker goes to Pepperdine?"

"No! I knew he went to school in California, but whoa. Good for him," Lucy said.

"I think he's one of those people who's good at everything he puts his mind to."

"Like you?"

I make a face at her reflection and deflect again. "If you never worked in a salon, how'd you make money while you were going to all those casting calls?"

"Bartending. My mother hated it, but I thought it was a blast. I was better than Tom Cruise in *Cocktail*." She flips the hairbrush like it's a liquor bottle, catching it smoothly on its way down. "I worked in a swanky lounge, and the pay was good. That's where I met my husband, actually."

I don't miss her slip, the way she refers to him as her husband instead of her ex, though I don't call her on it. It's hard to believe I've never heard this part of her history. "And then you got married," I say.

"And then I got married," she parrots. Sighing, she unclips the topmost layer of my hair and goes to work with the dryer. "My mother called the demise of my marriage before it was a week old. She wasn't impressed by a license signed in Clark County, Nevada." She turns off the dryer and brushes my hair out; it spills over my shoulders in loose, shiny curls. She stoops to study my bare face. "What are you going to wear?"

"Jeans, probably." I hear a feeble mewl and look to find Buddy circling my leg. I reach to pick him up. He curls contentedly in my lap, his weight almost unnoticeable.

Lucy pats his head. "I have the perfect top for you to borrow. Can I do your makeup?"

I nod, affection trickling from my chest, outward. Even considering everything she's done to aggravate me since I came back to Stewart House, I love her a lot.

"So," I say as she brushes smoky shadow over my lids. "Guess who called the other day."

She pauses. "Please tell me it wasn't the asshole."

"Aunt Lucy—"

"Callie. Based on what you told me last summer? Definitely an asshole, and I don't feel bad about saying so." She goes back to my makeup. "Did you talk to him?"

"Briefly. I asked him not to call again."

"Smart."

"I'm not sure he was trying to make trouble."

"Doesn't sound like he has to try. How often have you heard from him during the past year?"

She saw him at the reception that followed Chloe's wake; she approached him, red-faced and wild-eyed. As much as I wanted her to let him have it, a scene on the day meant to honor Chloe's life would have been atrocious. I managed to drag her away before she had a chance to crush him.

"A little bit last summer."

More than I'm proud of, is the truth. Nights I wasted away, high, staring silently at the blinking skyline while Isaac sat next to me, saying all the right things in all the wrong ways. The day of the Seattle Summer Triathlon, I banged on the Parks' front door, sobbing. Isaac scooped me up while his mom looked on, wringing her hands. He took me upstairs to the patio, where I spent the better part of an hour alternately screaming at him and begging him to help me.

"Help you *how*?" he kept saying, until he was crying, too.

Help me heal. Tell me the truth about what happened. Save me from the guilt.

But I didn't say any of that because I was hysterical and so full of self-loathing I couldn't form rational sentences. Still, we were so carelessly loud it wasn't long before Mrs. Park came up to see what was going on. She ended up calling my dad to come get me, a humiliating event he and I haven't spoken of since.

"And I saw him once around Christmastime," I admit to Lucy.

She sweeps peach blush over my cheekbones. "But not since?"

I shake my head, running my hand down Buddy's back.

She scrutinizes her work, *me*, with a tipped chin. "Is there still something between you two?"

"No. Not at all."

Last summer, I thought he was everything.

This summer, I know better.

"Good," Lucy says. "Because you'd be nuts to settle for him."

"You're just saying that because you think Tucker's dreamy."

She rolls her eyes, fishing around in her makeup drawer before unearthing a tube of mascara. She swipes the wand over my lashes, bottom lip between her teeth. "I think Tucker's good for you, whether you two are friends or otherwise. And I bet you're good for him, too." She swipes another coat of mascara over my lashes, then steps back to evaluate my finished look. She nods, satisfied. "You'll tell me if Isaac bothers you again?"

"Aunt Lucy, I can handle it."

"I know you can. But you shouldn't have to handle it alone."

When Tucker knocks on the door just after seven, I'm pacing the parlor, too anxious to sit still. I give my reflection a quick check in the hall mirror; I've gone with jeans, the nicest pair I brought, and a satiny blouse I borrowed from my aunt, the same blue as my eyes.

I swing the front door open, and Tucker steals my breath. The fading sunlight makes his hair look even lighter than usual, playing off his bronze skin. He's in shorts—suspiciously new-looking—and a butter-yellow T-shirt. He's all smiles, and he's reaching for my hand, pulling me out onto the porch and into him. I wrap my arms around him, close my eyes, and press my cheek into the softness of his shirt.

His hands sweep up my back. "I'm glad you're coming with me."

"I'm glad you asked." I poke my head through the doorway and call, "Aunt Lucy? We're leaving."

"Have fun!" she shouts from the kitchen. "Be good to her, Tuck!"

Tucker lifts a mischievous eyebrow and calls, "Always!"

He takes my hand as we walk to the Woody, then opens the passenger door for me, chivalrous. I'm not sure what to make of him tonight; I sense his nervousness, and frankly, it's making me *more* nervous.

"Will there be a lot of people at the bonfire?" I ask as he steers away from Lucy's property.

"Probably. Is that okay?"

"Yeah, totally. Where on the beach will it be, exactly?"

He glances at me, his face shrouded with sudden distress, because he knows, now, why I'd ask such a question. "Up shore, toward Shell City. Is that . . . ?"

I let go of a relieved breath. "That's fine."

I spend the next few minutes agonizing over how to behave when Tucker introduces me to his friends, giving myself a mental pep talk: *Stretch your smile to your eyes so you don't look like a robot, keep conversation light, don't stare at the surf—it won't rear up and take you under.*

In town, Tucker steers through heavy traffic, parking in an alley behind the Green Apple Grocery, one I've never even noticed. It seems every other space in Bell Cove is occupied by a car or a mass of people.

He keeps my hand as we emerge from the relative emptiness of the alley and join the crowd on the street. Most have congregated in the center of town, sprawled out on low wooden benches or colorful blankets. There's food everywhere: sandwiches thick with cold cuts, platefuls of creamy potato salad, ice-cream cones dripping in the day's lingering heat. The humid air is laced with brine and charcoal and excitement. Tucker buys hot dogs and fountain sodas from a vendor manning a food truck, and we snag the end of a prime bench.

I'm pretty sure the whole town—vacationers and locals alike—has turned out for this event. Tucker apparently knows everyone; he's waving and shouting hellos left and right. For a moment, I feel like an outsider, one of the fanny-packed tourists for whom Bell Cove is a stop on a summer exploration of the Oregon coast. Then, halfway through my hot dog, I spot Rex from the animal shelter, sitting on a plaid blanket with a woman and two small, dark-haired boys. It's obvious he recognizes me, and I smile. Moments later, I see Shirley, standing across the street with a group of comparably old ladies, plus Lucy. I wave to Shirley, then my aunt, suddenly an active participant in the celebration.

The fireworks begin as Tucker and I finish our food, while the sky is still lilac, dotted with clouds rolling in from the Pacific. The explosions of color are gorgeous, vibrant pinwheels of pink, yellow, white, and blue. I'm mesmerized.

When the air cools, Tucker wraps an arm around me, cocooning me in his warmth. I tear my attention from the sky to look at him; his eyes are dazzling, starbursts reflected in pale, pale green. They disappear as his lids fall closed, as he leans in and presses his mouth to mine.

I'm dizzy with the magic of it.

36

After the fireworks, we weave through the crowd, back to the alley where the Woody waits. It's a short, quiet drive up the coast. Tucker parks in a public lot, among a dozen other cars.

"You can leave your shoes in here," he says, kicking off his flip-flops and tossing them into the back seat. I place mine neatly on the floor mat beneath me.

We walk down the beach toward a distant, flickering bonfire. The sand feels nice on my feet, residual toastiness from the afternoon sun clashing with the crispness of the night. It's completely dark now, the sky robbed of its stars by a blanket of clouds, and the waves crest higher than I've ever seen in Bell Cove.

"When was the last time you went to a party?" Tucker asks as we near his friends.

"You mean besides the ones I threw myself in my bathroom at home? It's been a while."

"We can do our own thing if you want. You've met Drew and Brynn. The rest of my friends aren't even that great."

I smile. "I'll be the judge of that."

The bonfire looms closer. There are more people than I expected, more than the smattering of cars in the parking lot suggested. My apprehension progresses to full-fledged anxiety, and the desire to smoke hits me harder than it has in days.

A dark figure lumbers toward us. Drew, barefoot, in jeans, a cotton button-down, and a ratty cowboy hat. I can tell he's already a few drinks in by the way his feet drag through the sand.

"What's up, buddy?" he hollers, pulling Tucker into a one-armed hug while managing a quick assessment of me, head to toe, culminating in a cheesy grin.

Tucker throws an elbow into his ribs. "You remember Callie?"

"Callie Ryan . . . of course." Drew assumes a mocking tone that sounds remarkably like Tucker. "Don't flirt with Callie. Don't ask Callie for her number. Don't check Callie out—in fact, don't look at her for more than three seconds. And . . . Don't touch Callie in any way that might make her uncomfortable." He pauses to raise a brow at Tucker. "Did I remember it all, Morgan?"

Tucker gives him a shove. "Thanks a lot, wiseass."

I'm laughing—I can't help it.

Drew pushes him back, chuckling, then slings an arm over my shoulder. "Come on, Ryan. We've been waiting for you guys."

Partygoers ring the fire, perched on coolers and canvas beach chairs.

Almost everyone's drinking. It's weird, being surrounded by people—smiling, laughing people—after so many months of quiet seclusion. I breathe lungfuls of ocean air and manage my nerves.

Brynn comes skipping over, dressed in a red sundress. She's got a can of beer in her hand. She gives Tucker a sloppy hug before turning to beam at me. Despite my bare feet and wind-tossed hair, I feel more comfortable with her than I did at A Good Book, though a lot has happened since then. Also, she's visibly drunk, which lessens the intimidation factor. When she asks about the town's fireworks display, I tell her about it, like I'm chatting with any one of my forgotten friends back home.

When I finish, she links her arm through mine and says, "Time for some girl talk."

Tucker looks unsure about my going, but Brynn's already towing me along, and when his eyes meet mine, I give him an *I'll be fine* nod. He smiles, then gives his attention to Drew.

"We must get you something to drink," Brynn says.

"Oh, I'm good."

"Callie, it's the Fourth of July! What fun are fireworks without brews?"

Before I can put up a fight, she's procured a second can of cheap beer. She pops it open, then tugs me toward a log lying in the sand. She stumbles, nearly taking me down with her. Thanks to some help from my arm, she regains her balance, blots beer from the hem of her dress, and plops down. I do, too.

"I'm glad Tucker brought you," she says over the reggae music floating on the wind. She sounds mostly sincere.

I sip my beer. It's foamy and warm, not very good. "Me too."

"So you've got to tell me—what's it like living at Stewart House?"

"It's okay. Quiet."

"Quiet?" She gives a little shiver. "More like creepy."

"You think?"

"Oh yeah. Did Tucker tell you I saw a ghost there once?"

I shake my head, dubious.

"A couple of years ago we were all up there, you know—" she shakes her beer can and giggles "—and I saw something spooky out by the driveway. It was shimmery and white, kind of . . . indistinct? It even made this weird *ooohhh*-ing sound. Have you seen anything like that?"

I blink, certain her story's fiction. "I sure haven't."

"Well, be careful. People have died at Stewart House." She leans in, like she's about to give me a taste of some juicy gossip. "There was even a murder."

Goose bumps fan out over my arms. My bathroom . . . the blood.

Brynn shrugs, like *oops, I shouldn't have said anything,* but she's got a grin the size of Oregon plastered to her face. I can't decide if she's fake or flaky or snotty, but I'm pretty sure she doesn't know anything about any Stewart House homicides—not that I'd stoop to begging for information if she did.

I swallow a sip of beer and broach a new subject. "I hear you and Tucker have been friends a long time."

She switches gears easily. "Forever. He's awesome, right?"

I scan the crowd; he's standing on the other side of the fire with a group of guys, aglow in orange light. He must feel me looking because he turns my way, his expression a blend of curiosity and concern. Our eyes lock, and he lifts a questioning eyebrow. I nod. He winks. I smile. He laughs, and somehow we've developed a nonverbal means of communicating, like we're an actual couple.

I'm ready to ditch this party—with him.

"Yeah," I tell Brynn. "He is pretty great."

She swigs from her can, one gulp, two gulps, then three. She's a tiny person, but she can chug. "I hate that he chose Pepperdine," she says. "Though I can't say I was surprised. I wish he would've settled for Oregon State like the rest of us, but Tucker's never been cool with the idea of hanging around. I'm actually surprised he came home for the summer. Not that it matters—we've hardly seen him because he's busy with work and . . . stuff."

Stuff. Me, clearly. "I don't mean to—"

"Don't get me wrong," she says quickly. "You're obviously fantastic. He wouldn't want a girl who isn't. It just sucks, you know, when people you're close to move on with their lives. One of the drawbacks of growing up in a small town. You assume things will always be the same, and you're disappointed when they're not."

I feel a pang of sympathy for her. I've been spending a lot of time with Tucker; it's no wonder his friends are a little jealous. "I'm sorry he's been busy."

Brynn finishes the last of her beer and balances the empty can on our log. "Don't apologize. Things haven't been easy for Tuck. Benjamin's not one of those openly loving dads, and don't even get me started on his mother. But since he met you, he's been really happy."

Don't even get me started on his mother?

I have the sudden, nagging feeling that I'm missing something.

Brynn props a hand under her chin. Her eyelids are droopy. There's beer on her breath when she says, "Tuck never complains, but he never lets go, either. He's been different, though, lately."

I've rarely seen Tucker anything *but* happy, so I'm having a hard time merging this morose boy Brynn's describing with the person I've grown to know. But to think of our friendship as give-and-take instead of me take-take-taking . . . It dawns on me that I'm becoming half of a whole.

It's a scary notion.

At the same time, it's *not.*

Again, I look across the fire, but Tucker's not there. My heart falls because all at once, being near him is imperative, an elemental need.

He's behind me before I can look any farther, reaching an arm across my chest, sweeping my hair behind my shoulders. His breath is warm on my neck, his voice a tendril of smoke. "I've come to reclaim you."

Happily, I pass Brynn my half-full can and take a lap around the fire with Tucker. He introduces me to more people than I can count, referring to me as his "friend" in a tone that's protective and passionate and raw, and this thing we're doing, this thing I keep telling myself is casual, feels exactly the opposite.

After we've made the rounds, we find a spot of our own. "Do you want something else to drink?" he asks.

"I'm good. Are you drinking?"

He shakes his head. "I'm your chauffeur, remember?"

A whoop erupts from the crowd. Drew and a group of guys are opening huge, cellophane-wrapped packages of fireworks. "Morgan," one of them calls. "You gettin' in on this?"

"Nah, I'm cool."

"Oh, come on," Drew says. I hold my breath, waiting for the obligatory *you're so whipped* remark, but he refrains. "You sure?"

"Dude, I'm sure."

"You should go, if you want," I tell him. "I'll be okay here."

He takes a step forward, gazing at me with intensity that makes my face flush hot. "Fireworks are what I did before I brought girls to parties."

I cross my arms. "Just how many girls have you brought out here, Tucker Morgan?"

He tips forward, so his prickly cheek brushes mine. "One. And I'm not gonna leave her by herself so I can play fire with my caveman friends."

A thunderous boom sounds behind me, so horrifically loud it makes the earth shudder. I jump, then whirl around to find the source of the noise. Drew and his associates surround a shoebox-size explosive with a charred top. They're cracking up, as if fireworks are the world's greatest entertainment.

Tucker draws me close, until I feel the soft vibration of his laughter. "Maybe we should go for a walk."

"No, I'm fine."

He toys with the ruffled edge of my sleeve, leaning in, whispering, "Callie. Please?"

That kiss earlier, in Bell Cove. The burst of excitement, my craving for more . . .

"Okay, yeah. Let's go."

37

We walk far away from the strangers, the beer, and the too-loud fireworks. When we stop, the bonfire's barely visible, Tucker's friends hardly discernible.

"Wanna sit?" he says.

We sink onto the sand. I rest my head on his shoulder, wishing his arrival in my world meant I've atoned for mistakes past. I'm still not sure I deserve this kind of happiness, this sort of contentment, but I'm not about to turn it away.

He draws shapes on my arm with the tips of his fingers. "What're you thinking about?"

I work to condense my feelings into words that'll make sense. "Remember when you said you feel peaceful at the beach because your mom loved it?"

He clears his throat, an uneasy sound. "Yeah?"

"I want that. A sense of peace. You know?"

There's sorrow in the idle way he strokes my skin. "I bet you'll find it."

I'm not sure. Closure's hard to come by when my sister's ghost, my only shot at salvation, can't recall the night that changed everything.

Brynn's comment about Tucker's mother, her tone so full of revulsion, bounces around in my head. I don't care that she knows so much of his past; what's bothersome is that I know hardly anything at all. I sift a fistful of sand through my fingers and ask, "Tucker, when you said your mother took off . . . What happened?"

His hand goes still, and I worry I've crashed through a boundary I didn't know existed.

"Never mind," I say, fanning the air, as if my question is smoke I can clear away. "We don't have to talk about it."

"No . . . I just don't know a lot of the details. She was young. She wasn't happy with my dad. She thought he was holding her back, stealing her freedom or whatever. And then I was born, which made things worse. She went to visit a friend, and she never came back."

I try to imagine how a woman—a *mother*—could do such a thing. As depressed and dependent as my own mom has become, I know she'd never leave my dad and me.

There's a sonic boom from down the beach. Though we're too far away to hear laughter, I'm sure the bonfire crowd is in pieces, good and buzzed. They're a world away.

"Do you think being without her is the reason your dad's the way he is?" I ask.

"Uh, yeah. There's more to the story, stuff I've heard around town over the years, stuff my dad never wanted me to know."

"Like what?"

He gives a humorless laugh. "A bunch of shit-shooting I'm not sure I buy."

I lift my head to study his profile; his jaw is tight, his gaze trained on the waves. "You don't want to tell me?"

"It's not that."

"Then what is it?"

He turns to look at me, eyes piercing through the darkness. "You already have a hell of a lot going on. You sure you want something else to be sad about?"

"Tucker, you listen to me. I can do the same for you."

He stays quiet, though I don't push—I know how that feels. My patience pays off because at last he says, "My mother was tight with one of the Stewarts. Did you know that?"

"No," I say, taken aback.

"That's why my dad's never wanted me near the property."

I recall the time I found him poking around in the parlor, his vague curiosity about what's in the Gabriel, the rifling around he did in the attic yesterday. "Then why'd you choose to work for Lucy?"

He lets go of a sigh; his frame sags beside me. "My mother hung out at the house a lot when she was in high school. I thought there might be something left over. I don't know . . . something that might help me figure out why she was so messed up. A clue pointing to what happened to her, maybe." He shakes his head. "Stupid, right?"

He clings to Stewart House like I cling to Chloe.

Stupid is relative, I guess.

"It's not stupid," I say. "Not even a little bit."

He makes a gruff sound deep in his throat. "I'm over it now. I work for your aunt mostly because I need a job. Living in California isn't cheap, and my dad . . . Construction doesn't pay all that well. Anyway, I like Lucy, I like it up on the hill, I like working outside." He pulls his attention from the rising tide and gives it to me, staring so deep into my eyes I swear he can see my soul. He touches my cheek. "And I like seeing you."

His fingers on my skin make me weary of our heavy conversation, of the gloom that's settled over us. He's right; we shouldn't be hashing this stuff out—not tonight.

I lean in, and he meets me. He's so gentle, cupping my jaw as if I'm made of blown glass. He moves slowly, tentative and tasting of restraint, like I'll shatter if he's not vigilant. I pull back, resting my hands against the warmth of his neck.

"Hey," I say, sinking into his gaze, bright with surprise. "Why are you being so careful?"

"I just—I don't want to push you. You're so . . ."

Sad? Damaged? Crazy?

What am I, in his eyes?

He tucks a lock of hair behind my ear. "Fragile. Sweet. I'd hate myself if I upset you."

"Tucker, you won't. Not by kissing me."

He considers this, then smiles and eases me back, until I'm stretched out on the sand, my head cradled in his hand. I loop my arms around his neck and pull him close.

"Kiss me for real?" I whisper.

He does. And it's perfect.

It's a long time before he pulls away, hair tousled by the strengthening breeze. Hovering above me, he squints down the beach, looking troubled.

"What is it?" I ask.

"Hang on."

I do, waiting to see what's distracted him. The night is quiet but for the crashing waves and whistling wind.

"Did you feel that?" he asks.

"What?"

"Rain?"

"No." But his body is very effectively shielding mine.

He studies the sky, ominously dark now, rolling and rippling as if the clouds hold breath, and then, with a muttered, "Shit," he scrambles to stand. He grabs my hand and pulls me up, too. "It's gonna storm."

As soon as the words are clear of his mouth, a fat raindrop lands on my shoulder, followed quickly by another. He yanks on my hand. "Come on!"

We run, stumbling through the sand and the sudden, relentless downpour. By the time we've made it to the parking lot, empty now, we're drenched. Tucker unlocks my door and propels me in, then hustles around to the driver's side, where he drops into his seat, wet shorts squeaking across old leather.

"Well," he says. "That sucked."

He turns the ignition over and cranks the heater, then leans into the back seat. I hear the unzipping of a bag, his rummaging around, before he passes me a beach towel.

I dry my face and arms while he does the same with a towel of his own. I angle the rearview mirror in my direction. My hair hangs wet and limp around my face, and my makeup is ruined. I run the towel under my eyes, hoping to erase blackness that's making me look strung out.

The storm continues, soaking anything unfortunate enough to be stuck outside. Tucker rubs his towel through his hair as he watches rain pound against the Woody's windshield. "Guess I should've been paying attention to the weather. Sorry you got wet."

A bolt of lightning zigzags across the sky, followed by a rumble of thunder. I shiver, the drenched fabric of my shirt like a second skin.

"Hey," Tucker says, adjusting the heater vents so they're all aimed at me. "You okay?"

I nod. "Just cold."

He takes the towel from my hands and uses it to squeeze the water from my hair. Then he turns on the radio, a local country station playing twangy songs about lost love and apple pie and battered trucks. The heater fires up in earnest, pumping warmth into the small space. The car smells like Tucker: cedar and spice, chlorine, and something else, something very boy yet distinctly him. I focus on it, trying to quell my shivers.

Taking my hand, he tugs me closer. He weaves his fingers through mine as he always does, reverently, like this is the first and last time he'll get to touch me. The way my arm's angled makes my scar glow in the light of the dash. Tucker's looking at it, and I'm looking at it, and I've never hated it more.

"I got hurt after Chloe died. Right after she was found."

His gaze jumps to my face. "How?"

"We went out looking the night she went missing. We searched the beach for what felt like forever, and when we couldn't find her, Lucy called the police. They called in the coast guard. I wanted to stay, keep looking, but Lucy made me go back to the house because I was practically delirious. My parents had arrived by then—she'd called them, too. When the police finally came with news, it was morning, barely light. I was in my room—the room I used to share with my sister—but I could hear them talking to my parents and my aunt in the kitchen. My dad took it all in; he's good in a crisis, it turns out. But my mom fell apart." I drop my voice to a whisper. "I did, too."

Tucker's holding tight to my hand. "You didn't—"

"No. *No*. I couldn't have done that to my parents. Not after the news they'd just gotten."

"Then . . . How?"

"There used to be a mirror in that room, freestanding. Really pretty. I found out later it was an antique—an original to Stewart House. I don't even know how it happened. I shoved it, or fell into it. Lucy heard the crash and came running. She found me sitting in shards of glass, bleeding."

"Jesus, Callie."

"Yeah. My parents were beside themselves. Lucy had to drive me to the urgent-care center in Shell City so I could have my arm stitched up. And now I get to live with a constant reminder of those hours and how unbearable they were."

Tucker lays his hand against my forearm. Palm to fingertips, he covers the whole of the space, putting gentle pressure against my skin. "Brutal," he whispers.

"I know."

He looks from my arm to my face. "I really want to say the right thing, but I have no fucking clue what that is."

I shrug. "You didn't try to convince me that it's beautiful. That would've been the wrong thing."

He leans in, drops a kiss on my cheek, then moves beyond me, reaching over to open the glove compartment. He pulls out a package of candy—Jelly Bellies. He tears the cellophane and holds the bag out to me. I take a handful and sample them one by one, trying to discern flavors. Root beer, bubble gum, cherry. I hold my palm out for more, and Tucker obliges.

"Better?" he asks after a few minutes.

"I think so."

He covers my knee with a warm hand. "I bet your sister loved you a lot."

This, I know, is true. Our parents used to say that Chloe idolized me. She picked up my sport, read my books, begged to have sleepovers in my room. But our relationship was more than that. The adoration was mutual. Her spirit waited for me in Bell Cove even after her body was placed in the ground.

Our bond is that strong.

Stewart House is quiet and dark when Tucker pulls up, the rain just a drizzle now. He coaxes the Woody into park but doesn't kill the engine. Instead, he runs his hands around the circle of the steering wheel, eyes tracing the movement.

I'm sitting in uncomfortably damp jeans, but I'm reluctant to say good night. "You should come in," I say impulsively.

He gives me a look that's hard to read. "Yeah?"

"I mean, if you want to."

"Your aunt won't mind?"

"I don't think so, but it's late. If you'd rather get home . . ."

He grins, endearing, and yanks his key from the ignition. "I could give two shits about getting home."

I lead him to the parlor, where any well-mannered girl visits with a boy. I leave him sitting on the settee, across from the windowsill where

Daisy and Buddy sleep in a tangle of fur, while I hurry down the hall to change. On my way, I peek through my aunt's cracked bedroom door. She's out, her even breaths audible in the hallway.

In my room, I find my phone on the middle of the bed. In my rush to be ready for fireworks, I left the house without it, though I'm sure the last place I saw it was on my nightstand, plugged into its charger. Beneath it, there's a sheet of paper from the pad Lucy uses for grocery lists in the kitchen.

Isaac called, she wrote. *I thought you weren't in touch with him?*

I'm not, I'm not, I'm not.

Except, he doesn't understand the meaning of *We're done.*

When Isaac came to Bell Cove, he charmed Lucy, even though it had taken some persuading to get her permission for the visit. I told her he was our neighbor, a friend, because I still hadn't come clean to Chloe. Lucy didn't understand why I couldn't spend a couple of months away from this boy who'd only recently moved in next door, but I'd pushed because Isaac was pushing.

He rolled into town on a Saturday morning, parking his dad's Subaru in the driveway and emerging with a box of fresh doughnuts. Chloe was ecstatic—she'd raised her eyebrows at me over her orange juice as if to say, *See what he did for me?*—while the four of us had breakfast in the still-dilapidated kitchen.

Later, Lucy left for a meeting with contractors, and Chloe went for a run. Isaac and I sat outside on the porch steps to catch up. His mom had recently dragged him on an epic dorm-room shopping spree, which he described in his wry way before asking about the work happening at Stewart House.

"Slow going," I told him. "I think Lucy was expecting Chloe and me to have a clue about home improvement. We definitely don't. She's come to terms with the fact that she's going to have to bring in professionals to take care of the plumbing issues."

"I'd offer my services, but unless she has bikes that need maintenance, I won't be much help."

"Actually, there are a few in the shed," I said, pointing to the outbuilding. "They're rideable, but in rough shape."

"I'll take a look this afternoon. Has she been keeping up with her swims?"

"Yep. We've been going together, down to the ocean."

"Whoa. Extreme."

"Totally. Who needs a pool when you can freeze your ass off in the Pacific?"

He laughed. "You don't miss your swim team?"

"Sort of," I said, shrugging. "You know what I miss more?"

Isaac made a show of contemplating.

I poked him in the side. "You, dummy."

He kissed me then, because he'd missed me, too. I was glad he'd come, even though his appearance was complicating things where my sister was concerned. I hated that there was a secret between us, but it would work itself out. Chloe would understand.

Isaac pulled back, giving my ponytail a teasing tug. "I missed that."

"Me too—" I started, but movement in the yard grabbed my attention.

My sister, in running clothes, forehead glistening with sweat, standing near the tree line.

I scrambled back from Isaac, hissing, "Did she see?"

"Not sure . . . Maybe not?"

She was still looking at us, her expression murky.

"She saw. God. She's going to be furious."

"She was bound to find out eventually," Isaac said. His tone was so indifferent, anger flashed through me, hot and ardent.

He hopped up and jogged out toward where Chloe stood. I watched as he bumped his fist easily against hers, grinning, like this was a routine greeting between them. I watched as he said something that made her eyes clear, turned her gaze deferential. I watched him sling an arm over her shoulders and walk her back to the house.

By the time they got to the porch, she was laughing. Isaac had defused the situation, and maybe I should've been grateful—maybe she really *didn't* see—but I was fixated on his arm around my sister and the way she was looking up at him, enchanted.

I hated her for assuming his interest, and I hated him for leading her on.

Now, I hate him for trying to keep me from moving on.

He's a black hole—inescapable.

Meanwhile, Tucker is the brightest star, twinkling incessantly. His heat will thaw the cold, hard thing that's settled in the pit of my stomach.

I change into flannel pajama pants and a sweatshirt, then gather my hair into a ponytail. In the bathroom, I give my teeth a brushing and wash the smeared makeup from my face. When I tiptoe back to the parlor, I find him standing in front of the bookcase, regarding Lucy's collection of books and photos.

"Hey," I say quietly.

He twists around, then crosses the room and circles his arms around my waist. Leaning down, he murmurs, "Jesus, Cal. Why do you look so cute in pajamas?"

I let myself cozy up to him for a second, but his shirt is still damp. I hold out the dry one I dug up. "You can change if you want. This is too big on me, so it should work for you."

He steps back and peels off his shirt. He's topless for all of three seconds; not nearly enough time for me to admire him the way I want to, but God . . . I've seen him without a shirt more times than I can count, but this is different. Bare skin out of the context of the pool is bare skin I want to run my hands over.

I'm ogling him, degrading him, probably, but if he's noticed, he doesn't mind. He tugs the shirt over his head, then rakes a hand through his hair to return it to its state of perfect disarray.

I sink down on the settee, and he slips behind me. Curling against him, I close my eyes. I consider, for a half second, telling him about Isaac. About the recent calls and our muddied history, but he'll have questions and I'll end up flustered and that's no good.

Isaac doesn't matter. Not anymore.

Tucker tugs on the elastic holding my ponytail, releasing it. He combs his fingers through my hair, again and again, until I'm nearly rapturous.

"You have the softest hair," he whispers, wonderstruck.

Time passes. Minutes. Hours. Days, maybe, while we sit in contented silence. I breathe him in, knitting my fingers through his. His heart beats beneath my ear, a steady, quick *thrum, thrum, thrum* that'd lull me to sleep if I let it. How lovely it would be to drift off in his arms. But I like him so much now, I worry about wasting our time together. In just over a month, I'll be headed north to Seattle. He'll go south, back to Malibu.

"Tucker?" I whisper, mostly to keep myself awake.

His fingertips glide across my neck, back into my hair. "Hmm?"

"I can hear your heart."

"Yeah?"

"It's beating so fast."

He shifts, and I raise my head to look at him.

"Because I'm with you," he says.

I smile, then I press my mouth to his.

I woke up alone in the parlor, beneath a soft throw. It took me only a second to notice the single poppy set purposefully on the side table.

I missed Chloe.

Now, I'm walking the sidewalks of Bell Cove with Lucy. To free myself from Stewart House—from the shame of ditching my sister for a boy, again, the worry of a squandered opportunity to gather information, and the stress of wondering if I'll get another—I suggested we go shopping. My aunt was all too happy to take me up on my offer. She treated me to breakfast at The Coffee Cove, and now she's grilling me about last night.

"It was good," I tell her for the dozenth time.

"Just good?" she asks as we duck into a shop full of decor made of driftwood and seashells.

"Fine. *Really* good," I say, indulging her. "We watched the fireworks. I met some more of Tucker's friends. He came in for a while, after, and we hung out in the parlor."

She raises an eyebrow. "Oh, really?"

I run my fingers over seashells lining a picture frame. "It wasn't like that," I mumble, even though it sort of was.

"Speaking of boys, did you see the note I left on your bed?"

"Ugh. Yes."

"Why's he still calling, Callie?"

"I honestly don't know."

"I'm serious—I want you to let me know if he keeps it up," she says, like she's a mob boss with connections. She picks up a hurricane glass with a sterling silver base. It looks expensive. "What do you think of this? For the Theodore? I could sit it on the secretary with some sand in the bottom, and a pretty candle."

"Sure."

"I'll get one for the kitchen, too. Come help me pick out the candles."

We spend a long time standing in front of a shabby hutch lined with pillar candles. Lucy chooses a clean cotton scent for the Theodore, and I pick vanilla for the kitchen. When we're done, I wander outside and wait in an Adirondack chair while she pays for her finds. It's so nice today, and I'm headache-free thanks to last night's rain showering away the pollen. I close my eyes and sit, absorbing the sun until a shape passes in front of it, casting me in shadow.

I open my eyes, shading them with my hand. A small form stands silhouetted before me.

"Callie? I thought that was you."

"Shirley," I say. "Nice to see you."

"You, too, sweetheart. How's Lucy?"

"Good. She's just inside if you want to wait for her."

"I think I will." She eases herself into the chair beside me and says, "I saw you last night with the Morgan boy."

"Yeah, we've gotten to know each other since he started working at Lucy's." *Yard Boy.* I hide a smile.

"Such a nice young man. I taught his parents third grade. Did you know that?"

"No, I didn't."

"I knew their friend Nathan, too. Those three used to be cute as can be."

My interest is piqued. "Tucker doesn't talk about his mother a lot."

Her mouth sinks into a frown. "Not surprising. The rumors about her last days have probably caused him a lot of suffering. Not to mention his father."

I sit up, leaning right into her personal space, spilling over with questions, the most imminent being, *What rumors?*

Lucy breezes through the door, holding a paper shopping bag. "Shirley! What a nice surprise!"

Shirley pushes out of her chair, politely refusing Lucy's offer of a hand. The two of them make small talk for a few minutes, but I can't follow.

What rumors?

What rumors?!

After a century, they wrap it up. Shirley pats my arm. "Come see me in the shop, anytime."

She hobbles down the sidewalk. I follow my aunt to the Range Rover.

The questions I didn't get to ask gather like a flock of birds, frantically flapping their wings.

The next day, I spend a while in the Abigail, making the queen-size bed with linens Lucy ordered from an online boutique. The room is pretty much done, walls a dramatic ruby red, antique furniture, and a mishmash of books and candles placed atop flat surfaces. The curtains are my favorite, a striking red-and-white paisley that sets the walls off. Buddy and Daisy love to sneak in and play with their long-tasseled tiebacks.

A breeze wafts through the open window as I slide a pillow into its case, still warm from the dryer. The scent of the fabric softener my aunt uses is familiar now, homey, and I'm not sure whether to be calmed by that fact or unnerved.

Just as I've finished fluffing countless other pillows, a strange sound blows in from outside. A shout, muffled, maybe distressed. I go to the window and look out over the yard. I don't see Tucker or Lucy. The yard is quiet, still, and serene.

I go back to work, folding a knit throw to lay over the foot of the bed, lost in thought. My sister's elusiveness is bothering me. I waited out on the porch last night, but she never showed. Our last conversation was strained, she's frustrated by her missing memories, and I'm sure it looks like I ditched her for Tucker on Independence Day.

She's hurt. Or pissed.

Outside, a loud thud resounds.

I hurry to the window and scan the yard, listening hard.

Another shout . . . the shed. The door's closed but rattling on its hinges.

I run down the stairs, through the front door, then race across the lawn to the outbuilding, purposeful but rickety.

"Hey!" a voice calls from inside.

I press my hands to the wooden door. "Tucker?"

"Cal?" he shouts. "Finally—I'm trapped!"

I jiggle the handle; it's definitely jammed. "The door's stuck!"

"No shit. I'm gonna push. Pull as hard as you can, okay?"

I widen my stance and wrap both hands around the rusty handle. "I'm ready."

"One, two . . . three!"

I yank with all I've got. The door flies open, unchallenged. I reel backward and fall to the ground, hard, on my ass. Tucker materializes in the doorway, hunched, sweaty, winded. I expect him to laugh when he sees me sprawled in the grass, but he doesn't. He just stands there, hands on his knees, panting.

"Are you okay?" I ask, righting myself.

"No, not really."

He reels around and heads toward the house. I scamper after him, baffled and sort of offended; I just rescued him. I follow as he climbs the stairs to the porch and falls unceremoniously into a rocker, still breathless. I take a tentative seat in the chair next to his. He fixes a stare on me, his eyes a dull gray that's startlingly wrong.

He says, "I think I met your ghost."

Air whooshes from my lungs. "What?"

"I went into the shed to grab a shovel, and I swear to God, out of nowhere it got cold. Then the door slammed. *Slammed.* All on its own."

I nod, hoping that if I stay calm, he'll chill out, too.

"It wasn't the wind," he says. "It *wasn't* the wind."

"I know." It was Chloe—it must've been. But *why*? "Did anything else happen?"

"Beside the fact that I couldn't get the door open? There's no lock, Callie. Something was keeping it shut."

"How long were you in there?"

"I don't know." He shudders. "Too long."

I reach for him. His skin is clammy, and there are scrapes running the length of his arm. They're fresh, painful-looking. I twist his wrist for a closer look.

He glances at his wounds, then brushes my hand away, offering a startling explanation: "I tried to take the door down."

In life, Chloe was playful. Sometimes she was surly.

She was never mean.

Tucker gets up and stalks into the yard. The rigid slant of his shoulders makes me unsure about whether to follow. I loiter on the top step as he marches back and forth across the grass. Just when I'm certain I can't stand to watch him pace another second, he stops, looks at me, and says, "I should've believed you—the second you told me."

God, he still looks so shaken. "It's okay, Tucker. Seriously."

Time stretches long. The sun gleams overhead. Waves crash distantly. His face relaxes, and he opens his arms. I walk down the stairs and into them. He smells of wood shavings and freshly cut grass, deodorant and, faintly, sweat. He exhales, and I do, too.

"Distract me," he says into my hair.

I press my cheek to his heart, foraging for the right topic, settling on, "Lucy and I are almost done decorating the Abigail."

He laughs. "Thrilling."

"We painted the walls red. It looks good, actually."

"I bet. What else?"

"Oh! I ran into Shirley yesterday. From the bookstore? She mentioned you."

"Did she?"

"Yep. Your parents, too. She said she taught them third grade."

"That, she did."

"And she mentioned someone else. Nathan?"

The muscles of his back tighten beneath his damp T-shirt. "What about him?"

"Just that your parents were friends with him."

He pulls away, putting a rift of space between us. His expression is impenetrable.

"Is that bad?" I ask.

"Remember what I told you the other night at the beach? About my mother?"

I stand in the grass, thrown by his shifting mood, trying to link what he shared on the Fourth of July with what Shirley told me yesterday. "You said she knew one of the Stewarts? Nathan . . . Stewart?"

He nods. "My dad was tight with him, too, until they graduated from high school."

"You said your mom went to visit a friend. That she never came back."

He nods again, impatient now.

"That friend was Nathan Stewart?" As his name leaves my mouth, it hits me hard, how familiar this saga is. Tucker's mother went to visit her friend Nathan Stewart and was never seen again. Annabel Tate never returned from the Stewart property, either. And then there are the letters

I unearthed, signed with an *A*, speaking of loss and regret and a terrible mistake.

. . . *don't even get me started on his mother*, Brynn said.

. . . *caused him a lot of suffering*, Shirley said.

. . . *until they graduated from high school*, Tucker said.

I touch his shoulder. "God, Tucker . . . Was Annabel Tate your mother?"

He takes a swift step back. "What do you know about Annabel Tate?"

I blink, hurt by the space he keeps putting between us. "I know she went to Shell City High, like you. I know police officers think she jumped from the cliff out back. For a while, in the beginning, I thought she might be my ghost."

Something's wrong—the way Tucker's glaring, hard as marble, resentment carved in sharp lines and severe angles. "You have no idea what you're talking about," he says. "There's no proof she died by suicide—there're a shit-ton of people who think she was pushed. *Murdered*. And there're some who think she up and left town. Did you know *that*?"

"No," I whisper. "But the article I read said—"

"Don't," he says, his voice serrated. "The articles are wrong. *You're* wrong."

"Then help me understand!"

He drags a hand over his face, coming away with a fraction of composure. "My mother was last seen here, in the backyard, with her . . . I don't know . . . her *lover*." He nearly chokes on the word. "She was cheating on my dad, jerking him around. She wouldn't marry him, wouldn't even settle down with him. He was taking care of me, and she was screwing around with Nathan Stewart. He played my dad and manipulated my mother. A lot of people—my dad, my grandparents—thought he was dangerous. Thought he should've been held responsible for her disappearance."

"But it really could've been an accident."

"It was a fucking tragedy. So the next time you find a stack of love letters from her to *him*, I don't need to see them."

"Tucker—"

He throws up a hand, cutting me off. "I've gotta go."

He turns and stalks down the driveway to his car. I watch, speechless, as he climbs in, then slams the door with such force I expect the window to shatter.

Without a backward glance, he peels off, tires throwing dust and gravel into the breeze.

40

In the backyard, I lie on the lawn, watching the afternoon sun slide across the blue, blue sky.

I can't believe he left.

I think, maybe, I should be angry. I *want* to be angry, but all I feel is a sickening emptiness deep in my gut.

The grass makes my legs itch, and my cheeks have gone warm with a burn, but I don't move. I'm backtracking, combing over the facts, circling around to bits of conversation Tucker and I've had, thinking about what I've unearthed, recalling what I've read.

The article I found online didn't mention that Annabel had a child. I do the math; she disappeared in 1999. Tucker would've been an infant. That photograph in the Morgans' living room, baby Tucker and his mother, must've been taken weeks, maybe *days*, before Annabel vanished.

His mother . . .

I spring up from the grass and run into the house, into my room. I yank open the nightstand drawer. A's letters are there, secrets folded into pink stationery. I spread them out over my bed and pore over her words.

I broke what we had . . . but it was special. . . .

With every passing minute, I regret my time with him more. . . .

I carry my biggest mistake with me, every day. . . .

I'm not sure I can stay with him, trapped in a weak imitation of love. . . .

I need to know if we can reclaim what we lost.

Annabel wrote these letters to Nathan Stewart. Does that mean the person she regretted spending time with—the person she was trapped with—was Benjamin Morgan?

Was *Tucker* the mistake she carried with her?

I'm pushing my feet into shoes, cramming the letters into my pocket. I'm moments from heading out of my room when my phone rings.

I glance at it; I'm in no mood to deal with my dad, but if I don't answer, he'll worry.

I try to inject liveliness into my voice when I say, "Hello?"

"Callie. Hi, sweetie." I'm surprised—it's my mom.

"Hey. How are you?"

"Okay . . ." She stretches the word out, as if considering whether it fits.

I wait, easing the inklings of a tension headache by rubbing circles into my temples. Mom does the same thing; when she's zoned out at the kitchen table with a glass of wine, she presses her fingers to her head and kneads. I find it unsettling—not the movement, but the expression she wears: vacant and detached.

"Callie, hi," my dad says. I picture them at home, in the kitchen, with his phone on the countertop between them, set to speaker. "How are you? How's Lucy?"

"We're good," I say. And then, because the worry corkscrewing through my middle demands it: "Is something wrong?"

They take too long to answer.

"We're calling with news," Dad says at last. "Mom's going to go away for a while."

"I—what?"

My mom speaks, soft and lethargic. "Let's not sugarcoat it, Arthur. I'm going to a treatment center. Rehab, out on the coast. Daddy's tried to help me, and I've tried to help myself. But my drinking . . . It's beyond us."

A jumble of replies get lodged in my throat. It's not that her news is complicated or even unexpected—Mom drinks too much and, finally, she's ready to reclaim control—but still. I don't want her to have to go away.

"What if I come home? Dad, I can help out—no more smoking. Mom, we can spend more time together, you and me. You don't have to go to rehab."

"I do, sweetie. This isn't a problem you can solve, but I love you for wanting to try."

"Callie," Dad says. "Mom's going to be okay. This is a positive step."

"But what about you?"

"I'll be fine. When you both come home at summer's end, things will be different. Things will be better."

"It'll be a fresh start," Mom promises, but her voice breaks, and my heart squeezes.

There's a lump rising in my throat and my eyes have gone watery and, God, I know what they're saying is right and true—Mom deserves this;

it's a *good* thing—but all I want is a do-over. A trip back in time. A chance to save my sister. Because if I'd kept her safe, Mom would be healthy, sober, tending her garden. Dad would be happy, relaxed, busy with his classes. Chloe would have a triathlon under her belt.

She'd be here with me, loving Bell Cove the way I've come to.

I force my sadness down, back, *away*, afraid to let my parents in on how hard their news is hitting me—it's not like they don't have enough to worry about.

"I need to go," I say, steady, though my headache's burrowing deep.

"We love you," Dad says.

"So much," Mom says.

I end the call.

My first impulse is to get ahold of Tucker. I need him to affirm what my parents said: Rehab is a step forward, a fresh start is possible, everything really will be okay.

Except, Tucker left me.

I go into the bathroom. Wash my face. Towel it dry. Give my reflection a stern look. I will not sink back into sorrow—not when I've worked so hard to dig my way out.

In the kitchen, I search for Motrin, nearly stepping on Daisy, who skitters underfoot. She circles my legs, meowing cantankerously as I down two pills. It's weird, seeing her by herself. Buddy's become her shadow, batting at her tail and curling up next to her on the parlor windowsill.

God, now that I'm thinking about it, it's been hours since I last saw him.

My headache's forgotten as I tear the house apart looking for my kitten. Lucy helps, though she thinks I'm being silly. "Cats are independent," she says, peering under the bare mattress in the Savannah while I fling the closet doors open. "He probably found a quiet spot to nap. He'll come out when he gets hungry."

I'm not comforted, especially after I pull the bag of organic cat treats from the fridge, give it a good shake, and am rewarded only by the eager appearance of Daisy.

"He's gone," I say. "He must have slipped out an open door."

"Then maybe he's playing in the yard."

So we search outside. The porch, the shed, all the way out to the cliff. I wander the perimeter, near the woods, calling *Buddy! Buddy!* shaking the stupid bag of treats. As twilight approaches, Lucy and I reconvene on the porch. She's discouraged now, but she's wary, too, eyeing me like she's afraid I'll snap.

"He could be anywhere," I say, falling into a rocking chair.

My aunt squeezes my shoulder. "He's exploring. But he loves you. He'll be back."

At least she's conceded to the fact that he's missing. Too restless to sit still, I pop out of my chair and walk the porch, searching the yard for a glimpse of my little cat.

What will Tucker say when he finds out I've lost Buddy?

"Callie," Lucy says. "Why don't you go out for a bit? I'll stay here. I'll keep looking. When you get home—if Buddy's not back—we'll search together."

"I can't leave." I look into the rapidly darkening yard. "He's out there."

"You can't walk the porch all night. Take my car. Go to the pool. Swim for an hour. It'll do you good."

I lack the energy to argue. Besides, she might be right; my neck is stiff and my shoulders are tight and I won't stoop to smoking—not while my mom's on her way to a treatment center. A workout's the one thing that might release the pressure building inside me.

My drive to the pool's a blur. Before I know it, I'm plummeting into cool water, exhaling, sinking to the bottom. I push off and sprint down the lane, kicking wildly, pulling hard.

I'm only a few hundred yards into my swim when I realize it was a mistake to come alone. Solitude at the pool, the deafening silence and the monotonous back-and-forth, make it too easy to lament the ways my life is splintering: my parents, my missing kitten, Tucker. And Chloe . . . It's impossible not to think of her as I struggle through my workout, muscles straining, skin burning, like I'm swimming through gravel.

A sob rises in my throat. I throw myself into a flip turn.

I hate the clash of improvement and setback, opposing forces splitting me down the middle.

Will I ever just feel *normal*?

I pull up at the wall and yank my goggles off. Freaking Lucy. *Swim for an hour. It'll do you good.* No. I feel worse, winded and dizzy, and then a wash of grief crashes over me, so intense tears come even before I'm out of the pool. On the deck, I wrap up in my towel and sink onto a chair, grateful, at least, that no one's around to catch me losing it.

I cry until I can't cry anymore. Then I dress and drive home.

When I arrive, Lucy tells me Buddy hasn't returned.

I'm exhausted, teetering on a dangerous ledge. I go to my room and burn through what's left of my weed. Then, soaring with the stars, I climb into bed and stare at the ceiling, unseeing.

41

I sleep and stir and dream in fragments.

I see poppies, red and diaphanous.

I smell poppies, light and sweet.

I feel poppies, petals like tissue paper, tickling my skin.

Deep in the night, the moon hanging high outside my window, I wake with a start.

Chloe.

I slip out of bed and tiptoe barefoot down the hall. I'm foggy with lingering sleep, but I manage to sneak out the front door and silently cross the porch. The stairs are easy; I know which ones creak thanks to weeks spent traversing them. And then I'm jogging through damp grass until I reach a skyline of evergreens, extending my awareness, searching for my sister.

She's there, among the trees, just like my dream.

Droplets of condensation shimmer around her like a halo. She smiles, eyes creasing at the corners, and I'm overwhelmed with relief. She's still here. She's not mad about Tucker. She hasn't been avoiding me.

"Let's go to the poppies," she says.

She moves into the trees, drifting noiselessly through the underbrush, undaunted, claiming her forest. By comparison, I'm a freight train, crashing through the scrub, lumbering over fallen logs, sidestepping blackberry brambles. Forever passes before she pulls to a halt. I scramble to catch up, breathless when I reach her side. The sky is black, embedded with twinkling stars. Staring up at them makes me woozy.

"Look," Chloe says.

I drop my gaze.

Poppies.

Their red-orange buds are closed, hiding their pollen from the moon, but their delicate, honey scent permeates the misty air.

They're stunning.

Chloe drifts into the meadow. I follow, moving carefully to avoid crushing the flowers. When we've found the center, she sits. I do, too.

She says, "You seem sad."

I upset Tucker.

I lost my kitten.

Mom's in rehab.

The thoughts must leave my mouth to drift vociferously among the poppies because Chloe says, "Rehab? For what?"

"She's been drinking. Too much."

"But that's not like her."

It didn't used to be. Before last summer, Mom would have a glass of wine with dinner, maybe once a week. She'd go to UW faculty parties with Dad, and while he'd occasionally come home tipsy, she was always clearheaded, content to chauffeur him safely through the city. She'd go to her Garden Club's monthly brunches and come home sober, with anecdotes about how many mimosas the other ladies swigged. After Chloe died, though, one glass of wine a week became one glass of wine a night, then two or three, and then, in the space of a month, she was downing full bottles before bedtime. She wasn't subtle about it, either; I came down to the kitchen on innumerable mornings to find merlot-stained corks left overnight on the countertop.

"Dad says she needs help," I tell Chloe. "*She* says she needs help."

"When did this start?"

"Last summer."

She nods, somber, as if she were expecting as much.

"It's not your fault," I say reflexively.

She looks beyond me, beyond the poppies, into the blackened trees. "That can't be true."

"Chloe, what happened . . . you aren't to blame—not even a little bit."

"Then who is?"

You tell me.

A beat of silence passes. "I am, maybe."

Her gaze collides with mine and holds tight, like I fetter her to this strange night, this surreal place. She wants me to go on—her expression pleads for information, for understanding—but I don't know how to explain that *I'm* the reason she left for the beach. *I'm* the reason she felt compelled to swim alone. *I'm* the reason she exists the way she does.

Her death was an accident—but an avoidable one. Culpability sits with me. And Isaac, maybe.

"That night," I say, "*before*. We were in Lucy's yard. Please, Chloe. Try to remember."

Her eyes narrow as she focuses. I give her time, silently straining to relay what happened across the space between us, like my ability to commune with her spirit might have come with the added bonus of telepathy.

She has to remember; we have to talk about this.

Her face changes, clears, like steam wiped from a mirror. "We fought," she whispers.

I nod through the whirring in my ears, a drone that makes me light-headed.

"We fought over a *boy*," she says.

She's doing it—she's calling what happened out of the dark, reclaiming it as her own. Except, instead of finding strength in the knowledge, she's dimming, *fading*, as if the fight and the boy and the memories are stealing a share of her essence.

"Chloe?"

She's silent, a girl in a yellow dress, evaporating into a field of flowers.

I reach for her, the tiny diamonds in my ring twinkling like the stars overhead, but she wrenches away before I make contact. "You shouldn't."

My cheeks heat with the devastation of her snub.

The poppies murmur their disapproval.

She's luminous in the moonlight, almost transparent now, and I know with certainty: This will end. When she collects the pieces of her shattered memory and fits them back into an image that tells the whole story, the circle that's been broken for the last year will close. When she remembers, I can apologize. I can ask for forgiveness, and she can grant it, if she chooses. But for Chloe, remembering is the same as finishing her business—the same as saying goodbye.

A valve opens, releasing pain into my spine, forcing it through my neck, until it pools behind my eyes, surging and sloshing. I draw a sharp breath and press my palm to my forehead.

This is as bad as it's ever been.

Chloe's mouth moves, almost imperceptibly, but a breeze takes her words. The look in her eyes scares me: a discernible desperation that makes her appear untamed. She tries again: "I'm sorry. About Tucker. About the shed."

"I know," I say, weak, almost weepy.

Her eyes dim with worry. "Lay back."

I do, into flower buds that tickle my skin.

"I hate to see you in pain." She pauses, glancing skyward. When she speaks again, her voice is thick and sorrowful. "I'm not sure we should keep meeting."

We have to. I need the truth.

But I'm too miserable to form the words. My throat is parched, and the pressure in my head is inescapable. My vision comes in ripples and waves, like Stewart House's windows.

"Close your eyes," Chloe says.

Her face, pale and resigned, leaves an impression on my eyelids.

"Breathe."

I inhale.

I hear a rustling.

I taste copper, faint but metallic.

I feel dampness on my cheeks: tears.

My sister sweeps my hair away from my neck, as she did that first night in the bathroom.

A cool waft, an emphatic whisper, "Callie, sleep."

When I drift into consciousness, my head is too heavy to lift.

With my eyes closed, I struggle to roll over. A breeze strokes my cheek, the air misty and cool. My head rests on a hard surface—not my pillow. The pounding within it is regular and concentrated, vibrating the length of my bones, stiffening my joints.

I could throw up, but I don't have the strength to move.

I'm increasingly aware of birds' singsong, the almost constant kiss of wind on my clammy skin, the subtle taste of sea salt on my tongue. Without moving an unnecessary muscle, I open my eyes.

I'm not in my bed.

I shift. Red-orange flowers curtsy on long stems.

A fist of fear squeezes my stomach.

I'm alone.

In the woods.

No one knows.

I struggle to grasp last night's slippery memories. I left Stewart House. I followed my sister. We walked. Found the poppy meadow. We talked. And then she was gone.

Now I'm trembling, lost in an illness I can't shake.

It's early morning, I think. The indigo sky is just beginning to reflect light. I'm supposed to meet Tucker at the pool—even after the way he left me standing in the yard yesterday, I think he'll worry if I don't show up. And my aunt . . . She'll panic if I don't come home for breakfast.

I try to sit up. Pulling my knees to my chest, I rest my head on them. I close my eyes against surges of vertigo, swaying as if Earth itself is rolling beneath me.

I fall back to the ground. Sweat coats my face, but I'm covered in goose bumps, burning up, and freezing. I focus on breathing, on the simple act of inhaling air and blowing away what's left.

This is my fault.

I got high, then wandered out of the house.

Now I'm sick and stranded and scared.

How long will it be before someone realizes I'm missing?

42

My name tumbles into the meadow on a deep, smoky voice.

Sleep has dulled my headache, and it's easier to open my eyes now. The sky is brighter, more periwinkle than indigo. The sun, suspended in the east, warms my face.

"Cal! You out here?"

My throat is so dry and my head is spinning, spinning, spinning and I feel *awful*, but I prop myself up and rasp, "Tucker?"

The muffled crunch of underbrush, the snapping of twigs . . . He's hurrying.

I don't know how much time passes before he's kneeling over me, blocking the sun's light. He touches my hair, my face, presses his fingers to my neck. He's feeling for my pulse—an alarming realization that motivates me to sit up in earnest.

The joy I feel at seeing him is chocolate malts and easy swims and long walks, flawless kisses and firecracker smiles.

He goes still, gazing into my eyes for a long moment. The birds quiet their chirping, the wind dies down, the trees cease to swish their branches. We consume the space of the meadow, him and me, a closed circuit of energy.

Then, in one swift movement, he lifts me.

He trudges away from the poppies and, over his shoulder, I watch sunlight pour through the trees, drenching the flowers in light. It's beautiful and terrifying, a bizarre wonderland.

"What happened?" Tucker asks, stomping through the scrub.

I'm too full to speak, brimming with sadness and confusion and gratitude.

Despite what happened yesterday, he came back.

Perennial.

He lets me get away with silence because he's generous and kind and, I think, he knows me really, really well.

He treks on, and I feel every high step, every bend around a tree, every branch snagged on clothing. He doesn't slow, and though his neck grows damp with sweat, his breath never comes labored. He speaks continuously, barely a whisper, his words studded with worry. "You're safe. You can tell me what happened, whenever you're up for it. You're okay."

I look up at him as he makes an abrupt turn. "Tucker? I lost Buddy."

He gives a short laugh. "That's what you're thinking about? Lucy found him on the porch this morning when she was looking for you. He's fine."

"Really? He's home?"

"Shit, Callie. Tell me you weren't in the woods looking for him."

I can't tell him why I was in the woods—I don't understand myself. I rest my head against the softness of his T-shirt. I want to wrap myself in cotton; I want to wrap myself in *him*.

"Yesterday," I whisper. "I shouldn't have said anything about your mom. It's not even my business—I don't know what I was thinking."

"It's not important. Don't give it another thought, okay?"

He walks another few minutes before we break free of the trees, into the yard that surrounds Stewart House.

"You found her!" My aunt's voice, from the porch.

Tucker treks into the cooler air of the house and down the hall. He lays me on my bed . . . smooths my hair . . . touches my cheek.

"Where was she?" Lucy's close and either very angry or very upset. Cigarette smoke clings to her as their conversation meanders around me.

"The woods. The poppy meadow."

"Was she alone?"

"I didn't see anyone else."

"Do you think someone took her there?"

A pause. One of them pulls the sheet over me, right to my chin.

"I don't know."

"I should call her father."

"Her father? We need to take her to the hospital."

This. This is what brings me back. They're hovering over my bed. Tucker's driving a hand through his hair, and my aunt has her fists planted on her hips. "No hospital," I say, "and please, don't call my dad. I'm fine."

"You're not fine," Lucy says.

"Sleepwalking," I say, too tired to attempt a full sentence.

"Sleepwalking?" Tucker repeats, his tone hardened with skepticism.

"I have a headache." I close my eyes.

I want both of them to go.

"Let's let her rest, Tuck. If she hasn't improved in an hour, I'll take her to a doctor."

He sets his hand on my forehead. His palm is warm and calloused, so comforting I want to cry. He pulls away. Footsteps travel across the hardwood. The door closes.

When I wake, my headache has faded to a blunt rapping. Buddy's curled up on my pillow. I'm not sure how he got into my room, but I'm thrilled to see him. I kiss his little face all over before noticing ice water and two Motrin on my nightstand. I swallow the medicine and all the water.

I force myself out of bed and into the bathroom, where I gulp down another glass of water. When I finish, I sit on the closed toilet lid and stare at my filthy feet. I trampled through the woods *barefoot* in the middle of the night.

I lost myself.

Because of Chloe.

I stand too quickly; wooziness nearly takes me back down. Last night, this morning—there's no way allergies are to blame. There's something else to my symptoms. Something otherworldly, something unknowable, and that scares the shit out of me.

How much am I willing to risk to see my sister? To excavate her secrets?

I reclaim my equilibrium and strip out of my dirty clothes. I turn the shower on as hot as it'll go, letting the spray splash over me, then soap up, scouring my skin with a loofa. I scrub my hair and think of Lucy—how she must've felt not knowing where I was this morning. And Tucker—how he must have suffered seeing me weak and confused amid the poppies.

I am horrible.

Lucy's changing my bedding when I pad back into the bedroom with a towel wrapped around my middle. She tucks a sheet beneath the mattress before shaking out the down comforter and laying it back on the bed. I dress in a clean pair of leggings and a tank top while she fluffs pillows. I try to come up with a reasonable explanation for my behavior, but I have no idea how to justify disappearing in the middle of the night.

"You're taking the day off," she says, slipping a pillow into its case. She chucks it at the headboard and turns on me. "I want you to rest."

"Okay," I say, running a brush through my wet hair.

"You gave me a hell of a scare, Callie. What were you thinking?"

"I don't know."

"Not good enough."

"Aunt Lucy, I'm sorry. The truth is, I wasn't thinking at all."

Her expression is more imposing than anything I've ever seen out of her. Still, her voice wavers when she says, "I need to know where you are, all the time—especially at night. What if something had happened? What if . . . ?"

What if I died.

I wonder if she regrets inviting me to stay this summer.

"I'm sorry," I say again.

What I want to tell her is *thank you. Thank you for everything.*

She pulls back the bedcovers. “Buddy’s in the kitchen with Daisy. Don’t worry about him.”

I slip into bed and lie back on pillows that smell of fabric softener and home. Lucy bends to kiss my cheek and whispers, “Don’t ever make me worry like that again.”

She leaves me, quiet and alone.

I'm not sure how much time has passed when the door opens again. Heavier footsteps tread across the floor. My mattress shifts. Warm fingertips brush my cheek.

I open my eyes to Tucker and a surge of emotion foreign and powerful and *good*.

I'm not sure where we stand, though. He hurt me yesterday, and recalling what I put him through this morning makes my stomach roil.

Worry swirls in the celadon of his eyes. The only thing keeping me from bursting into tears is his hand on my cheek.

I push my mouth into my best imitation of a smile. "Hi."

His expression thaws, thank God, and he dives headfirst into an apology. "Callie, this is on me. Yesterday . . . if I'd stayed, if I'd talked to you, if I'd let *you* talk—"

"Hey, stop. Please don't feel bad about any of this. If it weren't for you . . ."

He opens his mouth, considers, and closes it again.

"Tucker, what?"

"I drove here this morning when you didn't show up at the pool. Lucy didn't know where you were. I couldn't find you anywhere. I was fucking terrified."

Blood courses through my veins, a sound like thunder in my ears. "Thank you," I say. "For coming. For helping me."

"Are you kidding? You were all I could think about." He takes my hand and threads his fingers through mine. He's nervous, I can tell, and he's stalling. Probably because he's about to poke new holes into our already-leaking boat. He takes a breath and says, "I need you to tell me, Cal. Were you in the woods alone?"

I trace a finger over the stitching in my comforter, avoiding his eyes.

Chloe, last night, waning and waxing as truths emerged.

"Shit, Callie. Who'd you go out there with?"

Not the ghost, he's thinking. *Tell me you weren't with the ghost.*

"I just—I needed fresh air."

"In the middle of the night?"

A sea of silence churns between us. He's still holding my hand—I'm clinging to his—and he's staring me down, daring me to, for once, be transparent.

"Tucker," I whisper. "She needed me."

"Who needed you?"

I can't say it aloud.

I *cannot* force her name free.

He wrenches his hand from mine, and all I can I think, over and over, is *Don't tell me we're done.*

"I'm trying," he says. "I'm trying so hard to be straight with you. To be open with you. I want to give you time. Earn your trust. But this morning? You can't disappear in the middle of the night. It's not fair to Lucy, and it's not fair to me and, shit, if you got hurt, what would that be like for your parents? People care about you. *I* care about you."

"I know. I care about you, too."

He shakes his head, disbelieving. "If we're never gonna get to a place where we tell each other important stuff, then I'm not sure I should keep coming around."

I close my eyes and see white spots. Cold creeps in, caressing my shoulders, leaching through my pores. Tucker sighs, rueful; I don't even realize I'm shivering until he tucks the comforter around me. He moves beside me, his back against my pillows, then loops his arm around my shoulders, charitably.

I dissolve into his warmth.

He rubs my neck, kneading tension away. "Am I being an asshole?"

"No. You're being passionate."

"Yeah, that happens sometimes, especially where you're concerned." He pauses, his hand still on my neck. His voice is quiet and heartbreakingly uncertain when he says, "There's something between us, right? I mean, I think there is, but maybe I'm assuming too much. Maybe you and me . . . Maybe we're just a distraction from what you've got going on at home."

A spark of indignation flickers inside me. I sit up and look him square in the eye. "It's impossible to distract me, Tucker. My sister is *dead.* I'm dangerously close to failing out of school. My mom's on her way to rehab.

My dad wants everything to be okay—" I inhale and finish, wobbly—"but *nothing* is okay."

He gathers me against him, and I cry, but it's not so tragic this time—nothing like yesterday's breakdown at the pool.

Tucker's here. I'm not alone, and I'm grateful.

When it's over, I'm rinsed clean, like the shore at low tide.

I ease back, feeling better, stronger, to find Tucker's bottomless gaze trained on me. His mouth sags in a frown; he looks deeply troubled, like my welfare agonizes him to the marrow of his bones.

"Chloe," I whisper. "Last night, I went into the woods with Chloe."

"Your sister is your ghost," he says. Somehow, he doesn't sound surprised. "Tell me how it works?"

"There's a connection between us," I say. "An energy. It's hard to explain."

"You talk to her?"

"All the time."

"And she talks back?"

I smile. "Yes."

"She knows? She understands she's . . . ?"

I nod. "At first, she didn't remember details. But she's recovering parts of the story. When she has it all, when she remembers, when we confront what happened, that's it. She'll have no reason left to stay."

He touches my neck, then lets his hand slip to my collarbone. Lower. It comes to a rest on my chest, a slight pressure against my ribs. He leaves it there, fingers spread, as if he's caging my heart inside. "You want her to stay."

He speaks with such tenderness, such empathy. I can't fathom having this conversation with anyone else.

"Of course. God, Tucker. It's been amazing, having her back."

He scans my face, hunting for clues. "But . . . ?"

I look at his hand, still pressed to my chest. "It's different now," I admit. "*She's* different. There's a wall between us—not a wall, maybe, but a screen. She's Chloe, but she's *not*. And when I'm with her, I lose part of myself. Last night, walking into the woods . . . I never would have done that if not for her asking. It's scary, surrendering like that."

"Cal, you probably don't want to hear this, but . . . You could stop seeing her."

"No, I can't. She waited a whole year for me to come back to Bell Cove—I can't disappear on her now. And anyway, I need her help. Something happened the night she died, something I don't understand, something she was a part of. I need her to remember. I need her to tell me about it."

"So help her remember."

"If I do, I'll never see her again."

He swallows, holding my gaze, and then, so gently, he says, "Is it fair to expect her to stick around, haunting a place she has no real tie to? I mean, does she want to be here? Is it good for her? Is it good for *you*?"

I've agonized over Chloe's well-being my whole life, but never more than these last couple of weeks. I run a hand over my face, grumbling, "Why do I feel like you're leading me to an answer I already know?"

He gives me a chastened smile.

"God, Tucker. I wish you could have met her. She was so much fun. Such a brat, but in the most endearing way."

His eyes go wide with realization. "Hang on—did *she* lock me in the shed?"

His exaggerated indignation sends me into giggles.

He grins, taking my face in his hands. “You have the best laugh,” he says, as if laughter is a sound I’ve worked hard at, a sound I’ve refined just for him.

Something like love bubbles up in me, new and thrilling and magical. “You make me happy,” I tell him, the absolute truth.

If I’ve spent the last year lost in a forest of grief, he’s the long, winding road out.

I’m leaning toward him before I consciously realize it. Our eyes meet. We share a warm breath. The strain, the weirdness, the doubt . . . forgotten. In this moment, Tucker and I are exactly as we should be.

I kiss him like my existence depends on his reciprocation. It’s hard to focus when he pulls me closer, impossible to form a coherent thought when he deepens the kiss I started, and then he’s everywhere: my head and my heart, running his fingers across my skin, teasing my mouth open with his. A girl I hardly remember, a girl who’s spirited and alive and overflowing with passion, moves over him, straddles his waist. He smooths his hands up my back and kisses me hard, and I’ve never felt such fervor, such unbridled emotion in my life. My senses are on overdrive; I’m impatient and needy and *hot*, like he’s shifting his sunshine to me, and just when I think I’m going to ignite, he slows us down, drawing back to shadow my cheek with his fingertips.

“I came here to check on you,” he says. “To talk to you. I didn’t expect this.” His mouth twists in a devilish grin. “Not that I don’t like this.”

I smile. “I like it, too.”

“We’re good together, Cal.” He traces the lines of my face: the slope of my nose, the bow of my upper lip, the curve of my cheekbone. I watch his eyes as they follow his fingers’ path; his expression is worshipful. “Tell me you feel it.”

"Tucker." His gaze finds mine, suspending time, unraveling a long thread of truth from my fragile heart. "I feel it," I say. "I feel it, too."

He kisses me again, and I kiss him back because being with him is something from a reverie, one where sisters aren't dead, futures aren't difficult, and ghosts don't haunt the living.

That's what I am in his company—*alive.*

"Callie." Like he can't help himself, he presses his mouth to mine, then breathes, "The door."

It's ajar, the way he left it when he came in. My aunt's a floor away at best, free to wander in as she pleases. She's the founder of the Tucker Morgan Fan Club, but I doubt she'll be down with him and me together in bed.

I slip away and hurry across the hardwood, then close the door and slide the lock into place. When I face him again, he's grinning, that infectious ear-to-ear grin I adore. He gives me a get-over-here nod. I'm crossing the room when my phone starts to ring, vibrating against my nightstand.

Dad, I think, preoccupied. *Worst timing ever.*

But what if he's calling about my mom?

What if something's wrong?

I make a grab for my phone, but Tucker's glanced at it, and I can see, now, that it's not Dad.

It's Isaac—his name is illuminated against the screen, bright and white, like a freaking marquee.

"Who's Isaac?" Tucker asks as I put an end to the ringing.

"No one."

He sits up. "Seriously?"

"Just someone I know. From before. I've mentioned him."

His brows pinch together, cutting fissures across his forehead. "Your ex?"

"The one and only," I say, making a poor attempt at laughing the whole thing off.

"I thought it ended badly?"

"It did."

"Then why's he calling?"

I sigh, sitting down. Tucker shifts away. The movement and its motivation sting. "He just does sometimes. I don't want him to. I've asked him not to."

"Was it serious between you two?"

"No. I don't know. . . . I thought it was."

"Huh."

"It's not a big deal."

He shakes his head, giving me a weary look because here I go again, holding back details that matter. "It must be a big deal," he says, his voice grating with hurt. "Otherwise, you wouldn't be talking around what happened between you and him."

Pressure is starting to build in my head, though this time its catalyst is different. It's pain borne of frustration, of my inherent failure to choose the right words at the right times. "Tucker, I'm trying. I swear I am."

"If he hadn't called—if I hadn't been sitting here—would you've ever brought him up?"

"Probably not," I say truthfully, and to my detriment. "I hate talking about him. I hate thinking about him. But he and I have a history, one I can't erase because I've met someone new."

"I'd erase my history if I could."

"This is different," I say with more heat than I intend. "There's a hell of a lot more to Isaac and me than the one-night stand you had your freshman year of college."

He rears back, like I hit him. "Then tell me. What is it about him that's got you so hung up?"

Why aren't I enough? is what he's asking, which flays me.

"It's complicated."

He huffs. "Well, let me simplify it. If it's important to you to stay in touch with him, fine. I'm not gonna tell you who you can and can't talk to. But if you're not cool with giving me anything more than *it ended badly*, that's on you. I know two-timing—I'm the *product* of two-timing. I'm not gonna wait around like my dad, hoping to be chosen first."

Heat scales my neck. "Tucker, please—it's not like that. It's not about choosing."

I know immediately that I've said the wrong thing; he deflates like a punctured balloon. *I choose you*—those are the words that should have come out of my mouth.

Those are the words I mean.

He slides off the bed, takes a step toward the door, then turns back. So softly, so miserably, he says, "I can't keep doing this."

Yesterday he stormed off, but today he shuffles out of my room, shoulders slumped, head down. I'm clutching the duvet with shaky hands, *crushed*, when I hear him close the front door with insufferable restraint.

I don't want to live without him in my world.

A moment later comes the petrifying realization that I might have to.

44

Days pass.

According to Lucy, Tucker's taking time off.

"He didn't tell you?" she asks before launching into an explanation about a vacation he's taking with his dad, a random fishing trip he never mentioned. He can't call, Lucy claims, because they're on a boat miles offshore. And she's not sure of the exact day he'll return, either, but he said he'd try to bring her fresh salmon when he does.

I haven't seen Chloe—not since the poppies. Without smoke to get lost in, I'm wide awake and circumspect. I miss her so much it's hard to breathe. I wrestle with how to help her remember and agonize over how to let her go. I worry about my mom, alone in rehab. I fret about my dad, alone at home.

And Tucker . . . *always* Tucker.

The last week's been lonely and monotonous. Early solo swims.

Breakfast with Lucy. Long mornings working in the Savannah, which will be yellow, or the Gabriel, which we've already painted a soft peach. Nighttime is the worst. I lie in bed, listening to Buddy purr, anxiously examining the careless words and reckless actions of this summer and last.

Today, I climb the attic stairs to sift through the last of the boxes, the ones we moved the other day, before we started painting the Gabriel. It's hot and terribly stuffy. Mid-July sunshine streams through the porthole windows, and dust bunnies dance in pillars of light. I'm sick of this attic, but I'm about to lose another afternoon trapped within its walls.

I set my mind to the work.

It's not long before my hands are filthy, thanks to dust and newsprint. My skin goes clammy. My tank top clings uncomfortably. I drag box after box, crate after crate, across the floor. I rifle through their contents—junk—then stack them in a rapidly growing tower to be moved downstairs and tossed.

I'm nearly done when I spot an unlabeled box deep in a far corner. It doesn't appear as old as the crap surrounding it, so I haul it to the middle of the room and pull its flaps open.

Inside, right on top, are four Shell City High yearbooks, the same editions I saw at the library weeks ago. I flip the book from 1998 open. It belonged to Nathan Stewart—his name is printed in black marker inside the front cover. I read a few of the messages inscribed to him: *Have a great summer! Keep in touch! Enjoy Europe!* They're superficial, bland, with the exception of one beautiful block of text on the back page. This letter speaks of soul mates and lasting love, the future and forever. It's signed, *Love, Annabel.*

I delve further into the yearbook, hoping to learn more. I find

Nathan's senior portrait and spend a minute studying it. Dark hair, brooding eyes, chiseled features. Classically handsome, like the men of old black-and-white movies—the ones who slick their hair and drink scotch and wear tuxedos. I pick him out of a photograph of the cross-country team, then find an individual shot of him midstride on a wooded trail, his legs long and lithe. Several pages back, there's a photo of him and two others: a boy who bears a striking resemblance to Tucker and a girl, blond and lovely.

Benjamin and Annabel.

Stuck between the final pages of the yearbook, I find one of those staged school-dance photos, tacky background with flowers and balloons, awkward poses, stiff smiles. SHELL CITY HIGH, SENIOR PROM, 1998 is stamped on the bottom. Nathan's on the right, wearing a tux, hair combed neatly. Annabel's in black, too, a velvet gown with a sweetheart neckline. A pink corsage is fastened to her wrist. She tilts her head toward his, her smile luminous.

She wasn't happy with my dad, Tucker said. *She went to visit a friend, and she never came back.*

Annabel must've been with Nathan in high school, at least at the end of their senior year. Yet, at some point, for some reason, she strayed.

I set the prom photo aside and paw through the other items in the box. I unearth an envelope packed with images of two dark-haired children—the children whose pictures I found the first day I went looking in the Gabriel. The day I found the ring I've worn all summer. As I flip through the photos, I watch the bright-eyed girl become a pretty teenager, plainly happy, usually surrounded by hordes of friends. She's labeled "Hannah" on the back of one picture—Hannah Stewart, the doctor Lucy mentioned my first night here, the woman who put this house on the market. I study an image of her brother, Nathan, straddling a motorcycle with HARLEY-DAVIDSON painted across its gas tank. He's solemn and intimidating and indisputably sexy.

Benjamin Morgan thinks he's dangerous.

Annabel Tate was seeing him behind Benjamin's back.

Makes me wonder where he is today.

At the bottom of the box, there are more pictures of Annabel and Nathan, casual, touching, smiling. There are pictures of Nathan and a younger Benjamin, too. They're playing volleyball on the beach, and they're in a parking lot, their arms draped over each other's shoulders, that same motorcycle in the background. And most surprising: a faded newspaper clipping with a grainy black-and-white photo of Benjamin Morgan and Annabel Tate. An engagement announcement. They're smiling woodenly, obligatorily.

She's wearing a ring—diamonds and plaited platinum.

My ring.

Months after attending the prom with Nathan, Annabel was betrothed to Benjamin.

I'm consumed by this mystery surrounding Stewart House, especially since the triangle created by Annabel, Benjamin, and Nathan is damn near equivalent to the triangle I once made with Isaac and Chloe. And *especially* since Tucker compared my behavior to his mother's: I don't want to be flighty and secretive and disloyal.

But I do want to understand Annabel Tate.

I gather the relevant photographs and the engagement announcement before hurrying downstairs, mentally cataloging the people I know in Bell Cove. My understanding of what happened between Nathan, Annabel, and Benjamin is like a beach ball riddled with holes. I need to talk to someone who can help me patch the punctures. Lucy will be as clueless as I am. Drew and Brynn are out of the question—their loyalty to Tucker outweighs any desire they may have to spill his family's secrets. Animal Shelter Rex doesn't seem like the type to gossip. Then, like the higher powers are rooting for me, a name flashes in my head. . . . *Shirley.*

I swing by my room to collect Annabel's letters, then head for the kitchen, where Lucy's testing breakfast recipes. I find a manila envelope in one of the drawers near the fridge, where she keeps pens and pads of paper and mailing supplies. She watches me slip the letters and photographs and newspaper clipping inside. I tell her I'm going on a bike ride and it's so obvious that her curiosity abounds, but she only nods. I haven't flaked and disappeared into the woods in a week, we're almost done with the second floor, and besides, I'm pretty sure she views my ventures into Bell Cove as forward progress.

Look at Callie, biking and socializing, inhaling fresh air instead of weed—she's healing.

She licks batter off a spatula, tells me to be careful, and asks me to swing by the Morgans' to see if Tucker's home from his trip.

Yeah, right.

When I reach A Good Book, I leave my bike against the planked facade of the store, tuck the envelope under my arm, and peer through the window. Shirley's behind the counter, ringing up a girl with a cute, angular haircut. A beefy guy waits beside her, fiddling with bookmarks that hang from a rack beside the counter. He knocks one onto the floor, and the girl pokes him before accepting the change Shirley offers.

I duck away from the window as they turn for the door, pretending to study the sticker affixed to the rusty handlebars of my bike. The bell on A Good Book's door tinkles as it opens, and then Drew and Brynn are a few feet away.

"Callie?" he calls.

Against my better judgment, I turn around. "Drew, hey."

Brynn, wearing a dress printed with tiny daisies and a pair of espadrilles, nearly knocks me over with her hug. "It's good to see you!"

Their presence brings such a powerful longing for Tucker; when Brynn unwinds her arms from my neck, I teeter, breathlessly sad. She's oblivious, but Drew's usual *I want a piece* demeanor is missing as he studies me from beneath the bill of his OSU hat.

"What're you guys up to?" I ask.

Brynn holds up a bag from A Good Book. "Shopping for magazines."

"Tagging along," Drew says.

I try to come up with something semisociable to say, then spout the only thing that makes sense. "How's Tucker?"

"Good!" Brynn says. "We saw him the other night. Grabbed pizza in Shell City."

I narrow my eyes, confused. "What about his fishing trip?"

She and Drew exchange a look that makes me wonder what Tucker told them. That we argued? That I'm hung up on my ex? That I'm too high maintenance to bother with? "Oh," Brynn says. "We went before he left."

My voice falters when I ask, "Do you know when he'll be back?"

She blinks. "Uh . . ."

Drew covers for her. "Shouldn't be too long now." And then, "Brynnie, why don't you go get us a table at The Coffee Cove? I'll meet you."

She frowns. "Why?"

"Because I wanna hang with Callie for a minute." Another glance passes between them, a wordless conversation that has her frown turning contemplative. Drew says, "Go on. I'll see you in a few."

She pivots and prances away.

He heads for a bench, then sits, stretching his legs out onto the sidewalk, where passersby will likely have to step over them. I join him. He doesn't look at me and he doesn't ask questions—he just lets the quiet fester. The atmosphere around our shady bench thickens until it's practically buzzing.

"I haven't spoken to Tucker in days," I say when I can't take the silence another second.

He glances over, as if only mildly interested. "Oh yeah?"

"Did he tell you?"

"Tell me what?"

"That he's pissed?" I'm not sure why I'm confiding in Drew, of all people. Maybe it's that he's known Tucker forever. Maybe it's the regret I feel at having judged him unfavorably when now he's being so decent. Maybe I'm desperate.

"He might've mentioned it."

"I have no idea how to fix things."

"Do you want to?"

"Of course I want to." There are a million reasons why: Tucker has the biggest heart of anyone I know, I hate that I hurt him, and I don't want to lose him. But all that feels intensely personal for a Bell Cove afternoon.

Drew stretches an arm over the back of the bench. "You want to talk about it?"

I shrug. "Everything was good, then it wasn't. He must hate me."

"Nah. He's definitely into you. Otherwise, he wouldn't be so bummed. Anyway, whatever happened can't be as bad as the bullshit he's put up with from Brynn and me over the years. He'll get over it." He flashes a flirty grin. "If he doesn't, you know where to find me."

I shake my head, hiding a smile. "I should go, but when he gets back from fishing, will you ask him to call me?"

"No problem."

When we stand, he engulfs me in a hug, thudding my back with his big hand, like a buddy, like a big brother. It's clear, now, why Tucker's been friends with him for so long.

"Thanks, Drew."

"It was good seeing you, Callie," he says before ambling down the sidewalk.

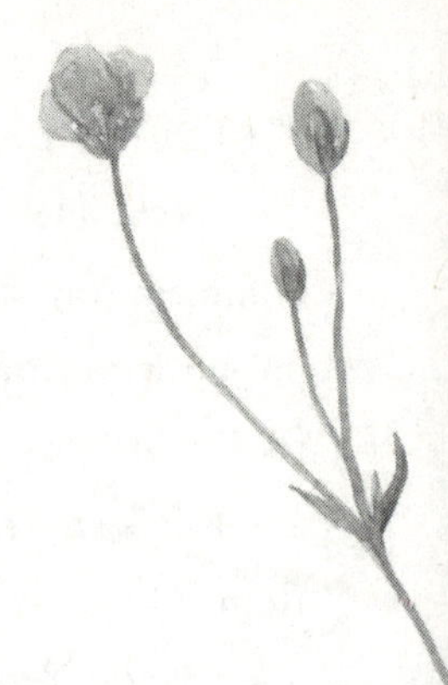

45

"Callie, hello," Shirley says when I step into A Good Book. "How's Lucy?"

"Good. I told her I'd check to see if you have new cookbooks."

"Not since last time she was in. I'll give her a call if I get any shipments, though. Is there something I can help you find?"

I approach the counter. "If you're not too busy, I thought I might talk with you for a few minutes." I open the envelope and fan its contents out. "I was hoping you could help me make sense of all this."

She makes a soft clucking sound and picks up the photo of Nathan, Benjamin, and Annabel. "I see you've caught wind of our small-town scandal."

"So you know about it?"

"All Bell Cove locals know about it." She gazes at me over the tops of her wire-rimmed glasses, impassive. "What is it you'd like to talk about?"

"You said you taught Annabel and Benjamin. Did you teach Nathan Stewart, too?"

"I didn't. There were two third-grade classrooms the year he and his friends passed through. My colleague had him, though I did have his sister a few years later."

I rest my elbows on the counter. "What were they like, Tucker's parents?"

Shirley's eyes narrow. She wants to know why I care.

"I found these pictures in the attic at my aunt's house," I explain. "I recognize Tucker's father and I'm curious, but I don't want to bug him with a bunch of questions."

Her expression becomes reflective. "Benji was a great kid. Mischievous, but in a way that made teachers laugh. Silly, but sweet as sugar. He was one of my favorites."

"What about Annabel?"

"Thoughtful, quiet, very bright."

It sounds like Tucker is a blend of his parents' best traits. I show Shirley the prom photograph. "Annabel and Nathan . . . ?"

"Were together for years. She was the best thing he had going."

"Why do you say that?"

She sighs, a reluctant sound, and folds her hands. "Nathan Stewart was spoiled. He had a reputation for being reckless, and he didn't have the best role model in his father. He and Annabel were serious, but they fought often, and they didn't seem to care who was around to pay witness. Once, here in this shop, I watched Annabel bat her lashes at Benjamin—I think he always had eyes for her—and Nathan caught her. They had it out on the sidewalk out front," she says, nodding toward the window. "I used to wonder if Annabel enjoyed pushing Nathan's buttons, toying with Benji, seeing how miserable she could make them both."

"But why would Nathan stay with her if she acted like that?"

"You know how young relationships can be," Shirley says. "Acutely passionate, occasionally codependent."

I drum my fingertips. I'd had Benjamin pegged as the villain in all this, a girlfriend thief, yet if what Shirley's saying is true, he might not have been more than a casualty.

I point to Annabel and Benjamin's engagement announcement. "How did this come to be?"

"Nathan went away the summer after high school, a family trip to Europe." She pushes her glasses up her nose and gives a dainty shrug. "Annabel found affection elsewhere."

"With his friend."

Shirley nods. "And then there was the pregnancy. Annabel's parents wanted her to marry Benjamin—they demanded it, if the rumor mill is to be trusted. They were traditional, old-fashioned, and in their eyes, a baby out of wedlock was taboo. Far as I know, Benjamin wanted a wedding, too. Even back when they were my students, he was protective of Annabel. Devoted."

"She accepted his proposal," I say, pointing to the newspaper clipping.

"But she didn't stop seeing the Stewart boy. People spotted them together in town when she was pregnant and even after Tucker came along."

This isn't surprising. Annabel's letters to Nathan were about finding their way back to each other. And Nathan . . . I wonder how culpable he was in all this. It sounds like he was betrayed by his girlfriend and his friend, but Tucker harbors so much hatred toward him; he all but blames Nathan for his mother's disappearance.

The shop door opens. A woman and a brown-eyed little boy stroll in. Shirley smiles and offers her help. The woman declines, and the two of them meander into the stacks, toward the picture books. Shirley turns her attention back to me, and I'm relieved—I've still got questions.

I point at the letters. "Do you think Annabel wanted to be with Nathan, not Benjamin?"

She sighs. "I'm not sure Annabel knew what she wanted. It was unfair of her, stringing those boys along. Unfair of her to walk into precarious situations when she had a baby at home."

"She was with Nathan before she disappeared. What do you think happened to her?"

A quiet moment slips by. Shirley stares at the scattered photos. Painstakingly, she shuffles them into a pile, tapping the edges on the counter to align them. When she looks up, her demeanor's cloudy. "I'm not sure we'll ever know."

"I've heard different theories," I say. "She fell, she was pushed, she left town in search of something new. Do you think she could've done that, left her baby—left *Tucker*—behind?"

Shirley's eyebrows arch. "I'm really not sure. But if I'm going by what Nathan did after, then I'd say he was likely involved in some capacity."

"What Nathan did after?"

"You don't know?"

A shiver rolls through me. "I have no idea."

She glances around the store, then she whispers: "Suicide."

"What?"

She nods. "Inside Stewart House. A week after Annabel disappeared."

I shake my head, dumbstruck. It's one thing for my sister to have died down shore from Stewart House, for Annabel Tate to have possibly died near Stewart House, but holy hell. Nathan Stewart died by his own hand, *inside* Stewart House.

Shirley touches her wrist, the only cueing I need.

The stain in my bathroom—it's his blood. It has to be.

I understand, now, why Tucker's convinced Nathan played a part in Annabel's disappearance; what he did could imply guilt. But it also points to some serious mental-health issues. Based on what Shirley's said, Nathan loved Annabel, no matter how imperfectly. When she vanished, he must have been devastated.

"What a terrible story," I say. "So much loss."

Shirley purses her lips. "You can see why not many Bell Cove residents talk about it. With Benjamin and Tucker still in town, it's better not to dwell. They deserve privacy."

I nod, thinking of the day I spoke to Tucker so flippantly about Annabel jumping from the cliff behind Stewart House. I wish I could travel back in time and slap a hand over past Callie's mouth, because if the situation had been reversed, if Tucker had disparaged Chloe and her death, I would have been inconsolable.

I owe him the biggest apology.

I turn to the sound of the woman and her giggling boy, arms laden with picture books. I thank Shirley, squeezing her hand before I tuck the photographs and newspaper clipping safely into their envelope. I'm preoccupied by lingering questions, but I take a second to browse the cookbooks. One with photographs of seafood on its cover catches my eye, and I buy it for Lucy. It feels good to do something impulsively nice for her.

After paying, I wave to Shirley and step out onto the sidewalk, where I run smack into the ample midsection of Benjamin Morgan.

"Callie?" he says.

I take a step back, excusing myself, working to wipe the shock from my face—he's supposed to be on a fishing boat with his son. "Hi, Mr. Morgan. How are you?"

"Benjamin," he reminds me. "I'm okay. Running errands." He holds up a Green Apple Grocery tote.

I shift, uncomfortable. I spent the last half hour discussing the tragedy he was unfortunate enough to be mixed up in, and now, here he is.

"I thought you were out on the water?"

"You did?"

"With Tucker?"

His sandy brows knit together. "I didn't go anywhere with Tucker."

"But my aunt said you guys were on a fishing trip—" Sluggishly, I realize what's going on, what an idiot I am.

Benjamin recognizes his mistake at the same time. "*Oh*, the fishing trip!"

My face flushes hot. "It's okay. You don't have to lie."

He squints up at the sun, then looks back to me. "He's at home, if you want to head over. I've got a few more stops to make, so now's a good time."

"He doesn't want to see me. He's upset."

Benjamin sighs. There's a barren sadness in his eyes, probably the same sadness that's been lingering since the summer of 1999. "He's been upset with me for a long time."

"Then I guess we're in the same boat—though, not a fishing boat."

He chuckles. “Whatever the type, you have time to bail before it capsizes.”

“So do you.”

“I don’t know about that. Tuck’s got a stubborn streak, especially if he feels wronged.” He smiles sheepishly. “Not that you did anything wrong. Whatever the case, go talk to him. His moping’s becoming tiresome.”

I could go to the Morgans’. Hash things out with Tucker. Admit to how much I’ve missed him. I *should*. I owe him the courtesy of my effort, if nothing else.

“Do you really think he’ll see me?” I ask Benjamin.

He shrugs. “I think if you leave him no choice but to hear you out, at least you’ll know you’ve done all you can. And since you’re asking for my input, I’ll tell you this: He’s been different since he met you. In a good way.”

I smile. “I’m going to go, but I’m holding you responsible if he turns me away.”

“I’ll take that gamble,” Benjamin says. “Good luck.”

46

I arrive on Beech Street, park my bike, and drag my feet up to the Morgans' front porch. I raise my fist to knock, but the door swings open. Now, after a week of *nothing*, I'm face-to-face with Tucker.

I'm struck by how tired he looks: eyes overcast, posture wilted, mouth set in a deep frown. He's wearing jeans and a faded baseball tee, white, its collar and sleeves royal blue. He smells of fresh soap.

My heart lunges for him.

"Hey," he says. He's holding a stack of clipped papers, and he's wearing shoes.

"Going somewhere?" I ask.

"Yeah, actually. I was coming to see you."

"Oh. Why?"

"Drew called. He said he and Brynn ran into you. . . ." His voice fades, leaving me to wonder what else Drew told him. He holds up his assemblage of papers and pulls the door wide open. "I've been wanting to show you this stuff. Come in?"

I nod and follow him inside.

The house is quiet. The blinds are low, and the TV's off. I trail him down the hall to his room. It's tidy and sparse, a full bed covered with a gray-and-white plaid comforter, a tall dresser, and a desk with a closed laptop. The closet door is shut, but I imagine it holds a dozen pairs of shorts and innumerable T-shirts. There are no posters of women in bikinis, no sports pennants or band flyers. Just a few black-and-white prints of the ocean, pleasant and peaceful.

"You can sit," he says, gesturing to the bed.

I do. He sinks down beside me.

"How was your fishing trip?"

He gives me a side-eye.

"You didn't fish," I say.

"I needed time away from work."

"You needed time away from me."

"No, Cal. I just—I needed to think."

"You could've called."

"Yeah . . ."

It's satisfying to know he has no justification for his behavior. "What did you want to show me?"

He pulls the clip from his papers and passes them to me. Bold letters are splashed across the top of the first page: *Physical Afflictions and the Paranormal.* "I've been doing some research. Your headaches? I think spending time with your sister is causing them."

I skim the first few paragraphs, a lot of scientific mumbo jumbo that's hard to understand. Stuff about currents and the transfer of energy. There are charts and graphs detailing studies on tension headaches and migraines, all angled lines and thick bars. There are control groups and participant testimonials. Mostly, subjects speak of pain when they feel they're in the vicinity of the paranormal or after an encounter. There are photographs, dark and gritty, but vague human figures are detectable. Ghosts.

"Where did you get all this?" I ask.

"Online. There's tons of stuff about it, but this study is the most comprehensive."

"You think it's legit?"

"I wouldn't have if I hadn't seen what's been going on with you, but yeah. It adds up."

I set the paperwork on the bed between us. "Lucy thinks my headaches are related to allergies—pollen in the air."

He hikes an eyebrow up. "I call bullshit. Does she know about Chloe?"

"No. And, also, I haven't had a headache in a week."

"Have you seen your sister?"

"Not since the poppy meadow. Since the night before—" *you left.*

Awkwardness swings between us like a pendulum, threatening to sever the remaining threads of our friendship. I hate that I can't reach for his hand or push his hair off his forehead. I hate that he hasn't smiled, not once, since I walked into his house.

"Are you going to see her again?" he asks.

"I have to."

"Even though she's making you sick?"

"Doesn't matter. I have to help her remember, Tucker. You were right: Being here, stuck in the in-between, it's not good for her. She needs closure. She needs to move forward. I do, too."

He lets out a breath. "I thought you were gonna be pissed."

"Why?"

He gestures to his research. "All this . . . I didn't think you'd be open to it. You're protective of Chloe, of what you guys have, and I get that it means a lot to you, seeing her again. Plus, you don't seem to like it much when people get in your business."

"You're not exactly 'people,'" I tell him.

He looks away, nudging my bookstore bag with his foot. "What's this?"

"Oh . . . I went to talk to Shirley about some stuff I found in Lucy's attic."

"What kind of stuff?"

I hesitate, remembering how upset he got the last time I brought up his parents. But I don't want to keep things from him—not today, not ever. I pull the envelope out of the bag and hand it to him. "Before you look inside, you should know that it's full of pictures. Pictures of your parents and Nathan Stewart. So, if you want to open it later, or not at all . . ."

He's already pulling the contents out. He sets Annabel's letters aside and rifles through the photos, silent. When he gets to the engagement announcement, he stares at it for a long time, his expression indecipherable. Then he stuffs everything back into the envelope and says, "Other than the letters, I've never seen any of that. My grandparents had pictures of her, but none of her with my dad. None of the three of them together."

"You can keep them. Show them to your dad, if you want." I slip

Annabel's ring off my finger and hold it out to him. "This, too. It was hers."

He's looking at it like it's a scorpion sitting atop my palm, not a ring of platinum and diamonds. "I don't know. . . ."

"I don't feel right hanging on to it, not considering its history. Put it away for now. One day, you might be happy to have it."

Warily, he takes the ring. He spends a moment inspecting it, brow drawn, before dropping it into the envelope. He sets it on the bed between us, on top of his research, then lets his gaze drift across the room, where it settles on the beige wall—on nothing. He stares, looking lost in the most wretched way, like he has no idea where he is or how he got here.

I think, maybe, I should go, but I can't make myself get up off the bed. Not while he's so shaken. Not while there's so much left unsaid.

I touch his arm. "Tucker, why didn't you tell me what really happened with your mother?"

"It's . . . complicated."

"I told you about my sister."

"Lucy told me about your sister."

"I've poured my heart out to you. I've *cried* in front of you."

He closes his eyes. When he opens them again, they reflect his pain. "I wanted to tell you," he says. "About a thousand times I almost did—that day in the yard when you showed me the letters, at the pool, on the beach, last week in your room—but you didn't look at me the way everyone else does. You didn't feel sorry for me. To you, I was normal."

I understand. I'm the girl whose sister drowned, after all.

"This summer," he says, "working at Stewart House, I thought I could solve the mystery. Figure out exactly what happened to her. Because the thing is, I want to believe she's alive. I want to believe she left because she couldn't take the stress of a baby and a life she hadn't planned for, and, like some fucked-up fairy tale, she's gonna come back one day and be a real mom. Or maybe she did die, but it was an accident—she fell and that's so, so shitty, but it's better than the alternatives." He clasps his hands, but not before I notice how they shake.

Fissures split my heart like tributaries. "What alternatives?"

He takes a breath, recovers, and meets my gaze. "Maybe Nathan Stewart killed her. He could've shoved her. He had it in him—he hated her for what she did with my dad. Or, maybe he had nothing to do with it. What if she jumped? She was overwhelmed and she was depressed and she was desperate. Maybe she thought death would be better than life with my dad and me."

"Tucker. If she went over that cliff intentionally, she was unwell, and that has nothing to do with you. She must've loved you so much, no matter how she was struggling on the inside."

"My dad's always thought Nathan was involved. I didn't understand why until you showed me those letters. I didn't know my mother was still in touch with him. He must've been *furious*. He opened his wrists a week after she disappeared. As far as my dad's concerned, that cemented his guilt. Doesn't matter, though. She's gone. We'll never know what really happened."

"Can you understand, then, why I have to see my sister again? I need to know what happened, and only she can tell me."

He studies my face for a long moment. I hope he sees strength, and resolve, and compassion. I hope he trusts me.

He must, because he says, "I can help, if you want."

My first impulse is to jump at his offer, but I've heard his words—*I'm not gonna wait around like my dad, hoping to be chosen first*—countless times since he stepped out of my room. I can't pretend that fight didn't happen.

"I thought you couldn't keep doing this?"

His face falls. "Cal, I shouldn't have said that. I didn't mean it."

It's so quiet in the house that when the air conditioner kicks on, its hum resounds like a roar.

"It's over with Isaac," I say. "It has been for months. What happened between us was messy, though, and there were a lot of repercussions." I touch the scar on my arm before lifting my gaze to his. "Isaac was there the night Chloe died. He's part of the reason she left for the beach. My guilt, my grief, a lot of it's tied up with him. So even though I don't have feelings *for* him, there are feelings—feelings that are hard to let go, even now. I should have told you about him, though. I'm sorry I didn't."

He lifts the envelope and papers from between us, sliding it all onto his nightstand before moving closer. "I get it," he says. "And you should stay in touch with him, if you want. I was such a dick last week—jealousy's not a good look for me. But I've got a handle on it." He touches my face, tentative, and my pulse leaps. His voice is low, gravelly, when he says, "I hated not seeing you. I only stayed away because I didn't know how to make things right." He leans in, resting his forehead against mine. "I want to be with you, Cal. Beyond this summer."

As I tip my chin to find his mouth, my doubts trickle away, until it's just him and me in the small space of his room.

Beyond this summer, he said.

I want that, too: a whole lifetime with him.

He nudges me back, until my head finds his pillow, then stretches out above me. His kisses are insistent and unrestrained, and I'm dissolving into his mattress. He runs his palm up my leg, over my hip, along my ribs, and I inhale unabashedly, slipping my hands beneath his shirt, smoothing them over the warm skin of his back.

I'm buzzing inside and out, wondering if I make him so uninhibited, so euphoric. When he sighs and murmurs, "You have no idea how often I think about you like this," I realize I do, and then it's easy to surrender to the longing that's building inside me.

He helps me out of my shirt, barely breaking our kiss, before ditching his own. And then my heart beats against his, and we're a mess of tangled limbs and needy kisses, and I'm obsessing over the softness of his skin and the minty taste of his mouth and the clean smell of his hair. I can hardly breathe, barely form a coherent thought, but when he whispers, "You're sure?" I nod without hesitancy, because *yes*, I am very, very sure.

I'm fumbling with the button of his jeans when I hear a rumble and feel a slight shaking of the house.

He jerks back with a muttered, "Shit!"

I scramble to sit up. "What?"

He gathers our discarded clothing with a quick sweep of his arm. He tosses me my top, then throws his shirt back on. "That's the garage door. My dad's home."

47

I'm pretty sure *this* isn't what Benjamin had in mind when he suggested I visit his son.

I yank my shirt over my head and run my fingers through my hair. It's snarled from Tucker's hands, from rolling around on his bed. His summery boy scent clings to my clothes, my skin. My face is so freaking hot, and my cutoffs are twisted around my waist. I dash across the room to the mirror hanging on the back of the door.

I look flushed, wild-eyed, and sloppy.

Tucker smooths a hand over his comforter as I swing the door wide open, as if that'll make us appear less guilty. Seconds later, we hear Benjamin walk into the house. It takes him half a second to appear square in Tucker's doorway, Green Apple Grocery tote in hand.

He looks in on us with a raised eyebrow.

I smile from the desk chair, ankles crossed, hands folded in my lap. Tucker's on his bed, leaning casually against the headboard, like we've been chatting about the weather.

"Glad you made it over, Callie," Benjamin says, propping a hand on the doorframe.

"Yeah, we've had a nice talk."

Out of the corner of my eye, I catch Tucker smirking.

"So I see," Benjamin says. His attention falls to the envelope on the nightstand and the photographs peeking out from its opening.

"What's that?" he asks, intrigue bouncing across his face.

Tucker glances at the envelope, circles of pink staining his cheeks. "Nothing."

"It doesn't look like nothing."

"Dad—"

"Tuck. Let me see it."

Tucker picks up the envelope, holding it to his chest, and shoots me an inquiring look. I lift my shoulders because, really, what choice do we have?

Reluctantly, he passes it to his dad.

Benjamin's eyes go wide as he looks through the photographs. When he withdraws the ring, I worry he'll keel over. He looks at Tucker, then back at the ring, then to his son again. "I gave this to your mother," he murmurs.

"Yeah. I saw the newspaper announcement."

"Where did you find all this?"

Tucker glances at me, floundering.

"I brought it over," I say.

"Where did *you* find it?"

I try hard to read Tucker's expression. His employer is a secret as far as his dad's concerned, and it's possible I'm about to create a problem for him. He shrugs.

"At my aunt's house."

Benjamin slips the ring onto his pinky finger, and then, eyes glazed, flips through the pictures again. "Why would she have it?"

"She kind of inherited it with the house she bought last year."

At this, he looks at me. "What house is that?"

"Uh . . ."

Tucker comes to my rescue. "The Stewarts' old place."

"Callie's aunt . . . This is the woman you've been working for?"

"Yeah."

Benjamin looks at the photos, at the newspaper clipping, at the glittering ring that fits only midway down his finger. "Can I have all this?" he asks me.

"Yes, sir. Of course."

He walks out of the room, groceries forgotten on the floor.

Tucker quirks a brow at me. "Wanna get out of here?"

He must be a Jelly Belly addict.

He bought a huge mixed bag from a local sweet shop during our walk through Bell Cove, and now we're sitting on a weathered bench in the town center. It's late in the afternoon, and the sun's warm on our backs. He's schooling me on flavor combinations—a lemon eaten with a coconut will taste like lemon meringue pie—and I'm laughing because he's weirdly fanatical about his Jellies. He's already picked out all the black licorice beans because, according to him, they're foul.

He passes me a crimson bean, then a white one with black speckles. "Strawberry jam and French vanilla."

I chew discerningly. "Um . . . strawberry shortcake?"

He nods, grinning, then ties the bag off, looking toward the stream of vacationers cruising the sidewalk, sunburned and windblown, toting rumpled towels and kites with tangled strings, heading home from a day at the beach. "So," he says, still watching the crowd. "In case you don't realize . . . I wasn't trying to take advantage of you back there. In my room."

I blink. "I know."

"I just—I thought you were going to . . . I don't know. Want nothing to do with me, I guess."

"Last week sucked."

He smiles. "But we're cool now?"

I kiss him, sugar-sweet. "We're cool."

He takes my hand, his eyes sweeping my face, and asks, gently, "How's your mom?"

"Still in rehab."

"What about your dad?"

"I think he's okay. I've talked to him a few times since my mom left. He's happy I'm swimming."

He draws me closer, kisses my hair. "He must be really proud of you."

I snort. "I don't know about that."

"Oh, come on. Think about how much you've changed." He jostles me with his shoulder, then teases, "I hardly remember the angsty girl who froze me out on my first day of work."

"Careful, or it might happen again."

"Nah. You like me too much now."

I run my fingertips over his knuckles, bones and muscle and tendons, mesmerized by his suntanned, work-scarred skin and the way he fits so perfectly within it. "Because you bought me a kitten."

He laughs. "Whatever it takes."

"What you said about my dad? I want him to be proud of me. My mom, too. When school starts, I'm going to get my grades up. I'm going to rejoin my swim team. I'm going to try to get into a decent college. I want a future."

"You have one, Cal."

I want a future with you, I think, wrapping my arms around him.

We stay that way for a long time, until the air cools and clouds roll in off the water. It's not long before tourists dressed for dinner wander onto the sidewalk.

"I should go," I say, pulling reluctantly from Tucker's warmth. "I need to get back before Lucy leaves for her book club. Want to come over and keep me company later?"

He flashes a delicious grin. "What time?"

48

When I get back to Stewart House, I find my aunt in the kitchen, where the air smells of oregano and spicy pepperoni. She bends to pull a pizza from the oven. “Was that Tuck’s car I heard? I hope he caught us some salmon.”

“Yeah, I don’t think the fish were biting.” I pull out the seafood cookbook I bought her. “But look—a consolation prize.”

Her face lights up. She abandons the pizza on the stove to take her new book from me, then leans on the counter, leafing through its thick pages.

“Aunt Lucy, do you mind if Tucker comes over later, while you’re out?”

“Not at all,” she says, looking over a crab cake recipe. “Lucky duck, finding romance in Bell Cove. I wonder if I’ll ever meet a nice man around here.”

"Tucker's dad is single."

"Does he look like Tucker?"

"He did twenty years ago."

"What's the deal with his mom?"

I slide pizza slices onto plates, then drag her to the table. I give her the abbreviated version of Tucker's story, finishing with, "Nobody knows for sure, but it's pretty commonly believed that Annabel died. That she fell from the cliff out back."

Lucy's pizza sits on her plate, mostly untouched. "*Our* cliff?"

I nod. "Some people think one of the Stewarts might've been involved."

She plucks a piece of pepperoni and nibbles on it. "I can't believe Tucker's worked here all this time and never said a word."

"He doesn't like to talk about it."

"He talks to you."

"A little. I talk to him, too. Sometimes about Chloe."

She beams, like this is the best news she's gotten all month. "If Tucker's the person you feel most comfortable with, then it's him you should confide in." She stands, dropping her napkin onto her plate. "Will you tidy up? I've got to get ready to go."

"No problem. Try not to get too crazy with the ladies."

"Try to keep Tucker in the parlor," she counters with a wink.

Lucy leaves just before seven. I clean the kitchen before taking a quick shower. I dress in jeans and a floral top, then spend forever in the bathroom, dusting my face with makeup, blowing my hair smooth. By the time I'm done, my skin's pink with the heat of the dryer. I stash it and my brush in the cabinet below the sink, then wander out the front door to cool off.

Twilight's fallen, and the sky is shrouded in clouds, leaving the porch darker than usual—except for a soft glow radiating from the south end.

Chloe's standing where we first reunited.

It's been a week since I saw her in the poppy meadow, since she remembered our fight, since her light dimmed.

A week since my last headache.

Her expression is taut with effort, as if it pains her to be more girl than ghost. Seeing her this way, drained, crushes me.

"It's been a long time," she says.

Has it? For her, have seven days dragged by like seven years?

You haven't been forgotten.

You will never *be forgotten.*

She stares at me, intently and immodestly, and something passes between us. An energy or an understanding. A pledge. She drifts closer. My skin prickles with the chill she stirs. "That night in the poppy meadow," she says. "Are you okay?"

"I am now."

"I didn't want to leave—you understand, don't you?"

I nod. "It's hard, maintaining this link."

"Hard for you?"

I wait a breath; I have to be honest about how our connection affects me, but God, I dread pinning her with guilt. "It makes me feel bad, Chloe. After the poppies, I could barely move. If Tucker hadn't come—"

"Tucker." She says his name like it tastes sour. "He's why I haven't seen you."

"No. You haven't seen me because the last time we were together, I lost myself."

Worse: I'm going to lose her all over again.

I chafe my hands over the goose bumps on my arms.

She must understand, because she says, "Let's walk."

"Not in the woods."

"No. Just the yard."

She moves down the steps, around to the back of the house. Unease makes my hands tingle, but I follow. I follow even though I'm not wearing shoes. Even though Tucker's on his way. Even though I have no idea where we're going. She leads me to the end of the yard, to the cliff that drops into the sea. The wind whips wild, whistling in my ears, stirring the ocean into a frenzy.

She stops a few feet from the edge. Her yellow dress looks muddied against the gloomy sky. The set of her shoulders tells me this is it—tonight, everything changes.

She turns; her woeful expression hurts my heart. "Callie," she says, rough with emotion. "I don't want to be like this. You can help."

I look at the darkening sky, battling tears. "Do you understand what will happen if I do?"

"No—I can't begin to imagine. But I don't think I'll get to see you anymore."

"You won't. You have to leave me behind."

"Will you be okay?"

I smile, pretending to be as brave as she is. "Eventually."

She nods. Her eyes are stretched wide, her mouth a hard line. She looks terrified, but she's not crying. She didn't cry in life, either—she persisted.

Thunder rumbles in the distance, a warning.

At the same time, Chloe and I look at the seething sky; we need to hurry.

She prompts, "There was a boy . . ."

I take a shaky breath. "His name is Isaac. He moved into the house next to ours at the end of last spring."

She watches me, rapt, like this is a story she's never heard—never lived.

"I liked him right away," I tell her. "And you did, too."

Recognition flares in her eyes. "He was into bikes."

I nod. "Sometimes you guys went out on rides together. He was helping you train."

The charcoal sky opens up, sending raindrops to spatter the dirt beneath our feet.

"By the time school let out," I go on, "it felt serious between Isaac and me, but I kept that from you. You were enamored and it was sweet, and I felt awful, being with him behind your back. But I'd already kept too many secrets, told too many half-truths. I didn't know how to go backward, how to fix what I'd screwed up."

Rain soaks my hair, my shirt. The ground is turning quickly to mud.

"He came to Lucy's—"

"With doughnuts," Chloe interjects.

I don't know if it's the weather or the night or the rescued bits of story, but all at once, she's hard to see.

I'm seconds from putting a stop to this—from begging her to stay.

Selfish, my conscience whispers.

"That's right," I say. "You ate the two with chocolate glaze, and I was annoyed."

She smiles, a classic Chloe smile—good-natured, unapologetic.

"Later that day, you went for a run. Lucy was out, too, so Isaac and I sat on the porch. I think you saw us kiss."

"I did," she says. She turns away, inching closer to the cliff. I pick my way across small, sharp rocks to stand at her side. She's quiet, washed out, fading away.

I'm a monster for hurting her all over again.

I lean out to look over the jagged edge. Waves surge, slamming the rugged rocks with unbelievable force. The water is blue-black, except for where it breaks.

There, it's white, frothy, deadly.

"Do you want to hear more?" I ask.

"I want to hear everything."

I take a breath and speak over the beating rain. "Isaac spent the afternoon working on the bikes in Lucy's shed. When he finished, you guys went for a ride. He was always talking about what a badass you were, and he felt as awful as I did, keeping secrets from you. At least, that's what he said. I've wondered if there was more to it. I've wondered if he saw you as more than my little sister."

"I tried to get him to," Chloe says.

I know this—I've known since the night she came into my room with news of his arrival—but hearing it now, set against her new awareness that I intentionally stood in her way, ignites a fire of shame. I tamp it down, brushing rain from my eyes, and press on. "When you came back, Lucy and I were making dinner. I was washing lettuce at the sink, and I saw you through the window. You were with him, standing where we are now."

A crack of lightning illuminates the sky. Chloe stares at the water—not the waves below, but farther out, at the nearly invisible horizon. She's right next to me, but her voice sounds far away when she says, "I told him I liked him."

"And then he kissed you."

"No," she says, resolute. "I kissed him."

I let go of a breath. . . .

It wasn't Isaac.

It wasn't Isaac.

"Chloe, why would you do that?"

Another clap of thunder rocks the coast. She looks at me, her eyes black pools. "Because you knew I liked him, and you went after him anyway. I wanted you to hurt because I was hurting."

I stole a boy from my starry-eyed little sister.

I reach for her, a gesture of apology. My hand passes through empty air.

I recoil as pain smashes into me.

Rain, wind, thunder, waves . . . Chloe, barely.

"Did he kiss you back?"

"No," she whispers, sounding so defeated I feel her mortification like it's my own. "He pulled away. And then he told me he thought I was cool, but like a friend. Like a little sister. He said he liked you—that you guys were together. I'd never been so embarrassed. So mad. So *hurt*. But then you came outside and said all those horrible things. You screamed—"

"That I'd never forgive you. That I hated you. Chloe, I know."

I relive those moments every night before I fall asleep. Every morning when I wake up. Sometimes randomly, unexpectedly, when I'm swimming or painting or cleaning or listening to Buddy purr. The last words I spoke to my sister were thoughtless lies fueled by bitter jealousy.

Her face is gaunt, and her shoulders are bowed, like an unseen force is bearing down on her. She's a glimmer. She says, "Did you mean it?"

I feel faint, outside myself. I betrayed her, and this is the consequence.

"Never. I saw what I saw, and I reacted without thinking. If I could take it back, I would."

Another bolt of lightning strikes the sky, followed closely by a rumble of thunder that shakes my spine. My joints ache and my head hurts so badly it's hard to remain upright.

"What did you say to Isaac after I ran into the house?" Chloe asks.

"I accused him of cheating. I called him a liar. I told him he had to leave."

"But it wasn't his fault."

"It didn't matter—I didn't let him explain. I just wanted him to go. As soon as he did, I went to Aunt Lucy. I told her what I thought I saw. She assumed Isaac was to blame, just like I did. And then we realized that you'd left the house and taken your wet suit."

"I biked to the beach," she says, vehement now, like the rest of the story is fizzing up and out of her, desperate to escape. "I was humiliated and so mad. I thought swimming would help. But I shouldn't have gone alone."

"I wish you hadn't."

"I thought I could do it—escape the current. Swim diagonally toward shore, like I've always heard. But it was too strong. So fast, I was out of breath. So fast, my muscles failed. I was so scared."

"So was I. Aunt Lucy and I tried to find you, but we were too late, and I'm sorry. For all of it, but mostly for not being with you."

"I forgive you—of course I do. Isaac, too. If he feels bad, he shouldn't.

He was never anything but decent." She flickers, a dying candle, then says, "Promise you'll do awesome things, Callie. Be good to Mom and Dad, and kick ass in the pool. Compete in a triathlon, just once, for me." She smiles, faint but mischievous. "Make sure Tucker's nice to you. Also, you should probably kiss him, like, all the time."

I'm half laughing, half crying, trying to imagine Bell Cove without her. "I will."

She raises a hazy hand and blows me a kiss. "Love you, Cal."

"Love you, too, Chloe."

I hold her gaze until she's almost transparent, blinking like an ebbing star.

No more questions. No more loneliness. No more wandering.

With a burst of frigid air and a flash of light that threatens to sever my sanity, she disappears into the darkness.

No more Chloe.

Below, the ocean rages.

A beam of light slices the yard.

Headlights.

Tucker.

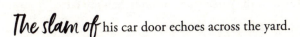

49

The slam of his car door echoes across the yard.

"Callie!"

He's streaking across the lawn. I watch him, dazed, toeing the edge of the cliff, trembling in the space that took my sister, my breaths fast and irregular. My head is throbbing, but when he stops a few feet away, I zero in with sharp focus. His T-shirt's spattered with rain, and his flaxen hair is windblown.

He throws out a frantic hand, but his voice is soothing when he says, "Cal, come here."

I hesitate, glancing at the water. I'm very high and very close to the edge. I sway, then catch myself.

"Jesus, Callie! Give me your hand!"

My senses are confused by the thrashing rain, my smarting feet, my clinging clothes, the waves, the thunder, the lightning, my *grief.* But when

I turn, I see Tucker. His cheeks are rosy, and he looks perilously close to tears. He extends his hand again. "Please, Cal," he says, laden with desperation.

I'm shivering, soaked through. My lucidity frays as my head pounds with nauseating intensity. "Chloe," I say. "It's over."

His expression softens with understanding. "I'm sorry. I'm so fucking sorry. But you have to move back."

I squint at him; he's the sun, and I'm a satellite reclaiming my orbit.

I'm stepping toward safety, toward *him*, reaching for his hand, when my foot slips in the saturated earth. Air leaves my lungs in a *whoosh* as I slam into the ground.

It's a blur—a backward slide, wind on my feet, my legs suspended in emptiness. I grapple, my fingers skidding through mud, grabbing for a root or a rock or a divot in the earth, something to halt my fall.

Tucker lunges, diving onto his stomach.

As the last of my hope evaporates, he grabs my hand.

My humerus jerks out of its socket; it feels as if my arm's being ripped from my body. I swallow a shriek as my eyes meet his, fraught, filled with terror. Heat radiates through my shoulder, my neck, my arm as Tucker adjusts his grip.

He groans, struggling to manage my oscillating weight. "Give me your other hand!"

I bite hard into my lip and swing my free hand up. He grasps it but can't hang on. My palm is wet. *His* palm is wet.

I look down—a mistake.

My feet dangle in a chasm.

Pebbles tumble into blackness.

Waves surge and crest.

I'm going to fall.

"Callie, don't look down—look at me! Swing your hand up again!"

It costs me, but somehow, we connect. He pulls, slow and labored, creeping toward safety. Gravel scrapes my torso and tears stream down my face as I kick, trying to lend momentum.

Finally, *finally*, I'm on solid ground.

Drenched and filthy, we scramble to our feet. I'm sobbing, shaking with superfluous adrenaline. My arm hangs limply at my side. The pain is excruciating, but I don't care because Tucker's shuddering so violently it's a wonder he's standing and, oh God, I want him to be okay—I *need* him to be okay.

He pulls me against him, fingers threading into my sodden hair. "Are you all right?"

"I—I think so."

I cling to him as long as I can, until he draws back to scan me for injuries.

His eyes fill with horror when they find my shoulder: A golf-ball-size lump protrudes where there's normally a smooth curve.

"Jesus," he breathes.

He makes me sit on the soggy lawn, cradling my arm, while he calls Lucy.

"She's hurt," he says into his phone. Then, tersely, "I don't know. Just come home."

She arrives as the clouds part, inviting the moon to peek at the night. She kneels in the grass, spouting questions like a geyser. What, when, where, how, how, *how*?

"I don't know," I say.

"It was an accident," I say.

"I'll be fine," I say.

Tucker keeps quiet.

Lucy examines my shoulder, cringing at the swollen knob. "You couldn't be *less* fine. You need to see a doctor."

"Aunt Lucy—"

"This isn't up for debate, Callie!"

I flinch because, holy shit, my aunt has never yelled at me.

Tucker squeezes my hand. "I should go," he says.

That's it. He's crossing the yard, pushing a hand through his wet hair, unlocking his car's door. I'm left empty, wanting; my heart longs to follow.

Just before he gets into the Woody, he turns to meet my gaze. His pale eyes are penetrating in the darkness. His mouth turns up in a slight, secretive smile, and I know . . .

Everything's going to be okay.

50

I drag myself into the house and sit in the kitchen while Lucy calls the urgent-care clinic in Shell City, where she took me to have my arm stitched up last summer. Buddy jumps onto my lap. I scratch under his chin with my usable hand, trying not to launch into a panic attack at the thought of returning to that clinic. But my shoulder throbs like a beating heart; I need to see a doctor.

Lucy helps me into the passenger seat of the Range Rover. Our trip to Shell City is quick because it's late and the coast is deserted. A bespectacled physician's assistant conducts an exam while my aunt looks on critically. He asks a lot of questions as he pokes and prods.

"I tripped," I tell him. "My friend caught me before I hit the ground. My shoulder didn't cooperate. Old swimming injury."

Lucy eyes me with blatant skepticism.

The P.A. resets my shoulder. I nearly bite my tongue off trying to keep a howl in, but as soon as it's done, the ugly knot is gone and I can move my arm without tearing up. Once I promise to use ice and stay out of the pool for a couple of weeks, I'm released.

Lucy's quiet during the drive home. It's not until we're headed up the hill to Stewart House that she says, "I want to know what happened."

"I told you. Tucker caught me when I tripped."

"What were you doing outside?"

"Taking a walk."

"During a thunderstorm? I'm not stupid, Callie."

I sigh, exhausted. "It's a long story—a private story."

She turns onto the gravel lane. Her mouth is a grim line, and her eyes are shrouded in worry. When she parks in front of the house, she kills the engine, then twists in her seat to face me. "I'm going to ask you a question," she says. "I want a truthful answer. Got it?"

I nod, trying to figure out why she's so worked up when, really, she should be relieved.

"Did Tucker hurt you?"

I gape at her. "*No.* Why would you think that?"

"Because he was the only person here. Because he couldn't look me in the eye when I showed up. Because your story about tripping is weak. What am I supposed to think?"

"You know Tucker better than that."

"I thought so. But the fact is, I misjudged Isaac. He broke your sister's heart—yours, too. What kind of aunt would I be if I had suspicions but didn't ask questions?"

"Isaac isn't a bad guy, Aunt Lucy. I know that now. And you can ask questions, but you can also trust me. Tucker was here when I needed him. I really did fall, and he really did help me. He would *never* hurt me."

Indecision skips across her face like a stone on smooth water. She's wrestling with conjecture, reassessing her instincts, reconciling the facts with the story I fed her.

And then her expression changes. Her mouth rolls into a smile, and she pulls me into a gentle hug. "I'm so glad you're all right."

As soon as Lucy goes to bed, I sneak up two flights of stairs to the attic, phone in hand.

I flip on the light, a bare bulb hanging in the center of the room.

I call Isaac.

He answers immediately, like all he's done for the last year is wait for me to get in touch.

"Please, Isaac," I say without preamble. "You have to stop calling."

"Yeah, I know."

I'm dumbstruck. I've prepared counterpoints for all the reasons he might offer for why we should try again, or why we should, at the very least, stay in touch. I sit down on the floor, tucking my feet beneath me. "You do?"

His response follows a long exhale. "I've been hanging on to something that's long over. It was good in the beginning, but after your sister died, you only came around because you felt obligated. I should've seen that."

"I didn't feel obligated—"

"I think you did," he says, not combatively. He speaks with fondness, as he always has.

I consider what he said. Did I see him last summer and seek him out again at Christmastime because I felt like I owed the universe allegiance to him? Some sort of warped penance for instigating the chain of events that led to Chloe, snared in a rip current, inhaling lungfuls of salty water?

"You're being very quiet," he says.

"I'm thinking."

"Thinking I'm right?"

I smile into the shadows. "Maybe. Except, why'd you try to stick it out with me?"

"Because I liked you. I think maybe I loved you and, God, I fucked everything up in the space of five seconds. I should've kept my distance with your sister. I swear to God, I didn't mean to lead her on. And then after, I let you keep coming around even though I knew your heart wasn't in it. I kept hoping that if you could stand to be in a room with me, then maybe what I did wasn't unforgivable."

In all the millions of moments I've spent in a spiral of shame and self-loathing, never once did it occur to me that Isaac might be coping with similar feelings.

"Isaac, what happened to Chloe . . . It wasn't your fault."

"I kissed her."

"*She* kissed *you*. You pulled away."

"Maybe not fast enough. Maybe I let her think there was something between us, even if I didn't mean to. Maybe if I wouldn't have come to Oregon, she'd still be alive."

"She swam in the ocean a lot of times before you showed up. It was an accident."

The line goes quiet but for his shallow breaths. When he speaks again, his voice is soft. "That's really what you believe?"

"I have to. Otherwise, I'll drive myself crazy what-if-ing. You have to believe it, too."

He sighs, watery and thin, and I picture him in Seattle, on the porch where we used to hang out. I wonder how many times he's cried over my sister. Over me.

"Thanks for calling," he says. "For giving me a chance to unload."

"Thanks for being so nice. For understanding."

We spend a few more minutes catching up, school and parents and late summer plans, surface stuff I'd give anyone, and then, amiably, we hang up.

It's easy to say goodbye.

I spend what's left of the night in Lucy's bed. Daisy and Buddy snooze between us.

I dream of my sister. She's wearing her yellow dress, as always, but the panicky draw I used to feel is absent. I'm an observer, watching her walk the beach, content. Exactly as I hoped she'd be.

I wake up early and indulge in a long shower. My shoulder's still sore and it takes forever to scrub the dried mud from beneath my fingernails, but I leave the bathroom feeling revitalized, like the day is full of possibility.

In the kitchen, Lucy's placed toast, fruit salad, and tall glasses of orange juice on the table. She's already seated, sipping coffee. I join her, laying my napkin on my lap.

"Your dad called while you were in the shower," she says, helping herself to a piece of toast. She butters it, and then she drops a bomb: "He's on his way."

My mouth falls open. If Dad jumped into the car to drive three hours to Bell Cove, then Lucy must've grossly inflated what she witnessed last night.

"I had to tell him what happened," she says. "He's worried, naturally. He wants to see for himself that you're okay."

"God, Aunt Lucy. What if he makes me go back to Seattle with him?" I'll miss Bell Cove, Lucy, Stewart House. I'll miss home improvement and long bike rides and swimming under the rising sun. I'll miss Tucker.

Lucy points her fork in my direction. "I'll do my best. I'll make sure he knows that what happened to your shoulder was an accident. I'll assure him you're safe and promise not to take my eyes off you for the next few weeks, but you have to do some things for me in return."

"Like what?"

"When you're healed, you have to get back in the pool."

I nod. Easy.

"You have to raise your grades next semester and start thinking seriously about college."

"Consider me back on the honor roll."

"Also, you've got to consider coming back next year. The B&B will be going strong by then, and I'd love your help with the summer rush."

"Done."

She grins. She has no idea how easily she's letting me off. Her wish list—swimming, school, seeing the B&B through—I'd do those things anyway.

"Aunt Lucy, thank you."

"You're welcome."

Out front, tires traverse the gravel drive.

"That's got to be Tuck." Lucy waves a hand at the front door. "Go on."

I fake nonchalance on my way out of the kitchen, but my stomach's simmering with nervous excitement. Through the window, I watch Tucker leave the Woody, hair like spun gold in the morning sunshine. He trudges up to the house, hands shoved into the pockets of his shorts, white T-shirt snug across his chest.

He radiates light.

I throw the door open and step onto the porch. The air smells of last night's rain, but the sky is clear, infinitely blue.

Tucker climbs the steps and reaches for me, fingers whispering over my shoulder. "Better?"

I smile up at him. "Better."

His arms come around me. He holds me like I'm made of snow crystals, but the heat of his skin is melting me. "I'm sorry," he murmurs into my hair. "For last night. For hurting your arm. I didn't want to go, but your aunt seemed . . ."

"I know. My arm is fine. And, holy hell, Tucker. Thank God you were here." I lean into him, running my hands up his back. "How's your dad?"

His shoulders rise in a shrug. "Okay. He sat me down this morning wanting to, like, *talk*. About everything you brought over yesterday. About my mother. About Nathan Stewart and his sister, Hannah, who still lives in Oregon, apparently."

"She does—Eugene. The house was in her name before Lucy bought it."

"That's what my dad said, too. I'm gonna look for her online. Email her. See what she can tell me about my mother and Nathan. See if she remembers anything from back when my mom used to hang out here. What do you think?"

"I think that's a good idea. What does your dad say?"

"That I should do whatever I need to do. He's trying, Cal. This morning's conversation was huge, and he was cool with me coming over here. That's something, yeah?"

"Definitely."

I take his hand and guide him to the two rocking chairs farthest from the door, where we first met. He scoots his chair closer to mine and reclaims my hand. "So your aunt . . . Do I still have a job?"

"Tucker, of course."

"She's not gonna send you back to Seattle early?"

"Nope. My dad's coming, though. He's driving here now."

"Yeah? Are you gonna introduce me?"

"Obviously. But there's a chance he'll want me to come home. Lucy said she could convince him that staying's best, but her power of persuasion comes at a price."

He tips his chin, hair falling over his forehead. "What's that?"

"She wants me to work on getting my grades up, and she wants me to consider college. She wants me to keep swimming."

"You were gonna do all that anyway."

"She also wants me to come back next summer. To help her with the B&B."

He flashes a heart-stopping smile. "I fully support that idea, but I'd better see you a hell of a lot between now and then."

My happiness is immediate and intense. He pulls me out of my chair and into his lap, enveloping me in his spice and cedar scent. He whispers, "Remember when I told you Bell Cove was the shit? Truth, right?"

"*Maybe*. But only because you're here."

He laughs and leans in to kiss me.

I meet him halfway.

Acknowledgments

I continue to count myself incredibly lucky to be part of the Swoon Reads family. Jean Feiwel and Lauren Scobell, thank you for fostering this remarkable community. Kat Brzozowski, I'm so fortunate to call you my editor. You were right—this book was supposed to be a sister story. Thank you for the nudge, the feedback, and the space to get it right.

Enormous gratitude, as always, to the entire Swoon Reads team, particularly Kelsey Marrujo and Emily Settle. Lauren Forte and Lindsay Wagner, thank you for lending your copyediting expertise to this book. Aurora Parlagreco, thank you for creating the most perfect cover. And to the Swoon Squad, you guys are the best, for too many reasons to list here.

Victoria Marini, your advice, knowledge, and advocacy have been invaluable for a lot of years now. Thank you so much for being in my corner.

Alison Miller, Temre Beltz, Sara McClung, and Elodie Nowodazkij, you've helped me grow as a writer and person. It's a privilege to call you friends. Thank you, thank you, thank you. <3

I've worked on *How the Light Gets In* longer than any other manuscript on my hard drive; as a result, it's been read in its various iterations by numerous savvy betas, over nearly a decade. So many people have had a hand in this book, and it's better thanks to each and every one of them. Special thanks to Amie Kaufman, Mandie Baxter, Lori Wilde, Heather Howland, Ann Rought, Christa Desir, Erin Bowman, Karole Cozzo, and Christina June for the essential feedback they've offered in the way of this story, not to mention their tremendous kindness and overwhelming enthusiasm.

Mom and Dad, thank you, as always, for your love and endless championing. Mike and Zach, while this is a book about sisters, I drew great inspiration from your combined childhood antics. ☺ Bev and Phil, thank you for being awesome in-laws, and a constant source of support. Andy, Danielle, Grant, Reid, Caroline, Sam, Kacie, Brynnlee, Michele, Gabe, Teddy, and Thomas, your cheerleading continues to mean the world to me.

Claire, you are a gift. Your smarts, your wit, and your kind, kind heart amaze me every day. I'm so happy we're sharing books now! Lulu, you have brought our family immeasurable joy. Always give supertight hugs, sing at the top of your voice, and giggle with your nose all crinkled up. Matt, thank you for letting me borrow your best qualities to bestow upon the love interests I make up. There's no way I could write romance without such a fantastic source of real-life inspiration. Love you!

Check out more books chosen for publication by readers like you.

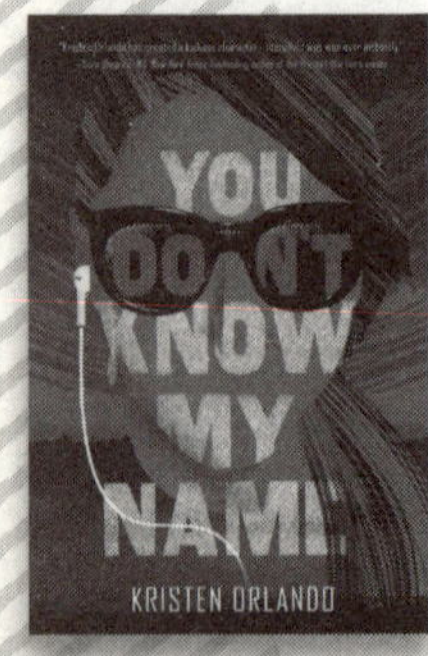